THE CHRISTMAS COLLECTION

VOLUME TWO

VICTORIA CONNELLY

CUTHLAND PRESS

The Christmas Collection is a compilation
of the following titles:
The Wrong Ghost
The Christmas Rose
Christmas with the Book Lovers

Victoria Connelly asserts the moral right to be identified as the author of this work.

Cover design by J D Smith
Author photo © Roy Connelly

ISBN: 978-1-910522-20-2
Published by Cuthland Press.

CONTENTS

THE WRONG GHOST

THE CHRISTMAS ROSE

CHRISTMAS WITH THE BOOK LOVERS

The Wrong Ghost

Be careful what
you wish for...

VICTORIA CONNELLY

In memory of my dear friend, Ellie, who left the party early but who danced more than most.

CHAPTER ONE

It was cold enough for snow. Beatrice Beaumont sat in the little nest she'd made for herself, gazing through the tiny diamonds of the leaded windows to the garden far below. The window seat was a secretive place. Tucked away at the top of the house in one of the wood-panelled rooms with sloping floorboards and a fireplace that hadn't been used for centuries, it was somewhere to escape to.

There were plenty of little places where Bea could have curled up with a book. The house was full of them. But something always pulled her back to this one. It was a little bit draughty up here on the fourth floor of Ketton Hall, she had to admit. The old house had a way of inviting the outside in, but Bea had made the little nook cosy with plump cushions in thick, comfy fabrics and had hung heavy damask curtains on either side of the window.

She had an old hardback novel in her lap, chosen from the vast collection in the house's own library. She ran her fingers over the gold embossed ridges of the spine and marvelled at the delicacy of the fine paper within. It had that inexplicably wonderful old book scent that she adored, but she had yet to read a single word of it. It had been written by one of her husband's ancestors and she'd been intrigued enough to borrow it, but her mind had drifted, her gaze soft on the landscape beyond the window.

For a moment, she wondered if George had read the book or, indeed, any of the books from the library. She wished she'd asked him. She'd never know now.

Her vision focused on the lake which was frozen at the edges, the reeds blowing and bending in the December wind. It had been unrelentingly cold in Suffolk this winter with frosts, hail, sleet and snow. Bea's fingers touched the old glass of the window, feeling its chill. She had quickly learned to wrap up warm, her slender form looking rounded from the many layers she wore. Elizabethan manor houses were not the easiest to heat and keep warm. They were draughty and creaky. Still, for all its faults, Bea couldn't deny that Ketton was beautiful. It was a true privilege to live in such a place even if the electricity bills were horrendous and the maintenance costs even worse. But it was home now, and had been for the past five years, and she really couldn't imagine living anywhere else.

She was just worrying that she might have left the plug-in radiator on in the bedroom when she saw her mother's car coming up the driveway. It was another advantage of being in the room at the top of the house – you could see when anybody was invading.

'Oh, heavens!' she cried, swinging her legs down from the window seat. She hadn't prepared afternoon tea and she'd said she would. Her mother would pick up on that, knowing that Bea had spent the entire day doing nothing but brooding.

Bea gently placed the book onto a little table, away from the window so that any pernicious rays of sunlight that might find their way through the moody winter clouds wouldn't do it any damage. It was something Bea had become acutely aware of since becoming a custodian of an ancient building. Light damaged. Mind you, everything seemed to damage the fabric of an old house. Water was possibly the worst culprit. Dust was another. Insects were also to be feared. And even the human hand could inflict harm with its natural oils and salts, and gloves were advisable when touching fragile textiles like tapestries and curtains. History was something you had to handle very gently.

Bea rushed down the stairs. Well, you couldn't exactly rush down them for they were treacherously uneven, worn away from centuries of footfall and they turned at every storey in this part of the house so that your journey was naturally broken. If you weren't in a hurry, it was tempting to stop by every landing window and peer out at the view. But Bea was in a hurry, if only to get to the front door before her mother did. Alas, she didn't make it.

'Ah, there you are at last!' her mother said without any sort of preamble once Bea had opened the door.

'I came as quickly as I could. I was at the top of the house.'

Valerie Maynard frowned deeply. 'Doing what?'

'Conservation,' Bea said. It was the sort of vague, old-building owner's reply that would fox her mother and prevent further questioning.

'Hi Bea,' Nicole, Bea's older sister, came forward and hugged her.

'It's so good to see you!' Bea said. 'It's been *way* too long.'

'I know. But I'm back now. For Christmas at least.'

Nicole had been working as a translator in France for the last few months and Bea had missed her terribly.

'I suppose you want your daughter back,' Valerie said.

'Yes. You do have her, don't you?' Bea said, looking around for the missing four-year old.

'She's in the car,' Nicole said.

'Why didn't you bring her in with you?' Bea asked anxiously.

'Because we wanted to make sure you were actually in before we disturbed her. She's sound asleep, you see,' her mother explained.

'Why wouldn't I be in?'

Valerie sighed. 'Well, forgive me for bringing it up, but there was that time when you took yourself off for a three-hour walk, wasn't there? And I had to come back later.'

'Ah, yes.' Bea remembered. She'd been having a particularly bad day and had had to get outside. She'd kind of forgotten that her mother was due back with Rose. She shook her head, appalled as she recalled the day.

'Well, let me get her,' Bea said now, leaving the house and walking across the gravelled driveway to the car. And there she was. Her beautiful red-haired girl, fast asleep in the back of the car, her plump cheeks gloriously pink.

'Hey there!' Bea whispered, gently unclipping her from her car seat.

'Mummy?'

'You're home, darling. Did you have a nice day?'

'I had cake!'

'Oh, lucky you!'

'And I ate all my greens.'

'Good girl.' Bea wrapped her arms around her daughter and lifted her out of the car, taking her into the house and popping her down in the hallway. 'I was just about to make tea.'

'Are the scones ready?' her mother asked.

'No. Sorry. I forgot,' Bea said, trying to sound as casual as possible. 'But there's a packet of chocolate digestives somewhere. I think. Or maybe I finished them.' Bea bit her lip. Yes, she seemed to recall finishing them when she couldn't sleep one night. She'd got up when the wind had been howling down the bedroom chimney like a banshee, and she'd sat by the Aga in the kitchen with a cup of tea and had miserably munched her way through the entire biscuit tin.

'You said you were making us tea and scones,' her mother said, tut-tutting.

'I'm sorry. The time...' She didn't finish her sentence. She didn't feel capable.

'Mum, Bea's probably been up to her eyeballs with her work,' Nicole said, throwing her a smile of support.

If only that was true, Bea thought, returning her sister's smile and mouthing a thank you. But, the truth was, Bea had just had a kind of wandering day, going from room to room, a little lost. She couldn't remember exactly what she'd done with her time now. Some days were like that. Even now. Even after a year.

Almost a year.

'Are you eating properly?'

'Yes, Mum.'

'You look skinny.' Her mother grabbed hold of Bea's face and turned it to the light. 'Your cheekbones are jutting out.'

'Mum!' Bea shook her away.

'I worry about you.'

'Well don't.'

'You really should think about coming home.'

Bea frowned. 'But *this* is my home.'

'This monstrous house will *never* be your home,' Valerie declared.

Bea's mouth dropped open in protest. In some ways, she knew her mother was right because there were days when she truly felt that she still didn't belong here – in those moments of insecurity usually brought on by gazing at the Beaumont family portraits. All those centuries-old faces, each looking so comfortable in their frames on the wall of *their* home. They seemed to glower down at her with accusation in their eyes.

Who are you, child? What are you doing in our *home?*

'I'm Beatrice!' she'd reply, knowing how ridiculous it was to talk to them. 'George's wife.'

She still remembered the feeling of apprehension she'd had when George, who'd just proposed to her, had shown her inside Ketton Hall for the first time.

'Well, here it is – the family pile!' He'd laughed. But Bea hadn't. It had all seemed so overwhelming. It still did at times. Sometimes, in the middle of the night, when she'd wake up to the creaks and groans of the old building shifting around her like a ship at sea, she'd wonder what on earth she was doing there. She'd feel so small and alone in the big four poster bed. And a part of her would long for a modern single bed in a modest room with floors that didn't undulate and walls that didn't bulge in the middle. But Ketton was her home now and she told her mother that.

'And it's Rose's family home too,' Bea added.

Her mother shook her head. 'It's too much for you to cope with on your own. I can't think how you're managing financially.'

Bea sighed. That was another thing about her mother – she'd never believed that her daughter was capable of earning a living in her chosen profession.

Messing about with flowers, Valerie called it.

'She's hugely successful, Mum!' Nicole rolled her eyes in sympathy with her sister. 'She has a massive YouTube following.'

'I really don't know what that means,' Valerie admitted with a weary sigh.

'Yes, well that's because you're out of date with how society works these days,' Nicole said. 'People don't have to have an employer and be sat at a desk for hours every day. They don't even have to leave home in order to make a living anymore. It's wonderfully liberating!'

Bea nodded. It was wonderfully liberating to be able to do the work she loved and have the luxury of being able to stay at home and spend so much time with Rose.

'But is it sustainable?' Valerie asked. 'How do you know that all these *followers* of yours won't just – I don't know – follow someone else or something?'

'Well, I admit, there are no guarantees,' Bea said. 'No job is guaranteed though, is it?'

'I worry about you,' her mum went on.

'You really shouldn't,' Bea told her, giving her a quick hug. 'I'm doing my dream job and Linenfold Flowers is doing really well. Honestly, I'm fine. *Everything's* fine. Now, come into the kitchen and I'll make those scones, okay?'

Her mother nodded and led the way.

Nicole sidled up to Bea. 'Don't listen to Mum.'

'She's rather hard to ignore.'

'I know, but she means well.'

Bea gave a weary sigh. 'Meaning well can sound an awful lot like disapproval sometimes.'

Later, having eaten fresh buttery scones together in the warmth of the kitchen, Bea watched her mother and sister leave, waving until the car turned round the bend of the driveway and they were out of sight. She shivered as she shut the great front door and locked it with a key the length of her hand. Having had the chatter of voices reverberating around its walls, the house seemed to be welcoming its silence back.

Bea walked into the living room. After feasting on both cake and scones that day, Rose was fast asleep on one of the big Knole sofas. She looked tiny on the large piece of furniture, half hidden by a tapestry cushion. Bea hated to disturb her, but it was bedtime and so she scooped her daughter up in her arms.

'You're really getting too heavy for this,' she whispered, kissing Rose's cheek.

Slowly, she made her way up the oak staircase, turning right at the landing where the stairs split in two. And there it was – the annoying squeak. She'd asked George to deal with it countless times, but he'd only ever laughed at her.

'It's an historic squeak. It's got its very own preservation order,' he'd told her.

She'd never known whether to believe him or not.

CHAPTER TWO

Winters in East Anglia could be brutally cold with winds coming straight across the North Sea from the Arctic, and the last winter at Ketton had been one of the worst on record. A red alert had been issued for an upcoming storm, with gusts of up to one hundred miles an hour predicted. It had been hard to imagine until it actually hit and the old house started to lose panes of glass to flying debris from the nearby trees. The sound was ferocious. Bea had never experienced anything like it. The wind in the living room chimney sounded like a thousand wild spirits being held against their will.

'I don't like this,' Bea had told George. 'Will the house be all right?'

'Well, it's lasted this long,' George assured her. 'It's survived countless storms, rampaging armies and my grandmother's assault with Laura Ashley wallpaper.'

Bea had laughed but, all the same, she'd made sure she and Rose didn't stand too close to any windows.

The day of the storm had been such a beautiful day too – a bit blustery, perhaps, that morning, but they hadn't let it stop them from enjoying the rare winter sunshine. George had packed a picnic basket. Bea had thought him crazy, but had watched in wonder as he'd made egg mayonnaise sandwiches, cutting the crusts off at the request of Rose. He'd even made lemon cake, filling the kitchen with its wonderful aroma. It had to be said that George was more of a ginger cake sort of guy, but he knew Bea loved anything lemony, and he got extra points for giving Bea and Rose the bowl and spoon to lick.

They'd then set out on their little winter expedition. To the lake.

'Are you sure this is a good idea with the storm coming?' Bea had asked.

'It's not due for hours!' George told her.

'But won't it be horribly cold out on the water?'

'Very likely!' he laughed. 'But we're all wrapped up, aren't we?' He plumped her scarf up around her neck and kissed the tip of her chilly nose.

There were little waves on the lake, making it feel as if they might be out at sea as George rowed them into the very middle. The rowing boat wasn't terribly big, but it was sturdy and Bea had taken blankets for padding and warmth and it really was very cosy indeed. It was the best way to see Ketton Hall too. It looked magnificent from the lake, framed by the water and the great oak trees in the parkland, dominating the landscape.

'Home!' Rose cried, pointing back to the house. Bea got her phone out and took a photo of her daughter. And one of George, his red-gold hair blowing under the old flat cap he favoured. She couldn't understand why he liked it so much. The tweed was practically threadbare and the colours faded and Bea was convinced that it smelled of wet dog even though the family hadn't owned one for years, but the cap had belonged to George's father and George was very attached to it.

They ate their egg sandwiches and lemon cake, the boat slowly turning so that the view kept changing.

'Good idea?' George said as he rowed them back after they'd all had hot chocolate from the flask.

'*Very* good idea,' Bea replied, leaning across the boat and kissing him.

Once safely on dry land, they all ran into the house as the wind picked up, hurling angry autumn leaves at them. Bea was glad when they were all safely inside. They'd made sure they had plenty of food in the larder in case the little country lanes became blocked by falling trees or cables, and they had matches and candles in case of power cuts. They were ready for anything.

Or that's what she'd thought.

It was a little after four in the afternoon and already dark when the storm began in earnest. George's phone rang almost immediately. It was Mrs Gilbert, a widow in her late-eighties who lived in a cottage at the edge of the estate. Her husband had worked as a gardener at the hall all his life and the two of them were like family to George. Bea knew that George missed the old man terribly and that he liked to look in on Mrs Gilbert every so often, taking her bits of shopping and lending a helping hand whenever he could.

'Is she okay?' Bea asked when George had hung up.

He shook his head. 'Mischief, her terrier's missing. I'm going to go and look for him.'

Bea scowled. 'You can't be serious. You're not going out in that?'

They both listened for a second to the howling wind.

'She sounds distressed, Bea. You know how she feels about that dog. It's all she has.'

'The dog will be fine,' Bea said. 'He's called Mischief for a reason, isn't he? He'll hunker down somewhere safe.'

But George wasn't listening. 'I won't be long. Stay in the Blue Drawing Room. If you close the shutters, the weather won't sound so scary. Light yourself a fire and cosy up with Rose, okay? Wrap yourselves up in that tartan blanket I got you.'

It wasn't a tartan blanket. It was a paisley throw, but Bea smiled at his thoughtfulness. He knew she felt the cold.

'I don't like you going out there,' she told him.

'Don't worry about me. Us Beaumonts are indestructible. Like our family seat.'

Bea sighed, knowing she couldn't stop him. He felt a duty to the old woman and he wouldn't settle until he'd seen that she and her dog were okay. He kissed the tip of her nose, popped his flat cap on his head and left before she could protest further. So Bea took Rose to the Blue Drawing Room where she settled with her colouring book while Bea turned on the lamps, closed the shutters and lit the fire. It was a pleasant room – one of the prettiest in the old house and she could imagine generations of Beaumont women curling up on cold winter nights while their husbands were out doing dangerous things like rounding up stray animals or fighting Civil Wars or whatever they had got up to in times past. She'd have to look it up. She wanted to learn more about the history of the house and the family she'd married into. Rose's family. She might not be related by blood, but her daughter certainly was.

Bea had flicked through a couple of parish magazines, an ancient copy of *Country Life* with a coffee ring stain on the cover, and two local newspapers. Rose had fallen asleep ages ago and Bea thought she should really take her up to bed, but she selfishly wanted her daughter there with her.

An hour passed. Then another. Where on earth was George? How could it take two hours to find a dog? Or had he found it and was now enjoying supper with their neighbour? Why hadn't he called her? He should have let her know what was happening. She rang his mobile, but it went to voicemail. She cursed and threw another log onto the fire. Ordinarily, sitting by a fire on a long, dark evening might well make Bea sleepy, but the great gusts of wind were keeping her wide awake as was the thought of George out there in the middle of it all.

Bea hated waiting. She wasn't a patient person at the best of times, but waiting for George to come home was agony. Part of her wished she could go out into the storm just to be with him, but she couldn't leave Rose. She looked across the room at her sleeping girl, her face amber in the light from the flames.

When the doorbell went, she assumed that George was just letting her know he was back as the door had been left unlocked for him. Bea rushed out of the drawing room, expecting to see him in the hallway, but he wasn't there.

'George?' She opened the old oak front door, but it wasn't George who greeted her. It was two police officers.

They asked if they could come in and she led them through to the main living room, away from Rose, doing her best to keep calm, but all the time wondering where George was. Perhaps they knew something. Yes, of course they did. That's why they were here. But why hadn't they simply rung? Or why hadn't George rung? Was he hurt? Maybe he couldn't ring.

Her mouth suddenly felt dry and her limbs very heavy – as if they didn't quite belong to her. She mustn't panic, she told herself as they all sat down. Nothing had been said yet. Nothing was certain. But it was, wasn't it? Why else would they be here?

'Tell me!' she cried.

And they did.

It was quick, they said. Very quick. One of the old trees on the main road into the village. He wouldn't have known a thing. No. It wasn't advisable for her to see him. He'd been taken away. They were so sorry for her loss. Was she all right? Was there somebody they could contact for her? It was best if somebody was with you at times like this, they said. Did she want them to make her a cup of tea? A hot, sweet drink was good. No? Well, if she was sure she was okay...

After the police had gone, Bea walked through to the drawing room and scooped Rose up in her arms, taking her upstairs to bed. Luckily, she didn't wake and ask where her daddy was.

Indestructible. That's the word George had used to describe himself. But he hadn't been, had he? He'd been small and vulnerable in the face of the storm.

She closed her eyes and leaned her head against the door frame of her daughter's bedroom and wondered about getting into bed with her right there and then. Not undressing, not washing, just trying to find oblivion next to Rose's warmth. But practicality prevailed. She should tidy the kitchen.

Bea made her way downstairs, the creak of the step George used to tease her about sounding loudly even with the noise of the storm still raging around the house. She'd tidy up and make herself a drink, she told herself. She wouldn't ring anyone tonight. She couldn't face it. It would all have to wait for the morning. She'd be okay. She'd hold it together. She had to be strong for Rose.

But, as she entered the kitchen, she saw the picnic basket they'd taken out on the lake that afternoon. And there on the worktop was the floral tin containing the rest of the cake George had made them. Bea could smell its wonderful lemony aroma and she saw the unwashed bowl and the spoon by the sink that he'd given her and Rose to lick clean. She could still hear his laughter as they'd indulged themselves.

'Is it good?' he'd asked.

'Yes,' Bea replied now.

And then she burst into tears.

CHAPTER THREE

It was almost a whole year since the night of the storm which had taken George from her. They say the first year after losing a loved one is the toughest – when you're marking all those dates on the calendar like birthdays and anniversaries that they're no longer there to celebrate for the first time. The seasons too. Bea thought that first spring was almost cruel in the way the snowdrops and daffodils dared to bloom without George in the world. Bea wasn't sure how she'd got through it all. She remembered the awful day when the tree had been completely removed. It was part of the Beaumont estate which meant that the cost fell to them. Bea would never forget the well-meaning young man from the contracting company knocking on the door and asking if she wanted to keep the wood. As if she'd ever be able to warm herself with wood from the tree that had killed her husband.

She'd taken a walk to the site once the tree had been removed. She wasn't quite sure what she was looking for. She didn't really want to turn the spot into a shrine as some people did with sites of road accidents, although she could understand the need to be at the place where a loved one had spent their last moments. But Bea knew that George wasn't there. His soul, his spirit – whatever it was that lived on – wasn't on the road where a tree had fallen. If anything, it was at Ketton Hall. Bea swore she could sometimes feel him there still, as if he were just in the next room, about to call her name. It was an odd feeling. Perhaps that was what happened to the owners of these old, ancestral homes – they never really left them, but became a part of their history forever, their very fabric, watching over the occupants and keeping an eye on things. It was a comforting thought.

To lose one's husband is a cruel fate at any time of year, but to lose him two weeks before Christmas had been particularly brutal. Her mother and sister had insisted that she and Rose spend the holiday at her old family home. Bea hadn't protested. But this Christmas, she'd been determined to celebrate the big day at Ketton, inviting her family there. For one thing, she needed to focus on her business, Linenfold Flowers, putting out as much Christmas content as possible. It had been running for four years now and, during that time, had evolved from providing beautiful floral displays and bouquets for the local community to creating a hugely successful YouTube channel where Bea ran online workshops and shared her passion for flowers.

Bea still couldn't believe the messages she received from all over the world. The floral displays she made and the tutorials she gave had fans in as far-flung places as China and Chile.

Now, she was busy creating tutorials on Christmas wreaths, and decorating one's home for the holiday season, and Ketton Hall proved to be the perfect backdrop. She'd already made a fabulous long garland which she'd wound down the length of the wooden staircase that led up from the main entrance hall, and she had great plans for the mantelpieces in two of the main reception rooms as well as making a wreath for the front door.

After dropping Rose off at school, Bea rushed back to Ketton just in time for the delivery van bringing her flowers and she helped bring the boxes into the downstairs parlour with the Elizabethan linenfold wood panelling which gave her business its name. Bea loved this moment of anticipation, trying to remember what she'd ordered and opening the boxes to reveal her bounty. Today, there were billowing clouds of creamy gypsophila, sprays of green-grey eucalyptus, white roses and pink pompon dahlias because one always needed a hit of colour in the depths of winter.

What was lovely was that Bea could also gather foliage herself, and the winter months at Ketton provided plenty of evergreens – the symbol of hope and new life – cheering the long, dark winter days. Bea loved nothing more than bringing in armfuls of holly and ivy from the garden and collecting fat pine cones and teasels and feathery grasses. Herbs were also a favourite. The bounty from the garden and grounds at Ketton never failed to dazzle her and she felt very lucky to have such a resource, although the local country lanes were also plentiful and she regularly gathered old man's beard and rosehips from the hedgerows.

The mistletoe had always been a challenge to collect. It was high up in one of the ancient willows. Bea remembered the adventures she'd used to have with George as they'd gathered it together. He'd hoist her onto his shoulders in an attempt to reach the plant while she'd cry that it wouldn't work, and he'd run around the orchard with her begging for mercy. Finally, a ladder would be brought from one of the outbuildings. It wasn't as romantic, but it was far more practical.

No matter what the season, Bea always found something to squirrel away, hanging and drying flowers from the beams of the house. She looked forward to gathering poppy heads once their delicate petals had fallen, and the sculptural flower heads of fennel always made a winter bouquet more ethereal.

For a few blissful hours, she worked quietly, stripping leaves and cutting the stems before placing them in big silver buckets. There was something wonderfully contemplative and restoring about working with flowers, she thought, not for the first time. Now, at thirty-one, she couldn't imagine any other life. The room was instantly transformed by their colour and scent, lifting her spirits. She couldn't wait to share them with her audience.

But the fun didn't stop with foliage and flowers. Not when it was

Christmas. The joy continued after the garlands and wreaths had been created with the addition of fairy lights, candles, baubles and anything else that shone and sparkled. Then came ribbons in rich velvets and wispy lace, and dried oranges and cinnamon sticks. The only limit was your imagination – that's what Bea liked to tell her audience. Enjoy yourself. Let go. Explore. Imagine. *Create*.

As she was filming a demonstration today, she lit the parlour fire and the candles on the mantelpiece to create a Christmassy mood. Great fat, white candles. Simple and stunning against the dark wood of the panelled room. They were the simplest of ornaments and yet added so much atmosphere. Of course, safety was paramount in an old house with so much wood, and Bea was careful never to leave any candles unattended. She wouldn't want to be responsible for her daughter's ancestral home going up in flames.

Finally, having organised the room and prepared all the flowers, foliage and decorations, she began to film a wreath-making video for her YouTube channel. She'd then edit a longer version for her paying subscribers. She loved making wreaths. There was something so very satisfying about circles. They were comforting and happy.

She started with a pre-made wire ring for speed, but often used willow which she would bend into shape herself. Then she would pad it with moss. George used to laugh at her as she raked up buckets full of moss from the lawn.

'Just you wait!' she'd tell him. And he'd always be amazed by the results. 'Free resources, see?'

'Good girl!' he'd say. Every owner of an historic home was always looking for ways to save money.

She thought of him now as she grabbed the first handful of moss from one of the buckets, pushing it around the wire frame to form the foundation of the wreath. This was the messy bit, the least creative bit, but so very necessary because the strength of the base was all important.

As she took her audience through the process, taking her time to show each stage, she tried not to think about that one special wreath she'd had to make for George. Her mother had told her not to, but Bea had felt that she'd needed to. It just seemed... right. She'd kept it simple with greens and whites. She'd even got the ladder out and climbed the willow tree to reach the mistletoe.

'Is that appropriate?' her mother had asked when she'd seen the white berries in the finished wreath.

'Completely,' Bea had replied.

And it had looked stunning. But Bea had never used mistletoe in a wreath again.

After she'd finished filming the making of today's wreath, she had a quick tidy up, marvelling at the way the winter sunshine bounced off the dark oak panelling at the back of the room. The fire had died down and she blew out the candles. The room instantly looked a little sadder.

She was just about to switch her ring light off when she saw something sparkling between the floorboards at the edge of the thick rug. At first, she thought it was a fragment of a broken Christmas bauble and she bent to take a closer look. No, it definitely wasn't a bauble.

'It's a ring!' she cried, her fingers reaching for it. The uneven floorboards of the room meant that there were sizeable gaps and the ring had become very firmly wedged. But Bea wasn't giving up and, after several attempts, she managed to free it from its woody prison.

She walked towards the window, the winter sunshine illuminating her treasure, showing the rich gold of the shank and the deep red of a stone she guessed to be ruby. It was a small ring, but there was something distinctly masculine about it. The shank was broad and the stone was a sort of flat oval in shape. Bea looked closer, hoping to find some inscription on the inside, but there was nothing. She looked around the room as if it might reveal the ring's secret and she wondered how long it had been lost there and how it could have been overlooked. But, then again, before she'd arrived at Ketton, the oak parlour hadn't been much in use and maybe the rug had hidden it from sight.

Bea gazed at the ring, wondering how old it was and whom it had belonged to. A visitor, perhaps? But most likely somebody who'd lived at Ketton. One of Rose's ancestors! It was exciting to think of that and Bea couldn't resist trying it on. It was too big for her little finger and her ring finger too, but it fit snugly on her index finger. Actually, it fit a little too snugly. She grimaced, doing her best to remove it a moment later, but it wouldn't budge. That would teach her, she thought. She'd have to leave it for now. At least it was safe.

After making a late lunch and cleaning a leak from an upstairs window that dripped after every single rainfall no matter how many times you fixed it, Bea went to collect Rose from school. She chatted incessantly all the way home. They'd been learning about Queen Victoria and Rose wanted to know if she'd visited Ketton Hall.

'I don't think so,' Bea said honestly, 'but your dad said that Elizabeth the First might have visited. Of course, every big house owner in the country claims that she visited them.'

'We're not learning about *her*,' Rose stated, obviously not interested in anything outside her curriculum. Bea grinned at her single-mindedness.

Later that evening, having had dinner and watched an episode of Rose's favourite children's drama before reading her a bedtime story and tucking her in, Bea returned to the kitchen. She stood for a moment looking at the bottles of mulled wine she'd bought in preparation for Christmas and, before she could talk herself out of it, she opened one and heated enough for a large glass in a saucepan on the Aga, throwing in a cinnamon stick for good measure. The smell was wonderful and the warmth of it on her hands when she'd filled a glass a few minutes later felt lovely and so comforting.

She took her drink through to the dining room, turning on the lights. It was a spacious room with a large mullioned window which looked out over the grounds towards the lake. Of course, it was dark now and she drew the heavy brocade curtains against the winter night as she sipped her drink, feeling the warmth of the wine spreading through her body.

Like the room she did her flowers in, the dining room was wood panelled. It had a large oak table at its centre, surrounded by chairs which were rarely used these days. Bea liked to use it on special occasions, though, setting the table with floral displays down its centre, and she was hoping they'd use it this Christmas.

But the reason she'd come into the room now was because it was full of old portraits of her husband's ancestors. She looked at them, pale-faced and staring down from their huge gilded frames. It had occurred to Bea to look at the portraits in the hope of spotting the ring she'd found. She still hadn't been able to remove it and she examined it as she took another sip of her wine. It was a beautiful thing. She sipped her drink, her gaze dissolving into the gold and ruby of the ring and, all of a sudden, she felt a huge wave of emotion engulfing her. Perhaps it had been making the wreath earlier that day and remembering the one she'd made for George's funeral or perhaps it was the mulled wine.

Or perhaps it was just time to cry.

Whatever it was, the tears came, blurring her vision and rocking her world. It always amazed her that memory could be jolted so swiftly and suddenly and, once again, just as you thought you were making progress, you were plunged into the depths of grief. But she'd learned that there was no way of hiding from it. You had to give in to it and so she did, putting her glass down on the sideboard and sinking to the floor of the dining room, rocking backwards and forwards in helpless agony.

She wasn't sure how long she was there for but, when it was over, she felt the strange weight of peace. Her eyes were sore, her ribs were sore, but her heart felt a little lighter. Just a little. Thinking of George, she looked up from her home on the floor, her eyes finding the portrait of one of his ancestors, her vision soft on the seventeenth century face. She touched the ruby and gold ring on her index finger.

'I miss you so much,' she whispered into the room. 'George. Can you hear me?' She took a deep breath. 'I wish you'd come back. I wish you'd come back.' She closed her eyes for a moment. Then she stood up, feeling a little dizzy. Cold too. Yes, it suddenly felt very cold, as if the winter weather had crept into the house and taken up residence.

And that's when she saw him.

A man. In her home. *Next* to her.

Bea stumbled backwards, her hand reaching out to grab the nearby oak sideboard in order to steady herself.

'Who the hell are you?' she cried.

'Who are *you*?' he asked, looking confused.

'What are you doing in my house? How did you get in?'

'I'm attempting to work that out,' the stranger told her, glancing around. 'But I believe you called me here.'

'What?'

'My name. You called my name.'

'I did no such thing.'

'You did. I heard you.'

'What are you talking about? I called for my husband. Not that it's any of your business because I want you to leave – *right now* – before I call the police.'

He shook his head and she noticed that he had dark red-gold hair that was long and tousled, curling at the collar of a white lacy shirt. His skin was pale, his cheekbones high, and he had piercing blue eyes that were fixed firmly on her. It was then that Bea noticed there was something very odd about this man. He didn't seem completely *solid*. She squinted at him. Was it her imagination or could she see the wood panelling behind him? *Through* him?

'What's happening to me?' she said, feeling quite faint. 'Oh, god! I'm seeing things that aren't there. I'm going mad, aren't I?'

'Quiet a moment, I beg you,' the man said, raising a hand. 'I'm still trying to ascertain... What precisely did you say?'

'What do you mean?' she asked, cursing to herself for conversing with someone who clearly wasn't there.

'You said you called for your husband?'

She nodded. 'I called his name.'

'And what is his name?'

'George.'

The man sighed. 'As is mine.'

Bea glared at him. 'What are you saying? I don't understand.'

'You're wearing my ring!' He pointed to the gold and ruby ring.

'This is yours?'

'Yes. I lost it. Some time before I left Ketton for the war.'

'The war?' Bea felt as if her head was swimming. Nothing was making any sense.

'You're wearing my ring and you called my name while next to my portrait. Look here!'

She glanced up at the painting of the seventeenth century gentleman she'd been looking at just minutes ago.

'That's you?' She looked from the portrait to him and back again. There was a striking resemblance, she had to admit.

'I never did like it, but Madeleine insisted we had portraits done. It is a Ketton tradition, is it not?'

'This conversation isn't real,' Bea told herself calmly, looking away from the stranger who said he was from the seventeenth century. Maybe her mulled wine was stronger than she'd thought. She'd created a strange narrative from having drunk too much and staring too long at the Beaumont portraits.

'But you called me here,' he went on. 'So this *is* happening.'

'No. *No*,' she insisted. 'I'm tired. That's all. I need to sleep.' She turned to look at him once more. He was still there, pale and hauntingly real. 'No. You're not there. You're *not!* I'm... I'm... not well.' Her hands flew to her face. Maybe she was coming down with a fever or something. 'I'm going to bed,' she told the man who wasn't there. 'And you're leaving. I mean, you're not actually going because you're not really there.' She grimaced. She wasn't making any sense even to herself. 'I'm going to bed. Yes.'

'Goodnight,' he said as she walked towards the door.

'Goodnight, George,' she replied.

CHAPTER FOUR

Bea woke up the next morning and, for a few moments, stared at the four poster bed that surrounded her. It still felt strange and luxurious to sleep and wake in such a grand bed, its wooden posts so ornate with their carvings, its headboard behind her and its canopy above her wonderfully comforting, giving her the feeling of being sheltered from the world, protected if only from a few of the draughts that found their way into the old bedroom.

And then she remembered the space beside her. Empty. Cold. She closed her eyes. Some mornings, it was so hard to get up and face another day without George. It didn't seem right somehow, to have so much life inside her and yet for him to be gone. For those first few painful days and weeks after he'd been killed, everything had been an immense chore and had seemed so wrong. Eating breakfast had seemed wrong, taking Rose to school and getting to see how cute she looked each and every day seemed like a kind of betrayal, and living at Ketton, inhabiting his ancestral home felt somehow improper. But, slowly, and with an immense amount of help from her mother and sister, Bea had come back into herself, finding a manageable routine for her and Rose. Of course, there were still days when everything seemed debilitating. Take last night, she thought. Since losing George, Bea had made friends with quite a few floors in Ketton Hall, collapsing onto them during her bouts of grief.

She swung her legs out of bed, her feet quickly finding her slippers and her hands reaching for the thick jumper that lived at the end of the bed. She pulled it over her nightdress, preparing for the journey to the bathroom where the radiator wasn't working. She'd have to add that to the endless list of things that needed attention at Ketton.

Putting all thoughts of the night before out of her mind, Bea got on with the business of the morning, washing and dressing, getting Rose ready for school, dropping her off, cleaning the kitchen and then venturing out in to the garden, breathing in the frosty air, and taking some lengths of ivy from an old garden wall. By harvesting the ivy, she was not only helping the wall to breathe a little but also obtaining free foliage for her work.

It was as she entered the hall with her bounty that she dared to stop outside the dining room. She'd been doing her best to forget the night before and all the silliness with the ghostly figment from her imagination. Ghost George, indeed! She blamed the mulled wine. She wasn't used to drinking and she'd had a sizeable glass. She'd also been in an emotional state. But to have conjured up a ghost – well, that was ridiculous! If her mother ever found out, she'd swoop in and have her packed up and moved out before you could say *Blithe Spirit*. Valerie Maynard had long worried about her daughter's mental state, living in the big old house on her own with just a small child for company. No, Bea had to stop this nonsense or risk losing her independence.

Leaving the ivy in the hallway, she slowly entered the dining room. She couldn't help feeling anxious, but silently chastised herself for her fear. It was just a room like any other and she took a deep breath as she crossed it to draw back the curtains, letting the morning light flood in.

The empty mulled wine glass was still there on the oak

sideboard, mocking her gently and she shook her head. She must remember to warn her mother and sister about the potency of the alcohol.

She crossed the room towards the portraits and looked at the one of the seventeenth century gentleman. He was certainly handsome with his red-gold hair, neat little beard, and blue eyes. She looked at the name underneath the painting. George Beaumont. Well, that wasn't really surprising, was it? There'd been a lot of Georges across the generations.

It was then that she noticed the ring that seventeenth century George was wearing in the portrait. Gold and ruby. She gasped. It was the one she was wearing now. Had she noticed it last night? She couldn't remember. She touched the ring lightly, staring into its deep red depths.

'I've found your ring, George,' she told the portrait.

'Yes. We established that last night,' said a voice behind her.

Bea screamed, turning around and coming face to face with the George Beaumont from the painting. And there was no disputing his presence this time. He was standing right in front of her in full daylight and she certainly hadn't had mulled wine for breakfast so she couldn't blame that.

'You're real?' she managed to say through ragged breaths.

'I think so.'

'No, no, no! Ghosts aren't real. They just aren't?'

'Oh, now you are just insulting me,' he said with a little smile.

'But that's what you are, isn't it? A ghost? I mean – look at you! You're not... you're not quite *there*. I can see the door behind you. *Through* you!' Bea clutched her head dramatically, watching as Ghost George patted himself.

'Yes. I see what you mean. There is something not quite right here.' He let out a laugh as his hand went right through his own body. 'How amusing!'

Bea was still in denial. Perhaps there was something about the room that wasn't right. A trick of the light or something. That could be it. And so she made for the door. George stepped aside to let her by.

'Are you leaving again?' he called after her, but she didn't answer him. Instead, she stood in the hallway for a moment and took a few deep, stilling breaths. She was still tired, perhaps, still emotional. She had to give herself some slack. Her imagination was in overdrive, maybe as a result of grief, she wasn't sure. But there was some rational explanation for what she'd seen in the dining room. That she was certain of.

Shaking her head in an attempt to dislodge anything even vaguely ghostly from her mind, she walked back in to the dining room.

And there he was.

'You're still here!' she said, swallowing hard, her disappointment evident in her voice.

'I am.'

'This can't be happening!'

'Why not?'

'Because – because I'm a rational human being, that's why!'

'Well, that may be so, but here I am,' he said calmly.

Bea took a deep breath. She could handle this... this... whatever *this* was.

'Okay,' she said, determined to remain calm. 'If you're *really* here – and I'm not at all convinced that you are – have you been here all night? Or did you go somewhere else? How does this work?'

He sighed. 'I really cannot say.'

'What do you mean?'

'I mean, I am still trying to work all this out myself.'

'But you're George Beaumont from the seventeenth century? Is that what you're telling me?'

'That is correct.' He gave a little bow as if apologising to her.

'And last night – that all really happened?'

'We met last night for the first time, if that is what you are asking.'

'And what you said – about me bringing you here – that's true too?'

'Yes.'

Bea was feeling distinctly odd, as if she was about to faint. She pulled out a chair from the dining table and sat down.

'Tell me again. How did I bring you here?'

George walked a little closer to her and she felt a sudden chill at his nearness. 'You made a wish, under my portrait, while wearing my ring.'

'And that's what brought you back?' Bea asked. 'Even though I was thinking of my husband?'

'I am sorry. It seems that I have upset you. But I had very little say in the matter.'

She looked up into his face. It was a kind face and Bea suddenly felt bad because, ghost or not, he appeared to have feelings and she'd done a pretty good job of trampling all over them so far.

'I haven't made you very welcome, have I?' she suddenly said. 'And I suppose this is your home after all.'

'Indeed, it is. Or rather, it was.'

'Even if you've not been here for a few hundred years.' Bea frowned. 'This is very strange for me. You see, I don't actually believe in ghosts, but I can clearly see you're here. Have you always been here? Hiding in the shadows? Watching everybody?'

'No.'

'Then where have you been all this time?'

George looked thoughtful for a moment. 'I am not altogether sure.'

'What's the last thing you remember?'

George focused his attention on the floor and Bea wondered what was going through his mind.

'I... I cannot recall.'

Bea noticed how pale he looked. But maybe that was just a ghost thing.

'And can you get back to wherever you came from or are you stuck here with me forever now?'

He gave a little smile. 'You are asking questions I cannot answer. I am sorry. But perhaps you can answer some of my questions?'

'Oh!' Bea was surprised. 'I suppose that would be okay. What do you want to know?'

'Well, your name would be a good start.'

She smiled. 'It's Beatrice. But most people call me Bea.'

'Bea. That's pretty.'

'And there's my daughter, Rose. Have you seen her?'

'No.' He frowned. 'I think it best that we keep my being here just between the two of us. You understand?'

She nodded. 'Yes. Perhaps that's best. She's only four.'

'And you say you lost your husband?'

Bea swallowed hard. It was still so difficult to talk about it. 'Nearly a year ago now.'

'I am sorry to hear that.'

'Thank you.'

'I believe I died before my wife too.'

'You're not sure?'

'Everything feels a little... foggy at the moment. But I remember my wife. Madeleine.'

'Oh, she's the one in the portrait here, isn't she?' Bea stood up and walked towards the paintings again, singling out the woman in the frame next to George's own portrait. 'She was beautiful!'

'Oh, yes!'

Bea gazed up at George's wife. She had a pretty round face with a high forehead and sparkling, intelligent eyes. Bea loved her soft dark ringlets and could see that pearls gleamed in her ears and shone around her neck. Her dress was a vivid yellow with lace around her décolletage and at her elbows. She was the picture of aristocratic beauty and elegance.

'She looks like a queen,' Bea observed.

'Ah, that was the fashion of the day,' George explained. 'Every royalist woman looked like Henrietta Maria, and every man like Charles, the king.'

Bea glanced back at George, noticing his lace collar and the length of his hair. He certainly did have something very stately about him.

'And what year are we in now?' he asked.

Bea told him.

His blue eyes widened. 'I had no idea. I mean, I had this vague notion that time had moved on, but nearly four hundred years has passed since I was here.'

'What does it feel like to be dead for that long?' Bea dared to ask. 'Have you ever come back like this before?'

'No,' he told her. 'All I know is that you brought me back and here I am.'

Bea took a moment to take this in. 'This is all so strange.'

'For me too.'

'Yes.' She gave a nervous laugh. 'A ghost. A real live ghost! Well, not *live*, as such. I'm not really sure how to describe you and I'm not altogether sure what to do with you.'

'Do?'

'Yes. I mean, if you're stuck here now, what do we do? How do we live together? Are you here forever? Do I need to feed you or give you a bed? What happens now?'

He shook his head gently. 'I do not need anything from you. I think I am just *here*.'

Bea narrowed her eyes. 'Just kind of floating around from room to room? I'm sorry, George, but I find that a bit creepy. I don't want you suddenly appearing in my bedroom!'

'Of course,' he said. 'I shall stay here then. Downstairs. Would that suit you?'

Bea sighed. 'A downstairs ghost,' she said. 'I suppose I can live with that. I mean, other than being dead and transparent, you seem quite normal.'

He gave a little smile. 'I shall take that as a compliment.'

It was then that the doorbell rang.

'Oh, heavens!' Bea said.

'Do not worry,' George said quickly. 'I will make sure nobody else sees me.'

Bea nodded and left the dining room to answer the door.

'Meter reader,' the man said, flashing his badge.

Bea let him in, leading the way to the kitchen where the meter was. It didn't take long and, as she led him out, they passed the dining room and he paused, glancing inside. Bea's heart almost stopped.

'Impressive place you've got here,' he said.

Bea laughed nervously. 'Yes.'

He looked around the hallway. 'Bit spooky, though. Got any ghosts?'

'What?' Bea cried.

'You know – these old houses often have a ghost or two rattling around, don't they? Seen anything like that, have you?'

Bea shook her head. 'Nothing but mice and spiders, I'm afraid.'

The man shook theatrically. 'Think I'd prefer a ghost to any creatures!'

And he left.

Bea let out a huge sigh and quickly returned to the dining room. 'George?' she called. 'It's safe to come out.'

But he wasn't there. She stood for a moment in the wood-panelled room. 'George?' She looked around, her eyes finally focusing on his portrait. 'Are you there?' She pursed her lips. She obviously still didn't understand the rules of having a resident ghost. 'Okay, George,' she said after a moment. 'I'll see you later.'

She left the room, feeling a little bereft. The thought amused her. Was she, perhaps, getting used to having a friendly ghost around?

CHAPTER FIVE

It was funny how very quickly life could change. One minute, Bea had been going through her daily routine in a kind of trance, trying to find the little moments of joy among the overwhelming sadness of her recent loss. And then George had come along. *Ghost* George, that was. He'd only been there for a few days, but he already felt like a major part of life at Ketton Hall. He wasn't there all the time, though. He had periods of rest. That's how he referred to the times when he wasn't around. He couldn't explain them, but he simply vanished, going back to wherever it was he had come from. And it was just as well really, Bea thought. It would be a bit much having a full-time ghost in the place.

But she really enjoyed his company. She hadn't realised just how lonely she'd felt since losing her husband. She had Rose, of course, and she saw her mother and sister regularly, but the long days alone at Ketton Hall had definitely taken their toll. Even Mrs Briggs, the cleaner who helped out two mornings a week, noticed the change in her.

'I can't put my finger on it,' she'd said after dusting her way around the living room, 'but you seem lighter. Yes, that's it. *Lighter*.'

'Do I really?'

Mrs Briggs nodded. 'And you know me – nothing *ever* escapes my attention,' she said, bending down to pick up a fluffy hard boiled sweet from the side of a cushion.

'Rose, I imagine?'

'I imagine.' Bea felt herself blushing; it was one of her chocolate limes.

But Mrs Briggs was right. Bea was feeling lighter and it was a good feeling. Was the heaviness of grief finally leaving her? Was that why Ghost George had been sent to her rather than her own George? Was it his job to bring a little joy into her life? If *her* George had returned, there would be the knowledge that he was in quite another dimension now and that, sooner or later, he could well return to that place.

Still, the thought of seeing her husband again wouldn't leave her and, one morning, having dropped Rose at school, she was tidying her floral arrangements away after filming a quick piece for social media when a thought occurred to her.

'George?' she asked as she ventured into the dining room. He seemed to favour that room. Maybe he liked being close to his wife's portrait. 'Are you there?' Bea called.

A coldness filled the room and Bea shivered as George appeared in the doorway.

'Good morning,' he said.

'Hello, George. How are you?'

'Very well. Still dead, of course, but I feel in good spirits.' He laughed. 'Good spirits!'

Bea laughed along with him. She liked his levity. It would be pretty awful to be stuck with a ghost who had no sense of humour.

'I've been thinking,' she began.

'About what, may I ask?'

'About how I managed to bring you back,' she confessed.

'It is nothing short of a miracle, I would say.'

'Yes, I know. But it's made me think. If I was able to bring you back, then surely I could bring *my* George back.'

'Your husband?'

'Why not?'

George looked a little anxious. 'Are you sure that is what you want?'

'What do you mean? Why wouldn't I want to see my husband again?'

A pained expression crossed George's face and he looked even paler than normal. 'Because he would not be your husband as such, Beatrice,' he told her gently. 'He would be – well – like me. Look, I'm barely here at all.' He did his old trick of putting his hands right through his own body.

'Ah, yes!' Bea said with a light laugh. 'I see what you mean. I hadn't thought about it quite like that.'

'I think you probably should.'

She nodded. 'But I'm so desperate to see him again. I mean, if I can. If that's an option. Even if it's not *all* of him.' She paused, aware that her heart was thudding anxiously. 'Do you think it's possible?'

'I think you could probably give it a try,' George said. 'If it is what you really want, and if you can remember what you did and what you said to bring me here.'

'Right. Yes. Of course.' Bea bit her lip, suddenly feeling unsure about it all. What if she did manage to conjure her husband back? Would he be pleased? And how would she feel, truly? It might possibly be a horrible mistake and yet...

'I want to do it!' she told George.

He gave a little nod. 'And you have thought about this for some time?'

'Yes.'

'Because it will not just affect you. You must think of those around you too.'

'You mean Rose?'

'Indeed. What if you let slip, perchance, that you have seen your husband?'

'I won't!'

'You may not be in control of your emotions.'

'But I've not told anyone about you, have I?'

'Yes, but I am not your husband,' George told her. 'You are not – how can I put this? You are not so excited about me being here.'

'Oh, George! I love having you here!'

'You do?'

'Yes! You've brought something really special back to Ketton.'

'And what is that, may I ask?'

'Joy.'

He smiled. She liked his smile. It was, in fact, just a little bit like her own George's had been with the right side of his mouth rising just a little higher than the left. Was that a Beaumont trait, she wondered? Or maybe it was especially particular to Georges. Whatever it was, she found it rather wonderful that a smile could travel down the centuries.

'And you feel that bringing your husband back would add to that joy?' George asked her.

Bea felt the sudden sting of tears as she tried to imagine her very own George back again. Even if she couldn't touch him, even if he lowered the temperature in the room with his ghostly presence, she wanted to see him. *Needed* to see him.

'Yes.'

'Then I will do all I can to assist.'

Bea took a deep breath. 'When do we begin?'

'When does your daughter return?'

'I have to leave to pick her up by three.'

'Then we have time now?'

'Yes.'

'And if this works – if you are able to bring your husband back – can you then continue with your day?' George asked. 'Will you be able to handle your emotions when you see Rose or, well, anybody?'

Bea nodded, but the truth was, she wasn't sure how she was going to respond. How could she possibly know until her George was standing there before her, semi-transparent or not?

'I'll be able to handle things,' she told Ghost George now.

'Then let us proceed.'

Bea was filled with sudden excitement along with the nerves she was feeling. This was really happening.

'Okay. What's first? What did I do to bring you back?'

'You were wearing my ring, were you not?'

'Yes.' Her fingers touched the ring now. She still hadn't been able to remove it, but it was fast becoming a part of her because she really liked wearing it. 'He had a wedding ring.'

'And where is that?'

'I'll get it.' Bea quickly ran upstairs, going into the bedroom she'd once shared with her husband. There was an old mahogany chest of drawers on which Bea kept her jewellery box and she opened it now. And there it was. The simple platinum band he'd always worn. He hadn't ever been a fan of yellow gold and so their wedding rings hadn't matched, but that hadn't mattered. What had mattered was that he'd worn it with pride and it had pained Bea when the undertaker had handed the ring back to her. Taking it out of the jewellery box now, Bea slipped it on. It was a little large, but she hoped it would still work its magic.

'Here!' she said, returning downstairs to show the ring to George who was still in the dining room.

'Very nice.'

'What else?'

'His portrait will be necessary,' George informed her.

'But we didn't have a portrait done.'

'No portrait?'

'We talked about it once, but we never had the money to spend on something so luxurious. I have lots of photos – you know – pictures? Do you think one of those will work?'

'I cannot say. But it is worth trying, is it not?'

Bea nodded and went in search of a photo. It didn't take long to find one of her favourites. It was in a glossy wooden frame on a table in the sitting room and it showed George out on the estate, his cheeks rosy and that irrepressible smile on his face. She loved the photo. It was so very George: outside, in his natural element.

She picked up the frame and took it through to the dining room to show Ghost George. But he didn't look impressed.

'It doesn't have the same... gravitas as a portrait, does it?'

'I know. But I love this one of him.'

'Well, he is very handsome. I can see why you became a Beaumont.'

Bea smiled at him. 'And is that it, do you think? The ring and the photo?'

'You will need the right words.'

'Yes, of course,' she said, placing the photo of her husband on the sideboard and nervously twisting his wedding ring. 'The words.' She took a deep breath. 'What did I say. I missed him? Yes. I said that, didn't I? I must have said that. And I wished he'd come back. I think that was it.'

George nodded encouragingly as she looked at him.

'Is that right? Do you remember?'

'I am afraid I was too busy concentrating on what was happening to me to remember much else.'

'Oh, right! Of course.' Bea must remember that this wasn't all about her. 'Let's begin then, shall we?'

George took a step back, giving her a little more room and privacy and Bea took another deep breath and began.

'George?' she whispered into the room. 'Can you hear me?' She touched the cool metal of his wedding ring as she spoke and gazed at his face in the photo. 'I miss you so much. I wish you'd come home.'

She waited. She could feel the thud-thud of her heart, but the only chill in the room was coming from Ghost George and the draught from the mullioned window.

'George?' she tried again. 'Will you come back to me?'

Again, she waited, aware of the gentle tick tock of the longcase clock in the hallway. But that was the only sound. There was no familiar voice greeting her from the other world. And there was no smile of greeting from the one she missed so much.

'It's not working!' she cried. '*Why* isn't it working?' She felt hot tears stinging her eyes. 'Why did it work for you and not *my* George? I don't want *you!* I want my husband!'

She felt a cold sensation on her right shoulder and realised that Ghost George had reached out to her in a gesture of comfort.

'Forgive me, Beatrice,' he said gently.

Bea began to cry, her tears full of frustration, fear and shame.

'I'm sorry. I didn't mean...' she began, but her sobs swallowed up her words.

'I understand.'

She mopped her eyes with the cuff of her cardigan. 'I like having you here. But I so want *my* George.'

'Perhaps...' George began, but then stopped.

'What?'

'Perhaps he hasn't been gone long enough.'

Bea frowned. 'Do you think that's the reason I can't reach him?'

'Well, I cannot say for sure. As I said before, I do not have all the answers you seek. I am sorry, Beatrice. Truly.'

She picked up the photo frame, gazing into her husband's handsome face. 'We could try again another time, couldn't we?'

George pursed his lips. 'Perhaps.'

'You don't think we should, do you?'

He took a moment to reply. 'I think it may be better not to.'

Bea sniffed back her emotion. It wasn't the answer she wanted to hear and yet something inside her told her that, maybe, it was for the best. How exactly would she handle the ghost of her husband returning? Would she be able to live her life and concentrate on her work and bringing up Rose while the spirit of her husband was roaming the rooms of Ketton? And what would happen if he disappeared? Could she bear another parting from him?

'Perhaps you're right,' she told her friendly ghost.

'I am sorry, Beatrice. I would to God there was something I could do.'

'Maybe – if you see him – you know, on the other side, you could tell him how much I miss him and, if he ever did want to come back...' Her voice dissolved into tears.

'Oh, Beatrice!'

George approached her and she felt a coolness on her left hand which was gripping the oak sideboard. When she glanced down at it, she saw that George had placed his hand on hers.

CHAPTER SIX

Something had awoken Bea in the middle of the night. There was a change in the atmosphere – she could feel it, sense it.

'George?' she whispered into the darkness of her bedroom. He'd agreed that he'd be a downstairs ghost, but maybe he'd sneaked upstairs. Or maybe it wasn't George at all. Maybe it was another ghost. Was that a possibility? And what if another ghost wasn't as affable as George? What if he meant to do her harm?

Panicking, Bea quickly turned on her bedside lamp, flooding the bedroom with comforting amber light. There was nobody there. Thank goodness. She sighed in relief. Maybe she'd imagined or even dreamed the whole thing.

She was just about to turn the lamp off when she heard a creak from outside her bedroom. The old house regularly creaked and groaned, but what she could hear now sounded distinctly like footsteps. Slow and regular. And George didn't make a sound when he walked.

She got out of bed, quickly grabbing her jumper to put on over her nightdress and thrusting her feet into her slippers. There was a wrought iron candlestick on a little table in the bedroom. It wasn't ever lit; it was purely ornamental, but Bea grabbed it now.

Just in case, just in case, she chanted to herself, and then she quietly crossed the wooden floorboards to the bedroom door. She always kept it ajar so she could hear Rose in the room next door if she awoke. She'd suffered from nightmares after her father had died and Bea had done her best to comfort her. But Rose didn't go creeping around the house in the middle of the night.

Taking a deep breath, Bea walked out onto the landing and that's when she saw him, half-lit by moonlight through the large mullioned window.

'Simeon?' she cried.

'Beatrice?'

'Of course, it's Beatrice! What on earth are you doing? You scared me half to death!'

'I've come to see you,' he said. The eerie light of the moon made his features sharp and burnished his sandy-coloured hair which flopped over his face. His hair had always annoyed Beatrice. It seemed affected and he was forever pushing it out of his eyes or twitching his head so he could see properly.

'Well, couldn't you have arrived at a more decent hour? I might have killed you with this candlestick!' she said as she moved closer to him.

Simeon gave a bark of laughter. 'It was Bea on the landing with a candlestick!'

'Very funny!' Bea said, shushing him. 'You'll wake Rose.' She bent to put the candlestick on the floor and hugged her arms around her body, aware of how bone-chillingly cold it was to be up in the middle of the night in an Elizabethan manor. 'How did you get in?' she suddenly thought to ask.

'Through the kitchen. George gave me a key.' Simeon said this as if it was the most natural thing in the world, but it didn't seem very plausible to Bea. A more likely scenario would be that Simeon had stayed at some point and taken a cutting of the key for himself. 'I was just making my way to the guest room.'

'Don't wake Rose, okay.'

'I'm trying not to wake anyone.'

Beatrice noticed that he was carrying a canvas bag. It looked a bit large for just the one night and she panicked. How long was he planning on staying? Surely he hadn't come for the Christmas holidays? The thought panicked Bea, but she didn't say anything. She wanted to get back to bed as quickly as possible.

'Can I get you anything?' she asked politely, not neglecting her role as host however unexpectedly it had been pressed upon her.

'I know where everything is,' he replied in a whisper.

Bea nodded. Yes, he certainly had that air of ownership about him. And that's when a thought occurred to her. Why was Simeon here? George had never disguised his dislike of his cousin and had never encouraged him to visit.

'He snaps at my heels,' George had once told Bea. 'He's always hated the fact that I own Ketton and he's just the lowly next in line.'

Of course, that was said before they'd had their daughter Rose so now she was the next in line to inherit Ketton when she came of age. Bea just hoped that Simeon understood that and wasn't here to make trouble.

Bea picked up the candlestick and the two of them walked along the landing, passing Rose's room.

'I'll see you in the morning,' she told Simeon and he nodded.

'Good night.'

He disappeared into the guest room opposite her own. There were plenty of rooms at Ketton, but this was one of the more pleasant, least damp ones with a view over the gardens at the back of the hall.

Bea returned to her room, replacing the candlestick and leaping back under the covers of her bed. She tried to think kindly of her husband's cousin. Maybe he was here for Christmas. After all, Ketton was part of his family's history and there was plenty of room, wasn't there? She sighed, pulling her blankets up around her and snuggling deeper into the warmth of the bedding. Christmas was a time for giving and sharing, wasn't it? And sharing a little of Ketton with Simeon was the least she could do.

~

The next morning, Bea found herself tiptoeing round the house so as not to disturb the sleeping Simeon. Rose was less anxious, trotting along the landing, pretending to be a horse. But nothing seemed to wake him and they left the house for school, Bea scribbling a quick note beforehand which she left on the kitchen table telling him to help himself to breakfast.

When she got back from the school run, there was still no sign of Simeon and so Bea got on with her day, setting up for a live video demonstration in the dining room.

'George?' she whispered as she dusted the table, ready to make her display.

'Beatrice! Good morning.'

Bea smiled as George appeared under his portrait, his form gently materialising out of thin air.

'Something rather unexpected has happened so you might need to keep a low profile,' she warned him.

'Oh?'

'Cousin Simeon arrived in the middle of the night.'

George's eyebrows rose a fraction. 'And I take it from your expression that he is not altogether welcome?'

Bea raked a hand through her hair. 'I don't mean to sound... unkind, but don't you think it odd to just turn up in the dark and break into someone's home?'

'He broke in?'

'Well, he had a key, but I find that equally unnerving because I don't think my husband would have given him one.'

'I see,' George said. 'And where is this cousin Simeon now?'

'In bed. I think he's here for Christmas, but I'm not sure.'

'You look worried.'

'I am. I can't help thinking...' she stopped, experiencing that uncomfortable fluttery feeling in her stomach again.

'What? Tell me,' George said gently.

'I can't help thinking that he's not here to pay a social call.'

'Beatrice?' Simeon's voice called from the hallway.

Bea glanced at George.

'Do not worry,' George told her. 'I will make myself scarce.'

Bea watched as the figure of her friend slowly dissolved into nothing just as Simeon's head popped round the door.

'Simeon!'

'Not disturbing you, am I?' he asked, his hair flopping over his face.

'No, of course not,' Bea said, glancing into the recently vacated corner of the room just to make sure George was no longer visible. 'Have you had breakfast?'

'Just grabbed a coffee.'

'Well, we can do better than that, I'm sure,' Bea said, leading the way out into the hallway and through to the kitchen.

It turned out that Simeon had quite the appetite and ate absolutely everything Bea could find from buttered toast and marmalade to scrambled egg, fried bacon and a croissant spread thickly with peanut butter. She watched as he scraped the jar clean of its contents, knowing she'd have to explain to Rose that there wasn't any left for her tea.

It was as she was making him his second cup of coffee that he cleared his throat.

'So,' he began. 'You may have heard that I've been away. Africa.' He said this with the haughty tone of someone who wants to sound important. Bea didn't rise to the bait, but waited for him to continue. Sure enough, he did. 'I rather thought things would have been sorted out some time ago. While I was away.'

Bea put his coffee down in front of him. 'What things, Simeon?'

His eyes narrowed and he twitched his head to the side so that his hair flopped out of the way.

'My dear lady,' he said in the kind of condescending tone that instantly had Bea's skin itching in discomfort, 'we're talking about Ketton.'

'What do you mean?'

'My inheritance.'

Bea swallowed hard. So her instinct last night had been right. Simeon wasn't here to celebrate Christmas or to check up on her and Rose. He had no interest in how they were coping. He'd come to George's funeral and she remembered him standing next to her to greet the guests in that important way he had, taking over any room or event he possibly could. Actually, Bea had been glad of his presence; it had taken some of the pressure off her on that dreadful day. But she also remembered the hug he'd given her when his hand had taken in a little more of her body than a sympathetic relative should have.

No, he wasn't there to spend the holidays with them, to play happy families or to ask about their welfare. As always, he was only interested in himself.

'We didn't have much of a chance to talk at the funeral, did we?' he continued, sipping his coffee. 'Not the right time either for this sort of thing, though, I suppose. Anyway, I've given you ample time now, I think.'

Bea pulled out a chair opposite him, feeling that she needed to sit down for what was obviously a confrontation.

'Ample time for what?' she asked.

'I was expecting to hear something from the family solicitor. I would have got in touch myself only one doesn't like to bother these people for fear of being landed with a massive bill.'

Bea gritted her teeth. It was typical of Simeon to express such a fear.

'And what did you think they might have to tell you?'

'When I inherit, of course,' he said, giving a light laugh that sounded horribly hollow and threatening to Bea.

'You think you're inheriting Ketton Hall?'

'Well, of course I do. That's the way it goes, isn't it? I'm the closest male relative to George.'

Bea shook her head.

'Male-preference primogeniture, my dear Beatrice,' he said as if explaining to a child. 'You *must* be aware of it.'

'Yes, of course I am. Only you're horribly outdated, I'm afraid.' Bea did her best to keep her tone friendly and light although she was seething inside. 'In case it slipped your attention, George left a child to inherit – Rose – and his will clearly leaves the Ketton estate to her.'

'But she's a girl!'

'Simeon, even the royal family doesn't subscribe to the whole male inheritance thing anymore!'

'But the family name. If Rose inherits and marries, the name will be lost forever.' He was shouting now.

'I imagine, if Rose ever marries, then she'll keep her name and pass it on to her children. The name won't be in any danger,' Bea assured him. 'Of course, she might link it with her husband's or take his name. Who can tell? You and I might not be around to dictate things and it wouldn't be our place if we were.'

'This is ridiculous!' Simeon said, quite pink in the face.

'I'm afraid it's you who's being ridiculous.'

'What? By believing in tradition?'

'Your notion of tradition is outdated, old-fashioned and – well – just plain greedy! This house is not yours.'

'Yes, well, we'll see about that!' Simeon stood up from the table, scraping the wooden chair loudly on the flagstone floor.

'The will is legal and binding,' Bea warned him. 'It was George's express wish that Rose inherits. You'll be wasting your time and money contesting anything.'

'Well, my lawyer might think differently. He'll have something to say to you about all this, I'm sure.'

He left the room.

Bea got up from the table and began to clear Simeon's breakfast things away. Her heart was racing. She felt angry and nervous and hated that he'd made her feel so uncomfortable in her own home even though he'd only been there for a few short hours.

As she left the kitchen and walked into the hall, she saw Simeon at the top of the stairs. He was holding his bag. Bea felt a surge of relief. He was leaving. She watched as he charged down the stairs and headed straight into the dining room and, for one awful moment, Bea felt sure he was about to start removing paintings or grabbing a chair or two.

'Ketton's collection stays here,' Bea warned him as she entered the room after him.

'Don't worry! I don't want your mouldy old portraits,' he said with a sneer. 'But know this. I have more right in my little finger to be standing here, *living* here, than you do or *ever* will. You can't even take care of this place properly. There's damp and decay everywhere. It's a disgrace!'

Bea felt her whole body turn cold at his words even though she knew they were cruel exaggerations.

'Please leave,' she said, her voice managing to remain calm.

'I'm going.' He tossed his annoying hair out of his annoying face. 'But this isn't the last you'll hear from me.'

Simeon left the room, knocking into her shoulder as he did so.

Bea closed her eyes for a moment and took some deep breaths, waiting for the sound of the front door opening and closing. She moved to the window and watched as Simeon's car sped away.

'Did he call my portrait mouldy?' George asked behind her.

'Oh, George!' Bea leaped with surprise as her friendly ghost reappeared.

'Sorry! I could not help overhearing some of that. He does shout rather, does he not?'

'Yes he does. And he didn't exactly call your portrait mouldy. It was more of a generalisation which included all the portraits.'

'That is even worse!'

'He's an idiot and you should never pay attention to idiots.'

George moved to look out of the window. 'So, he has gone?'

'Yes. For now. And I'm hoping for good. But I feel so bad that he just won't accept the situation. He's my husband's nearest relation, you know?'

'Well, I hope you do not mind an observation, but he had all the manners of a Roundhead.'

Bea grinned. 'Perhaps you could be on hand to give him a ghostly fright if he dares to turn up again.'

'It would be my pleasure,' George told her.

Bea sighed. 'You know he's threatening legal action. He believes he's the rightful heir of Ketton.'

'But he is not?'

'No, Rose inherits. I know that might seem a little odd to you. Wasn't it always the eldest male heir that inherited in your time?'

'It was indeed. But I understand that times change and, if it were up to me, I would most certainly vote for your daughter over that nasty cousin. "Mouldy old portraits" indeed!'

Bea smiled, but she still couldn't banish her fear.

'Oh, George! What if he's right? What if I can't take care of this place on my own?'

'You are doubting that you can?'

'No. Well, maybe a little. It's such a huge job, isn't it? It can seem overwhelming sometimes. It was different when my George was here. We were a team. We could face all the challenges together. But now it's just me and costs are rising all the time and there's an endless list of things that need doing and no money to do it with. The last thing I want to do is to let George down and hand our daughter a house that's practically falling apart.'

'It must be a worry for you,' Ghost George said. 'I wish there was something I could do to help.'

'That's kind of you. I don't suppose you're any good at fixing old gutters, are you?'

He gave a sad smile, but then a serious look crossed his face. 'I suppose the Ketton jewels are long gone?'

Bea started. 'Ketton jewels?'

'You know the sort of thing. Necklaces, brooches, rings and things. All those pretty baubles you ladies like. There was quite a collection in my time. Madeleine took great care of them. But they are, I fear, the kind of things that get stolen or sold down the centuries.'

'I'm afraid I've never heard of them,' Bea said. 'My George certainly never mentioned them.'

'I only have a vague memory of them, but I remember that Madeleine hid them during the war for fear of robbery by the Roundheads.'

'So they were valuable?'

'Oh, yes! There was gold and silver, rubies, emeralds. Take a look at the portraits here. They will give you some idea.'

Bea walked across to the wall of ancestors and looked at them with a new interest. George stood next to her.

'Madeleine always loved pearls. Pearls and rubies,' George said.

'So I see.' Bea stared up at the portrait, admiring the pearl necklace and drop earrings. She moved to the next portrait - a lady she guessed to be from the mid-sixteenth-century. This Beaumont ancestor was wearing a heavy gold necklace set with rubies or garnets, Bea wasn't quite sure which. But it was certainly beautiful.

'Maybe they've all been sold,' Bea said.

'It would not surprise me. Jewellery and art are the first things to go, alas.'

They stood side by side for a moment, gazing from portrait to portrait.

'I'm just wondering,' Bea said at last.

'Yes?'

'What if they were left here? What if Madeleine died without telling anyone where she'd hidden the jewels during the Civil War and subsequent generations never found them? Do you think that's possible?'

George looked pensive. 'I suppose it could be,' he said at last. 'I fear I never came back from the Civil War so I do not know what happened to them.'

'Oh, George! I'm so sorry.' She gave him a sympathetic smile, wishing she could comfort him in some way. It wasn't every day that somebody told you that they'd died in a war almost four hundred years ago.

'So,' Bea went on, 'if Madeleine hid the jewels and they weren't found by the Roundheads or any later Beaumonts then they might still be in the house somewhere. Is that what we're saying?'

'Do you think we should look for them in case they are still here?' George asked.

Excitement suddenly surged through Bea and she nodded enthusiastically. 'Yes! We absolutely should!'

CHAPTER SEVEN

The next day, Bea was still feeling pretty shaken by the whole Simeon experience. She was so angry that he'd felt he had the right to not only enter her home without warning, but to threaten her within it. But she did her best to put him out of her mind. After all, she couldn't be in control of his thoughts or actions, and it was a waste of her time and energy to be worrying about what he may or may not do next. Besides, she was able to distract herself rather wonderfully with the thought of the Ketton jewels.

George's revelation about them had kept her awake for half the night as she mentally searched each room in the manor house, trying to think where Madeleine Beaumont might have hidden the family treasure during the English Civil War. It was hard to imagine what she must have endured being a woman on her own in a large house. Bea had been reading a bit about those times and, after taking Rose to school, she met up with George in the hallway and he told her some more about it.

'Wives were left at home, often with young families to protect,' George revealed. 'And the men were away fighting. And I mean, all the men – not just gentry. The fields were empty of their workers and

crops were left to rot. The whole country was plunged into chaos.'
She saw a look of anger crossing George's pale face as he remembered
it all. 'Homes were pillaged. Roundhead soldiers were merciless,
taking anything of value and doing endless damage. I heard reports of
deer being killed in parklands and lakes being drained and trees
being cut down and sold or just pulled up for the sheer hell of it.
They wanted to completely destroy estates. Other animals were let
loose. Carnage and chaos. That's what it was.'

'It sounds terrifying,' Bea said.

'It was. I hated leaving Madeleine, knowing that Cromwell's men
could turn up at any moment and do God knows what.'

'And did they?'

'They most certainly did. They took mostly food and horses. We
got away lightly. So much damage was being done elsewhere and
some people were left only in the clothes they stood up in. Madeleine
still had Ketton – a roof over her head. So many women had to fight
for their homes, resisting attack.'

'Yes, I was reading a bit about that,' Bea told him. 'Mary Bankes
held Corfe Castle in Dorset for the king.'

'I remember hearing the stories at the time,' George said. 'She and
her daughters threw stones and hot embers over the battlements at
the Roundheads below.'

Bea took a moment to take it all in. It sounded like a truly
horrifying time to live through. 'But why fight at all?' she asked at last.

'For loyalty to the king and monarchy, for tradition and to protect
our homes and families,' George said matter-of-factly.

'And the Parliamentarians – what were they fighting for?'

George gave a hollow laugh. 'You are asking the wrong person if
you want an unbiased answer.'

'Yes, I guess I am. But I know enough to believe that your King
Charles was not a good ruler.'

George looked a little shocked by her declaration.

'He disbanded parliament and raised taxes and spent too much
money. But I know it's more complicated than that.'

'Yes, it is not an easy subject to understand,' George agreed. 'Indeed, families were torn apart by it with fathers and sons and brothers fighting on opposing sides.'

'That's awful!' Bea said, imaging how heartbreaking that must have been for everyone involved. 'So that's when Madeleine hid the Ketton jewels – during all the fighting?'

'Yes. She wrote and told me as much although she was careful not to give too much away in case her letter was intercepted,' George said.

'But she didn't tell you where they were?'

'If she did, I have long forgotten.'

Bea sighed. 'I spent a good deal of last night trying to work out where I would hide something if I had to.'

'And where would you?'

'I don't know. Behind a painting? Under a floorboard? Probably the first place people would look.'

George glanced around the hallway now, peering into each of the rooms that led off from it.

'Any obvious hiding places?' Bea prompted him. 'You probably know this place better than I do.'

'Hiding places,' he repeated her words slowly, thoughtfully. 'Hiding places.' He turned around, glancing up the stairs and then his gaze returned to the ground floor and he walked into the dining room and crossed towards the window.

'What is it?' Bea asked, joining him and looking out onto the landscape which sparkled with frost. It had been a cold night, but the sun was out now and the world looked as if it were bejewelled with diamonds.

'Where would be the last place somebody would look?' George asked.

Bea shook her head. 'I don't know.'

'What about outside? We must not assume that Madeleine hid the jewels inside Ketton Hall.'

Bea glanced at George and then looked outside. 'But the estate is vast! Where would we begin?'

'I was thinking of the lake.'

'No! You can't be serious!'

'Not the *middle* of the lake. Perhaps somewhere accessible. Some shallow spot where a box or bag might have been lowered.'

'But surely it would have been found by now if it was accessible?'

'Not if no one knew to look for it.'

Bea wasn't feeling convinced. Still, she couldn't not look for something if there was the slightest possibility that it might be found.

'You asked my opinion,' George added. 'The lake is somewhere I would think to hide something because I believe nobody would think to look there.'

'Okay then. I'll take a look,' Bea told him, going back out into the hallway and opening a cupboard where the coats and boots were kept. She grabbed her warmest hat and then pulled out her heavy wax jacket, pausing for a moment as she looked at the other coat hanging there with the familiar flat cap on top of it. She swallowed, her hand reaching to touch them both – the rough wool of the hat, the smooth wax of the coat. One day, shortly after she'd lost George, she'd snuggled into this very coat just so she could feel his arms around her and she'd taken his cap to bed with her, laying it on the pillow beside her. It was ironic really. She'd teased him mercilessly about that cap – his horrible old hat, she'd called it, telling him even the moths refused to feast on it. But, when he'd died, she'd needed it by her.

'Beatrice?' Ghost George prompted her from behind. 'Are you all right?'

'Yes!' she said, quickly closing the cupboard door and throwing him a smile.

Crossing the hallway to the front door, she turned to face him.

'Are you able to come outside?' she asked. She'd never thought of it before but, now that the opportunity presented itself, she rather liked the idea of having his company with her.

'I am not altogether sure,' he said, looking anxious. 'And, perhaps it is not the best of ideas. For fear of being discovered.'

'Right.' Bea nodded. 'Well, wish me luck. I'm not quite sure what I'm looking for, but I'm going to give it a go.'

'Good luck!'

She opened the front door and stepped outside. The air was bitterly cold and her breath came out in dragon-like puffs as she made her way to the lake. This was not what she'd had in mind when George had first mentioned the Ketton jewels. She'd naively hoped they'd be tucked in the back of some easily accessible wardrobe somewhere. Indeed, she had yet to look properly around the house. But maybe George was right and the house was too obvious a place.

Trudging across the lawn, she soon found herself at the head of the lake. The little rowing boat was moored there. It hadn't been touched since the day of the picnic. The day of the storm. Bea looked at it now, almost seeing George sitting inside it, with that infectious grin of his as he took the oars. Bea hadn't been able to venture out in the boat since – not even on the most glorious of summer days. It reminded her too much of that last perfect time when George had rowed them out onto the water for their winter picnic.

She paused, looking out over the lake. She tried to get into Madeleine's mindset. Where would she have hidden the jewels? Would she have had a boat? George seemed to think they'd be close to the edge – somewhere accessible. But how deep was he thinking? And would it have survived? If it had been a wooden box, surely it would have long rotted. But would a metal box have fared any better? Would it have sunk into the years of silt and sludge and have slowly corroded away? Bea had no idea about this sort of thing, but she walked carefully along the banks, looking into the inky, icy depths.

There was a little jetty half-way around and she stopped there, kneeling down on the slippery wood, but she couldn't see anything of importance and so she moved on, her head down as the wind picked up. She was looking forward to getting back inside. Maybe she'd light a fire in the parlour and make another video for her channel. George had watched her as she'd made one yesterday. He'd been fascinated by the whole process as he'd leaned against the wood panelling in the corner of the room, careful to keep out of shot while she'd talked to her audience. She'd done her best to describe the internet to him, but he simply hadn't been able to understand.

'There are people in that device watching you?' he'd asked.

'Sort of. They have devices of their own which hook up to mine so they're able to watch me.'

She had wondered if she should include George in one of her videos. What would it be like if she could capture him on camera? Just imagine the hits she'd get. The first real internet ghost. The traffic to Linenfold Flowers would soar. For a few moments, she dreamed about the fun of it all and the possibilities. But she quickly realised that such a video would be all about George and not her flowers, and she'd been so careful to build a business that she believed in. It was hers and she was immensely proud of all she'd achieved – without the need for a ghost.

She smiled now as she tried to imagine George talking to her audience, but then put it out of her mind. She should be concentrating on the business in hand.

She stopped by a clump of reeds by the lake and peered in again. How much had it changed in the centuries since Madeleine had been chatelaine? The landscape too. As she thought of her predecessor, she realised that she had something very fundamental in common with this seventeenth century Beaumont – they'd both lost husbands. They'd also both been left to cope not only with the running of Ketton Hall but with raising its heir on their own. But what must it have been like for Madeleine to have lost her husband to war? Bea could only imagine the pain she must have endured. Imagine watching your husband riding off to fight many miles from home and never returning.

Bea turned and looked at the hall as an icy blast of air hit her full in the face and she began to feel the soft kiss of snowflakes on her cheeks. What was she doing out here, she asked herself? This was the very definition of a wild goose chase. Bending her head down, she walked back along the shore of the lake, entering the hall a few minutes later.

George was there to greet her in the hallway.

'No luck?'

'No.'

'There is an ancient oak tree in the grounds, I believe?' George said.

'Yes.' Bea knew the tree well.

'Perhaps the jewels are buried underneath it.'

Bea frowned. 'Wasn't it an oak tree that Charles the Second hid in during the Civil War? Although that's possibly after your time, depending on when you died.'

'Yes, I cannot recall that event myself.'

'When were Cromwell's men here at Ketton?' Bea asked.

'1644.'

'Right. I think the whole king in the oak tree was a little after that.' She took her phone out of her pocket and quickly looked it up. 'Yes, the tree incident was 1651.'

'That information is in your... device?'

'Almost everything's in this device,' Bea told him.

George shook his head. 'I still do not understand.'

Bea smiled at him, but then sighed. 'The thing is, George, I'm not sure I fancy grabbing a spade and digging in the frozen earth. It's snowing now too.'

George looked out of one of the hall windows. 'I have to agree it would not be much fun.'

'I think we should look indoors. Try and think of all the places Madeleine might have hidden the jewels that's aren't obvious.' Bea glanced up the stairs. 'How about the attics.'

'Is that not "obvious"?' George asked gently.

'Possibly,' Bea agreed. 'But we could start there and at least rule it out while we're thinking of other places.'

The two of them made the journey up the stairs to the top floor of

Ketton. The attics were somewhere Bea generally tried to avoid. They were filled with an accumulation of stuff that was either unwanted or broken.

'Oh, George! It could be anywhere,' Bea announced as they entered. 'If indeed it *is* up here!'

'Yes, it is a little daunting.'

Bea walked further in, noticing the endless boxes and wondering what was inside them all. Had her husband known about all this? Surely it was a fire hazard to have so much stuff up here. Maybe she should have a good sort out. Perhaps even a sale if she found any interesting items. Yes, that was an idea. Old country house auctions were popular, weren't they? It might help to raise some much-needed funds for some of the repairs that needed doing.

'Why do people keep so much stuff?' she asked, idly dragging a finger across the dusty surface of a chest of drawers. She opened the top drawer, but there was only a dead bluebottle inside. As well as a chest of drawers, there was a wardrobe. The door was hanging off its hinges and there was nothing but a stack of old newspapers inside and a pair of split Wellington boots. Bea shook her head. Why go to the trouble of storing old papers and broken boots inside a defunct wardrobe and carting it up into the loft?

It was then that she saw a long wooden box. It looked too big and ordinary to contain anything valuable, but Bea opened it just in case.

'It's a croquet set!' she announced. George took a step closer to look.

'Croquet?'

'It's a game you play outdoors,' Bea told him, touching one of the mallets which was time-worn and smooth. 'It's a shame these aren't in use anymore.' She put the lid back on the box, but made a mental note to come back for the croquet set later.

Moving on, casting her eyes over a rusting child's tricycle, an artist's easel with a broken leg and a hideous collection of dolls with nightmarish faces, she wondered if there was anything up here that remotely resembled treasure. But she didn't feel ready to give up.

Spotting another box, she opened it to find a collection of marvellous old ladies' hats. They were a little tatty but utterly charming and she tried one on, grimacing at the musty smell of it.

'Very attractive,' George told her.

Bea smiled and took the hat off, returning it to the others. 'I don't think we're going to find any gold or jewels up here. It's mostly just junk.'

'Yes. I suppose it is.'

They glanced at one another, smiling in sympathy and then they returned downstairs. Bea washed her hands. She felt grubby and cobwebby after the trip to the attics, her hair was a mess, she'd broken a nail and she was feeling a little dispirited too.

'I am sorry, Beatrice,' George told her as she made herself a cup of tea in the kitchen.

'It's not your fault.'

'You look disappointed.'

'Well, you can't promise a girl jewels and not deliver,' she said, grinning at him.

'I wish there was somewhere else we could try,' he said, glancing around the kitchen as if Ketton's great treasure might be lurking in one of the cupboards.

'There must be. This is a huge house and I'm not ready to give up yet. We've only just started.' She sipped her tea. 'I wish you drank tea, George. I make a really good cup.'

He smiled. 'I miss food.'

'Do you?'

'Yes. It is a strange thing not needing to eat or drink.'

'I suppose it must be,' she said, pausing to think about this for a moment. 'What do you miss the most?'

'You mean what kind of food?'

'Well, yes. But generally too.'

He took a deep breath and Bea couldn't help wondering how his whole body worked. He seemed to need to breathe and yet he didn't need to eat. It was all so confusing.

'What do I miss?' George began. 'I miss my wife and my children. I miss walking around this place. I mean *really* walking – when I could feel my body and the floorboards under my feet and touch the fabrics in the house, the bedroom curtains and the tapestries. I miss my friends coming to dinner and the idle conversation we would have. And then the not so idle conversation about the nation and politics. I miss a glass of good wine and a plate of good food. I miss feeling the warmth from a fire on a cold winter's night and the thrill of galloping across the estate on my horse, Merlin.'

Bea smiled. She loved the insight into his life. She'd have to try and remember it all.

'And I miss being alive! *Truly* alive. Not this half-life I seem to be living now where I am barely here at all.' He motioned to his transparent state. 'I cannot feel properly. I cannot tell if it is hot or cold. I do not get hungry or thirsty. I am not here and I miss being *here*.'

Bea smarted at the emotion in his voice. 'Oh, George!'

He shook his head, suddenly looking embarrassed. 'Listen to me moaning on when I had such a good life!'

'You have every right to moan. I would too if I was half-transparent and couldn't enjoy a glass of wine anymore!'

He laughed at that and then a serious look crossed his face.

'Beatrice!' he suddenly said.

'What is it?'

'Why did I not think of it before?'

'Think of what?'

'The priest hide!' he said.

'The what?'

'The priest hide or priest hole, I believe they are sometimes called. There was one here at Ketton. The Beaumonts used to be Catholic and, during the reign of Elizabeth, the family used to hold secret and illegal masses, and the priest would have to be hidden away if a search was made of the house. If they were found, they could face torture and even execution.'

Bea gasped. 'The more I learn about English history, the more I fear it!'

'It was definitely not a good time to be a Catholic.'

'So where's this priest hide?'

'Downstairs, I believe. A room with lots of beams.'

'And you think the jewels might be in there?'

'I think it very likely. It is a good hiding place and Madeleine would have known about it.'

Bea felt a surge of excitement coursing through her. 'Let's start looking!'

CHAPTER EIGHT

George led the way to the parlour – the room Beatrice used most often for her filming. It was wood panelled all the way around.

'There were beams in the walls,' he told her.

'You think they're behind the panelling?' Bea asked.

'Perhaps. Is the panelling later?'

'I don't think so, but I'm no expert. George knew more about this house. I'm still learning, I'm afraid. But I know that different generations would modify rooms, adding on to older structures so it's likely that the panelling has been put on top of a much older wall.' Bea put her hands on her hips and surveyed the room. 'You're not suggesting we start taking it off, are you?'

George glanced around. 'That does seem a little extreme.'

'Shall we check some more rooms before we start dismantling any?'

'Perhaps we should.'

They left the panelled room, going to one next door.

'Maybe this was it,' George said, nodding to the walls which were a mix of old Tudor brick and wooden posts as well as sections of panelling.

'You think so?'

'It looks right.'

'So, what am I looking for?'

'Anything that looks like it might be hiding a place behind it.'

'The walls, you mean? Not the floor?'

'I think it was the walls.'

Bea frowned. The walls looked pretty solid to her. There didn't seem to be anything obvious, but then that was rather the point, she realised. A priest whose life was in danger wouldn't want his hiding place to be easily discernible as soon as you walked into a room.

Unconvinced, Bea moved slowly around the room, reaching out and touching the walls with her hands. The old red bricks were rough. Some were darker than others and Bea marvelled at the different textures. She'd never really paid much attention to them before. To her untrained eye, it had just been an old wall in a house full of old walls. But she took her time now, her fingers touching the vertical posts that had been holding the house up for so many centuries, but nowhere could she discover a likely hiding place.

'Are you sure it was this room, George?' Bea asked in frustration.

He looked pensive. 'I was sure this was it.'

Bea walked around the room one more time. 'It all looks pretty solid to me.'

'Yes,' George said. 'It does. But I am quite sure...' he stopped. He didn't look sure at all, Bea couldn't help thinking, but she didn't say anything. 'I thought the panelling went all the way round like in the other room,' George continued.

'Maybe it did. Houses change over time,' Bea pointed out, pressing a hand to the one wall which was still panelled. Surely, if any wall was going to be hiding something, it would be the panelled one. 'The rest is bricks and posts. I don't think it's possible to hide anything behind those.'

'Push them,' George said.

'Push what?' Bea was confused.

'The vertical posts.'

Bea wasn't at all sure George knew what he was talking about. How could pushing a post do anything? Still...

Bea reached out a hand and pushed the middle of the nearest post. Nothing budged.

'Try the top and the bottom,' George suggested.

Bea did as he told her, moving from post to post.

'That one,' George suddenly said, pointing to one near the back corner.

Bea pushed it. 'Nothing's happening,' she complained and she was just about to give up when the post moved at the top. 'George!'

'Keep pushing!'

Bea pushed again, harder this time and something wonderful happened – the post moved out towards her at the bottom like a seesaw.

'George – it's working!' Bea pushed for all she was worth and, as the post swung towards her, she grabbed it underneath and lifted it until it was a horizontal plank above her head.

'This is it,' George said, stepping closer. 'This wall – it used to be covered by panelling, I am sure of it. It would have been removed before the priest went inside and then put back to hide the entrance.'

'It's a very good hiding place,' Bea said, peering inside the cavity. 'I can't believe I've never seen this before. Did my George even know it was here?'

'Possibly not.'

'But it's very dark. I think I'll need a torch if I'm going in.'

Bea left the room and hurried to the hallway cupboard where a torch was always kept, returning a moment later and shining it into the hole in the wall.

'Are you sure this is where the priest would hide? It's not very big or easy to use,' Bea pointed out, wondering how she was going to get inside.

'It was meant to be hard to find. You would not exactly build a nice comfortable door that was easily accessible.'

'Point taken,' Bea said, taking her jumper off and turning herself sideways to get inside the wall. The old bricks were dusty and cobwebby and she wasn't sure how far back the hide went. Bea had never counted herself the most adventurous of sorts, but she had to admit to finding this all rather thrilling. She was actually squeezing herself through a wall.

'Be careful!' George called.

'There are steps,' Bea called back as she lowered herself down them. 'It's not very wide, but it goes back a little way.'

'What can you see?'

'Not a lot at the moment,' Bea called back from her crouched position. 'It's quite narrow. About three foot across, I'd say. It goes back a little bit further, but I can't quite stand up fully.' Bea flashed the torch around, noting the same brick and post construction of the walls in the hide as there had been in the main room. The wooden floorboards were wide and dusty and, also, disappointingly empty of anything.

'There's nothing here,' Bea called back up to George. 'I don't suppose there's a priest hole within a priest hole or something?' She pushed one of the walls with her hand, but it felt pretty solid.

She climbed back out into the room, brushing herself down and sighing.

'Any other priest holes in the house?' she asked

'It is possible, I suppose. Many houses had several. But we only ever knew of this one.'

'Well, it was a good idea of yours and I'm surprised we haven't found anything in here. It's a great hiding spot. Maybe Madeleine did use it, but then moved the jewels after the war.'

'I am sorry, Beatrice.'

'It's okay. Ketton's managed this long without the Beaumont jewels. I'm sure we can survive. Still, it would've been nice to find them.'

～

Bea was busy for the rest of the day, making some floral arrangements and Christmas wreaths for a local hotel. It was work she enjoyed. Although she loved making her videos and connecting with her virtual audience, there was something immensely satisfying about real-life customers who gave you face-to-face feedback. You could see their honest reactions to your work, hear their comments in real time and find out what they particularly liked. For Bea, that was an invaluable part of her business.

After her delivery to the hotel, Bea picked up Rose from school and, once home, they had tea and then curled up in front of the fire in the Blue Drawing Room, each with a book – Bea's was a novel and Rose's was a colouring book which she was attacking with her felt pens. Bea loved their quiet evenings together, the shutters closed, and the thick curtains drawn against the cold evening, the gentle tick of the mantel clock and the flames of the fire cheering the room. Sometimes, Bea would feel herself drifting off and often thought of tucking herself up in bed at the same time that Rose went which was far too early really. But winter nights did that to a person, she found. It would be so easy to hibernate.

The clock ticked around and Bea took a reluctant Rose up to bed.

'Can't I finish my book?'

'You want to colour the whole book before you go to bed?'

'Yes!'

'Well, that's not going to happen, is it?'

Rose pouted, but soon forgot about her disappointment when Bea escorted her to the bathroom and started to brush her hair.

'Tell me about the imps,' Rose said.

Bea smiled. The imps were characters that George often told stories about and they had captured Rose's young imagination.

'What made you think about them?' Bea asked.

'I thought I saw one.'

'Where?'

'In the dining room. Something moved in there.'

Bea panicked, wondering if Ghost George had made an

appearance in front of Rose, but she soon dismissed her fear. He'd said he wouldn't do that and she trusted him.

'Well,' Bea began, 'the imps are the things you hear rustling in the grass and moving under the furniture. They're the things you see only in the corner of your eye. You never get a good look at them for they move swiftly. But they're there all the time, living in the shadows of rooms, watching us, teasing us. Some people say it's the imps that hide things and move things.'

'Like keys and socks!' Rose interrupted, remembering her father's words.

'That's right. And felt tip pens and important papers. They never steal them. They just move them a little.'

'Why?'

Bea shrugged. 'Who can get inside the head of something as naughty as an imp?' She put Rose's hairbrush down and nodded towards the toothpaste, watching as her daughter picked it up together with her brush.

'And are they real, Mummy?' Rose asked after she'd finished brushing her teeth. 'Like fairies and ghosts?'

Bea bit her lip, not quite sure how to answer. 'What do you think?' she asked instead.

'I think they're real,' Rose declared as they left the bathroom for her bedroom.

'Well, let me know if you ever see one, okay? Imps, fairies or...' she paused, 'ghosts.'

'Okay,' Rose said, completely taking it in her stride that she might, indeed, see any of these at some point.

After tucking Rose in bed and kissing her goodnight, Bea tidied the kitchen and then slowly walked around the house, switching off all the lights. She then went upstairs to her bedroom, grimacing as she hit the squeak. It was getting worse and really set her on edge.

Tomorrow, she vowed. She'd do something about it tomorrow.

CHAPTER NINE

But Bea didn't do something about the squeaky step the next day because it was two weeks before Christmas and that meant one thing: it was the first anniversary of George's death – a day she'd been dreading. She hadn't marked it in her diary. She hadn't needed to. The date would be forever seared upon her heart. But her sister must have made a note of it because she rang first thing.

'Hey, you!'

'Hi Nicole.'

'How are you?' Nicole asked. 'Silly question. I'm sorry.'

'It's okay.'

'But... how are you?'

'I'm good,' Bea said. 'I'm up. I'm not hiding under the bed covers or hitting a bottle of vodka before nine in the morning.'

'And Rose?'

'She's getting ready for school. I don't think she realises. I don't want her to think about it to be honest.'

'Probably wise.'

'She's coping really well. At least, I think she is. She's not had a nightmare for a while now and, when she talks about her dad, it's always with warmth and affection and not sadness.'

'Children are pretty resilient, aren't they?' Nicole said.

'I guess they are.'

There was a pause.

'What are you doing today?' Nicole dared to ask.

'I'm making a hand-tied bouquet for a client, but then I thought I might go for a walk.' She sighed. 'Actually, I thought I might visit Mrs Gilbert.'

'Oh, Bea! Are you sure that's a good idea?'

Bea scrunched her fingers up into a fist. 'I don't know. Probably not. But I've not seen her since the funeral. George would want me to visit, I'm sure. And I feel ready... I think.'

'Well, you know best,' Nicole said. 'Do you want me to come over?'

'Aren't you working?'

'Well, I've got a boring business book I'm meant to be translating, but I can take a couple of hours off.'

'You don't need to. I'm fine. Honestly. And I have...' She stopped just in time. She had been about to say that she had George to keep her company.

'What do you have?'

'I have the Christmas decorations to think about. Rose will be breaking up from school soon and you and Mum will be coming over and I want the place looking perfect for Christmas.'

'Just don't overwork yourself. You need to take it easy,' Nicole told her in her best big sister voice.

'No I don't,' Bea countered. 'I need to work. I need something to focus on.'

It was Nicole's turn to sigh. 'I do worry about you.'

'Oh, don't start turning into Mum!'

'I'm not, really. I know you can look after yourself. You're a brilliant mum and an amazing creator.'

'Can I hear a but approaching?'

'But you need to slow down. Have a day off. Get away from Ketton if only for a few hours. When was the last time you did that?'

Bea hated to admit that her sister was right. She couldn't actually remember the last time she'd spent a day away from Ketton let alone gone on anything as self-indulgent as a holiday. Holidays always seemed so very unnecessary when you lived in a grand stately home. It seemed excessive to spend money staying somewhere else. But Bea had to admit that the thought of getting away did occasionally cross her mind.

'You're thinking about it, aren't you?' Nicole pressed.

'Maybe.'

'Well, perhaps we should talk about that sometime. Maybe have a holiday together. Somewhere warm and sunny.'

Bea smiled as a rattle of hailstones hit the window she was standing by. Warm and sunny sounded pretty seductive in the middle of an English winter.

They said their goodbyes and hung up and Bea left the house with Rose a few minutes later.

By the time she got back home and her client had collected the arrangement Bea had made, it was mid-morning. George didn't seem to be around and Bea was quite glad as she wasn't sure she was in the mood to talk to him. Not today. But there was somebody she felt she should talk to so she put her hat and coat on, stuffed her feet into her warmest boots and plunged her hands into her thickest gloves for the walk across the estate to the little cottage.

Bea avoided the icy track from the hall, choosing to crunch through the snow between the hall and the lake before skirting a little wood and coming out onto the main village road a few minutes later. The Suffolk countryside was looking a cold, steely grey today, but at least the hailstones had stopped.

And there it was. The little cottage. It was a simple building of brick and flint with a neat garden at the front behind a white wooden gate. Bea had only been there once before. Mrs Gilbert had asked her and George to afternoon tea shortly after their wedding and George had been delighted to show off his new bride.

Bride. The word rattled around her head. She'd been a bride for a day, a newly-wed for – well, however long one was a newly-wed for, and now she was a widow and would be one forever. The thought pressed down on her chest, making her feel as if she was suffocating. Perhaps it wasn't a good idea coming here today, she thought. Maybe she should just return home.

But she couldn't because it was then that she spotted Mrs Gilbert at one of the downstairs windows. Bea had been seen.

'Beatrice!' Mrs Gilbert exclaimed as she opened the door a moment later, her wrinkled face creasing even more in surprise. 'Oh, my dear – come in. Come in!' She ushered Bea inside and encouraged her to take off her hat and coat. Bea also removed her boots, knowing that Mrs Gilbert kept an immaculate home. 'What are you doing out on such a cold day? Did you see that hailstorm? It sounded like a thousand tap dancers up on the roof!'

Bea nodded as she followed Mrs Gilbert through to the living room. There was a fire on the go and Mischief looked up from his place beside it before deciding that Bea was welcome. But she felt awkward around the little dog. It was hard to look at him and not curse him for escaping that night. There was a part of Bea that wanted to have a serious conversation with him.

'What did you think you were doing going out on a night like that?' she'd ask him. *'You know when you run off like that you're putting other people at risk searching for you?'*

She shook her head. She was being ridiculous, but that's how she felt. Grief made you think of ridiculous things.

'How about a cup of tea?' Mrs Gilbert said and Bea nodded, glad of the distraction. 'You sit there while I make it.'

Tea. It was one of those strange English customs that fulfilled so many purposes – it was an invitation to stay a while, a nod to civility, a calming process. Whatever the occasion, whoever you were with, a cup of tea seemed to slot right in.

Bea could have sat down and thawed out by the fire, but she moved across to the sideboard on the other side of the room. It was covered with a shoal of silver photo frames and Bea took her time looking at each one. There was Mr and Mrs Gilbert on their wedding day. What a vision she was. And there she was holding a baby. And there was a photo of that baby now a father and holding a baby of his own. How time passed, Bea thought, glancing over the other pictures. This was the Gilbert version of the Beaumont family portraits in Ketton's dining room. A little less grand, perhaps, but no less precious.

'Here we are,' Mrs Gilbert said, coming into the room with a tray after a few minutes.

'Please, let me,' Bea said, taking it from her and placing it on a little table near the fire.

'Thank you, dear. My wrists aren't as strong as they once were. A touch of arthritis, I fear.'

Bea nodded sympathetically and they both sat down on armchairs opposite one another. Mischief glanced up at the tea things, but obviously didn't smell anything that suggested he'd be getting a treat and so closed his eyes for a little nap.

'This is our favourite thing to do these days,' Mrs Gilbert said. 'Taking it easy by the fire. We have a little walk in the morning. Not as far as we used to go, mind, but it's important to get out in the fresh air, isn't it? One would seize up completely if one didn't keep moving.' She gave a little chuckle as she leaned forward and poured the tea and Bea helped herself to a spoon of sugar.

'You're keeping well?' Bea asked

'Mustn't complain,' Mrs Gilbert said. 'That's what they say, isn't it? Mustn't complain. Although some people do, like that Mrs Bempton in the village. I dread finding myself standing next to her in line in the post office for fear of hearing all her latest complaints.' Mrs Gilbert chuckled again. 'So there you are. I mustn't complain. I'm still here.' She grimaced, seeming to regret her choice of words. 'I'm sorry,' she said quickly.

'It's okay.'

There was a pause before Mrs Gilbert spoke again. 'I know what day it is.'

'Yes.' Bea nodded.

'Is that why you came to see me?'

'I've been meaning to for a while,' Bea confessed. 'But I wasn't ready. I'm sorry it's today. But it felt – right somehow. A kind of connection perhaps.'

Mrs Gilbert nodded and gave a faint smile, but Bea could see that there were tears in her eyes. 'I wanted to reach out to you. So many times. But I thought I'd be the last person you'd want to see.'

'That's not true!' Bea assured her.

'You're in my thoughts. You and Rose. *All* the time. Is she okay? And you – how are you?'

'I'm...' Bea put her teacup down and stared into the fire. How did you explain to someone that, even after a year, you sometimes had days when you felt you'd made no progress at all? Would they understand? Mrs Gilbert was a widow but, at her age, it was to be expected. That, of course, wouldn't make it any easier. Losing a partner... 'I'm getting through each day. Sometimes, that's all I can manage.'

'And that's enough,' Mrs Gilbert said gently. 'It will get easier. With time. I know everybody will be telling you that, but it does. It was that way with me, at least.'

Bea nodded, not trusting herself to speak at that point.

'But I should never have called him,' Mrs Gilbert said, mopping her eyes with an oversized hanky as her tears began to spill. 'It's the greatest regret of my life!'

'It's not your fault,' Bea assured her.

'Oh, yes it is! If it hadn't been for me—'

'You mustn't think that way.'

'How else *can* I think?'

'He wanted to help. You know what he was like. He'd probably have gone out to check on you even if you hadn't called first.'

'You think so?'

Bea nodded as she picked up her teacup again. 'He liked to keep an eye on you.'

Mrs Gilbert sniffed loudly which caused Mischief to glance up. 'Mischief wants to say he's sorry too.'

Bea managed a smile at that and the tension in the room eased a little.

'I'm always here, you know,' Mrs Gilbert went on. 'If you need to talk.'

Bea was holding on to the fragile china teacup so tightly now that it was a miracle it didn't crack between her fingers. The truth was, she was glad she'd come and she felt a little comfort that they'd managed to talk about the dreadful night that had hung between them for a whole year, but she needed to go now.

'Listen...' Bea stood up. She was still holding the teacup and quickly placed it down with a clatter. 'I should go. Rose...' She glanced out of the window into the snowy lane. It was ages until she had to do the school run. Mrs Gilbert must know that. But she couldn't stay a moment longer. It was all too much.

Mrs Gilbert seemed to understand and didn't make a fuss. 'Thank you for coming and don't forget what I said. I'm always here.'

Bea nodded and then left the room as quickly as was polite, grabbing her hat and coat and pulling her boots back on. But she paused at the door, suddenly feeling horribly rude. She turned. Mrs Gilbert was standing behind her, her eyes red and teary in her pale, wrinkled face. Bea moved towards her and hugged her and, for a few moments, the two of them stood there in the silence of the tiny cottage hallway, their arms tight around each other. No words were spoken; none were needed. But they'd finally reached a place of peace with one another and that was everything.

That evening, as Bea was tucking Rose up in bed, stroking her daughter's red-gold hair, it suddenly occurred to her that George had been gone for a quarter of Rose's life. That was a long time, wasn't it? Was she beginning to forget him? Would she grow up without any memories of him? The thought terrified Bea and she determined that she'd keep the memory of George alive. She would tell Rose stories about him – how they'd met at a summer fete held in the grounds of Ketton, and how he'd managed to spill half a glass of ginger ale down her dress after tripping over an escaped runner duck. She'd tell Rose how he'd proposed to her on the boat in the middle of the lake and how he'd managed to hide a bottle of champagne in the water under the jetty. Yes, she'd tell Rose all her stories about George and, together, they would never forget him.

Later, climbing into her bed, her head was full of memories of him, playing like a wonderful movie in her mind's eye. She never wanted it to end, but sleep was beckoning and she leaned out of bed to switch her lamp off.

'Goodnight, George,' she whispered into the dark room hoping, somehow, that he was able to hear her.

CHAPTER TEN

The next day, Bea vowed to do something about the squeaky stair. She'd had enough of it. So, after dropping Rose off at school and gathering some fresh evergreens from the garden, she walked up the main staircase, stopping at the squeaker which was just three steps down from the top of the first landing. There was something distinctly odd about this step, she thought, her hand stroking its length. It looked the same as all the others and yet it felt different. Bea couldn't quite explain. It was just a feeling.

Bea put a foot on it, listening to the squeak on the left-hand side. There were other squeaks in this staircase, but none quite as pronounced. She wondered how long it had made this noise for. Possibly decades if not centuries. Generations of Beaumonts had been wound up by this squeak. The thought amused Bea. Well, no more, she thought. She was going to fix it. She'd watched a couple of YouTube videos, had grabbed some tools and believed she knew what she was doing. But as she bent to examine the step, she noticed that the whole thing felt loose. She frowned. Why hadn't she noticed that before?

Placing her hands under the top of the step where the squeak was, she gave it a little shove. Nothing happened. She then pulled it up a little. It felt stiff, but it was definitely on the move and Bea cried out in alarm when the whole step rose. Was that normal? She peered into the gap it had revealed which went both back and down as far as she could see.

What was this? Another priest hole? Did they hide them in staircases? Or was this just a quirk of an old house? She didn't really know, but thought the best thing to do was to forget her tools and go and fetch a torch instead.

A couple of minutes later, she was back at the open stair. She removed her bulky jumper to give herself a better chance of fitting into the space. It did look odd and rather eerie, she had to admit as she switched her torch on, and it was a little nerve-wracking to lower herself down into it. Once inside, and quite sure that the floor underneath her wasn't going to give way, she shone her torch around. Like with the priest hole in the panelled room, there were beams and bricks and it smelled musty and strange. Had anyone ventured inside here since the sixteenth century? That is, if it was another priest hole. Had her husband George known about it? Surely he would have shown it to her if he had.

She climbed back out the way she'd come in.

'Oh, George! Where are you when I need you?' she asked, wondering where her friendly ghost was.

'Beatrice?' he said, suddenly appearing behind her.

She turned. 'George! Where have you been? I've not seen you for a while.'

He looked a little awkward. 'I had a feeling.'

'What feeling?'

'That you might need a little time alone.'

'Oh. You mean...?'

'Yes. I sensed it.'

'It's a year already.'

'The first year is the hardest.'

She nodded, not really sure what to say, but the wonderful thing with Ghost George was that she didn't have to say anything. He just seemed to understand her without the need for words.

'But look at this, George!' she said, pointing to the staircase. 'I think it's another priest hole.'

George bent to look into the cavity in the staircase.

'Did you know it was here?' Bea asked.

'No.'

'Well, I'm wondering if Madeleine did. I'm going in!'

'Is that a good idea?'

'It's okay. I've already been in and it's perfectly safe. And this could be what we've been searching for! Madeleine's hiding place.'

'You think so?'

'I'm hoping so,' Bea said, lowering herself into the hole again.

'Be careful!' George called after her.

'I'm always careful!' Bea shouted back, banging her head on a beam as she flashed her torch around for a second look.

'Can you see anything?'

'Just bricks,' Bea said, examining the poky hole that she couldn't quite stand up in. 'No, wait...'

Up against the far wall was a large piece of material that looked like an old damask curtain. She'd overlooked the first time she went in, but she approached it now. It was dusty and Bea didn't really want to touch it, but curiosity got the better of her and she reached out to move it.

She gasped.

'What do you see, Beatrice? Tell me!' George called from outside.

'There's a box.'

'What sort of box?'

'Wood. Beautifully engraved. I'll bring it out.'

She popped the torch under her arm and lifted the box. It was heavy despite its relatively small size, but she made it out into daylight to where George was waiting anxiously.

Bea placed the box on the windowsill on the nearby landing, her fingers gently touching the exquisite detail of the carving which covered it.

'It's beautiful!' she whispered in awe. 'I'm almost afraid to open it.'

'But you must!' George said.

She laughed at his impatience and slowly opened the box, thanking her lucky stars that it wasn't locked.

'It's a book,' she said. She felt a slow, sinking feeling as she lifted it out.

George nodded as he saw it. 'A Bible,' he said. 'They were often kept in special boxes.'

Bea smiled. She didn't want to appear ungrateful at having found something so beautiful and obviously treasured. It was a part of Ketton's history after all. But it wasn't quite what they'd been hoping to find. Tentatively, she opened the thick leather cover, her fingers gently tiptoeing over the fine pages of print.

'It's a lovely thing,' she said. 'Do you remember it, George?'

'I do. It belonged to my father.'

'Really?'

'It feels strange seeing it again.'

'And do you suppose it's been hiding in this secret place since the Civil War?'

She heard him curse, but couldn't quite make out the exact words. Something seventeenth century and scandalous, no doubt.

'What is it?' Bea asked him.

'It just makes me think about Madeleine being here without me to protect her,' he told her and then he frowned. 'How did she find this priest hole, do you suppose?'

'Probably the same way I did – a squeaky floorboard was driving her crazy.'

George grinned. 'That sounds quite plausible. Madeleine hated squeaks!'

Bea laughed at the notion of squeaky floorboards linking her to one of her husband's ancestors.

She was just about to return the Bible to its box when she decided to place it on the windowsill instead and pick up the box again.

'It's quite heavy even without the Bible in it,' she said.

'And well made. A jewel in itself.'

Bea looked at him and then at the box. 'I don't suppose...'

'What?'

Bea put the box down and then started to prod it. 'I wonder...'

'Wonder what?'

A moment later, a tiny little click was heard and the base of the box lifted a fraction.

'What is that?' George asked coming forward.

'I think it might be hiding what we're looking for.' Bea slowly lifted the wood which gave a little creak as if in protest before revealing its secret in a hidden compartment underneath.

Bea gasped. 'The jewels! Look!' Suddenly, her eyes were filled with gold and her vision blurred with tears of joy and disbelief.

'You found them, Beatrice!'

'I can't believe it! They've been here all this time!'

'You doubted it?'

'I – I didn't know what to think!'

'Madeleine kept them safe for you.'

'Yes! And look how beautiful they are. I've never seen anything like them.' She blinked her tears away and focused on the tangle of necklaces, rings and bracelets nestled together at the bottom of the heavy wooden box. She dared to pick up one of the necklaces. It was cold and heavy in her hands, but gleamed as brightly as the day it had been made. That was the magic of gold – age didn't tarnish it.

'Oh, George! I wish you could see all this!'

'But I can,' George said from behind her.

'I meant *my* George,' Beatrice explained. 'It seems so unfair that I get to find all this and not him. Do you think he knows – somehow?'

'I cannot say.'

'No. I know. But I hope he can. I hope he can sense it somehow.'

Bea held the necklace up to the light. It was studded with fat rubies which gleamed and glowed.

'I remember Madeleine wearing that one,' George told her. 'It was a favourite.'

'I can see why. You had matching rubies,' Bea said, motioning to the ruby ring of George's which she was still wearing. He smiled at that. 'And look at this!' From the tangle of gold, Bea gently extracted an emerald ring. 'And this!' Another necklace caught her eye – this time set with pearls.

'The Ketton jewels. Hidden under the stairs!' George gave a laugh. 'My clever Madeleine. Cromwell's men would have had those for sure had they found them.'

'But what should I do with them now? They're much too grand for someone like me to wear and they'll no doubt cost a fortune to insure properly.'

'I thought you were going to sell them,' George said.

'Yes. I thought so too. But that was before I actually found them. Before I *saw* them. It's very easy to sell something in theory. I suppose they really belong in a museum so everyone can admire them. Somewhere wonderful like the Victoria and Albert in London.'

'But they belong to Ketton,' George said.

'Yes.' Bea carefully put the pearl necklace down. This was all rather a lot to take in.

'Well, you need not make your mind up now,' George told her. 'Why not enjoy them yourself as Ketton's new owner? After all, they are yours, Beatrice.'

Bea smiled at the notion. *Hers.* These beautiful jewels belonged to her. Enjoy them, she told herself, echoing George. Jewels were meant to be enjoyed and wasn't Christmas just around the corner? If you couldn't sparkle at Christmas then when could you?

CHAPTER ELEVEN

When Beatrice's husband George had been alive, he'd insisted on the Christmas tree arriving on the first of December. Bea had always tried to dissuade him.

'It's too early!' she'd cry. 'It'll go brittle and the needles will drop.'

But he'd never listened and the great tree would be placed in the hall in all its statuesque glory. The rule, as far as George was concerned, was the bigger the better and he never brought any tree home that was under ten foot tall.

'What's the point of having an entrance hall like this if you don't fill it at Christmas?' he'd say.

Well, Bea hadn't been able to focus her thoughts on her family Christmas until that dreadful first anniversary had passed. She'd allowed a few days to elapse afterwards, being careful to place an order for a tree to be delivered on the day that Rose's school broke up for the holidays. That weekend, the two of them brought out the boxes of decorations. There were more each year as Bea was a perfect magpie when it came to ornaments and could never resist adding to their collection. Then there were the home-made decorations for neither Bea nor Rose could ever pass up the opportunity to be creative with felt tip pens, paper, scraps of material and ribbon.

This year, Bea had chosen a smaller tree, placing it in the Blue Drawing Room which felt more cosy and homely than having it in the hall. Maybe they'd return to a larger tree next year but, this Christmas, she needed to do something different, drawing her family close in a room that was comforting and familiar with the fire blazing in the hearth and the thick curtains drawn tightly against the long winter nights.

She and Rose had agreed to decorate the tree in traditional Christmas colours: gold, silver, red and green. But then they'd found some pink baubles, and the blue peacock decorations were just too beautiful to keep hidden away, and the big fluffy white snowflakes they'd made together the year before just *had* to be included too. So, once they'd finished, they declared it a rainbow tree for every colour featured and made the whole thing glorious.

'So, what do you think?' Bea asked George later that evening once Rose was in bed.

George gazed at the tree and shook his head. 'I cannot believe you bring a living tree *into* the house.'

Bea laughed. 'Blame Queen Victoria. She started it.'

'Well, there is something unique about it,' George confessed.

Bea nodded as she took in the warm white lights she'd chosen and how they made everything twinkle. It was an exceptionally beautiful tree this year, she had to admit.

'But you would have brought evergreens into the house, wouldn't you?' Bea asked.

'Of course. They represent everlasting life.'

'That seems to be working with you,' Bea observed with a smile.

'Your evergreens seem to be a bit more...' George stopped as he gestured towards the garland Bea had made for the mantelpiece, 'sparkly.'

'Ah, yes. We do love a bit of sparkle these days.'

'And I am coming round to it.'

'Good!' Bea crossed the room and threw a couple of logs onto the fire. 'Listen, George, my mum and sister will be arriving tomorrow for the holidays so it's going to be difficult for us to – well – talk.'

'I see,' he said. 'Do not worry. I will not scare anybody unnecessarily.'

Bea laughed. 'I'll try to sneak away every so often, though, so we can see each other, okay?'

He nodded. 'Are you looking forward to Christmas?'

She gazed wistfully into the bright colours of the tree. 'It will be nice to spend time with my family. But there will always be somebody missing.'

George took a step towards her. 'It will get easier.'

'With time. I know.' She gave a little laugh and George smiled and, for a few moments, they stood side by side, admiring the tree. Bea liked their quiet moments together. It was lovely that they were comfortable enough in each other's company not to need to talk all the time. They were, she thought, true companions now.

'I was just thinking,' Bea said at last, 'what a shame it is that you don't eat. My mum and I make the best roast potatoes and my sister, Nicole, makes a pretty fabulous Christmas cake each year. I'm sure you'd love it.'

'I was actually known for my love of cake!' he admitted.

'My George was too.'

For a moment, she wished with all her heart that she could introduce her George to this George standing with her now by the fireplace. What would they make of one another, she wondered? She'd love to know. Two relatives separated by almost four hundred years. It was quite extraordinary. Maybe she'd find out one day. Maybe Ketton had a few more surprises in store for her. She did hope so.

'Did you know that it was Christmas Eve that we had our first son?' George suddenly revealed.

Bea gasped. 'No. I didn't know that!'

'Clever Madeleine. Is there anything more magical than a Christmas baby?'

'Very few things, I'd say.'

George nodded in agreement and then his eyes took on a wistful look as he gazed into his own past. 'My Henry.'

'Not George?' she teased.

'No. Not that time!'

Bea grinned. 'I'm a bit vague on the Beaumont family tree. How many children did you have?'

'Six. Two died young.'

'I'm so sorry.'

George nodded. 'And you just have Rose?'

'Yes. Our heir.' Bea watched George for his reaction. 'How do you feel about that? I mean honestly?'

'A woman inheriting?'

'Yes. I know it was different in your time.'

'But times change, do they not?'

'They do.'

'And change is good.' He nodded. 'Yes. Change can be good.'

They stood, side by side, watching the flames of the fire. It wasn't until a few moments later that George gave a cry.

'Oh, no!'

Bea flinched at the panic in his voice. 'What is it?'

'I – well...' he pointed to his legs which seemed even more transparent than usual.

Bea gasped. 'George! What's happening?'

'I seem to be disappearing.'

And it was true. Right before her eyes, George was fading. Everything below his knees had already gone. It was the oddest sight.

'Is this just – you know – you going for the night?' Bea asked him.

He shook his head. 'This feels different. I think I may be going. For good.'

Bea swallowed hard. 'But I'm not ready for you to go. Not yet!'

'But I cannot help it. I am so sorry, my dear Beatrice, but I think this may be goodbye.'

'No – George!' Beatrice reached towards him, but there was nothing to hold on to. He was fading fast. 'Don't leave me!'

'You are strong, Beatrice!' he told her as his waist faded into oblivion. 'Stronger than you think. You can cope with whatever life throws at you.'

'No. *No!* I need you here with me!' She watched in distress as his arms and torso slowly vanished.

'Ketton is lucky. So lucky!'

'George!' she cried as his face slowly faded before her very eyes. 'Please come back!'

She waited a moment, looking around the room, hoping against hope that he might appear in one of the corners while panic surged through her at the thought that she might never see him again.

'George?' she whispered, her eyes filling with tears.

But there was no sign of him and Bea was left alone in the room, staring helplessly into the empty space that George had left behind.

CHAPTER TWELVE

Beatrice didn't have much time to dwell on George's departure before Christmas slammed into her with the force that only the festive season has. First, Rose's school broke up for the holidays and then Bea had to get the house ready for the arrival of her mother and sister. It was a chore she didn't mind. She liked preparing the guest rooms with fresh bed linen, cosy winter blankets and heaps of cushions. She loved making special little floral displays for the bedside cabinets and decorating the dressing tables until everything was looking homely, festive and sparkly.

There was shopping to do. Food, drinks and last-minute gifts. She also had several floral displays to deliver to local businesses in time for the holidays and a Christmas video to record for all her viewers.

Once the shopping, deliveries and video were ticked off her list, Bea spent several happy hours making a couple of batches of mince pies and wrapping all her gifts. Gift wrapping was one of the things she looked forward to most about Christmas – choosing the wrapping paper and ribbons and decorating each present so that it was totally unique. This year, she'd gone for a gold and ruby theme to match the beautiful ring she'd found and to echo the richness of the Ketton jewels. She'd bought crimson velvet ribbon and made little decorations from tiny gold baubles and berries to slot into the elegant bows she tied around each present. The result was wonderfully opulent.

It wasn't until her mother and sister arrived that Bea felt she could finally stand still and breathe a little. They came armed with presents and Bea watched as they gently placed them all under the Christmas tree in the drawing room, Rose smiling in delight at the scene.

Bea then retreated to the kitchen to make hot chocolate. Her heart suddenly felt very heavy. It was as if the last few weeks were catching up with her. It had been an unusual time. First, she'd found the ring, then Ghost George had arrived, then there'd been the first anniversary of her George's death and the meeting with Mrs Gilbert. Add cousin Simeon, the Ketton jewels, the priest holes and then Ghost George's departure and it wasn't any wonder that she was feeling overwhelmed.

After heating up the milk on the Aga, Bea pulled out her favourite Victorian metal tray featuring hand-painted birds and berries – perfect for Christmas. She remembered the day she'd discovered it at the back of a cupboard, dusty and unloved. That was one of the joys of living at Ketton Hall. You never quite knew what you were going to uncover next.

Hot chocolate made, Bea took the tray through to her waiting family. The scent of the Christmas tree filled the Blue Drawing Room and everything looked soft and mellow in the lamplight as she entered. Her mother and sister were sitting by the fire and Rose was on the floor by the Christmas tree, bewitched by the prettiness of the presents underneath it.

'Hot chocolate, everyone!' she announced and there was an instant chorus of approval as everyone grabbed a mug from the tray.

'Ah!' Nicole sighed in pleasure a moment later.

Rose giggled in delight as she sipped hers and Valerie smiled contentedly. Nobody said anything for a good long while. All were happy in companionable silence, sipping their drinks to the soundtrack of the crackling fire.

'You've done a beautiful job with the room, Beatrice,' Valerie said at last.

'Thanks, Mum. I know the tree's smaller than usual, but I wanted to have it in here for a change.'

'I prefer it in here,' Nicole said.

'Me too!' Rose chimed in.

Bea smiled. She still felt a little guilty at going against one of her husband's traditions but, then again, she kept having to remind herself that Ketton was her home and she had to be able to make her own choices about how she lived in it. And maybe they could have a tree in the hall next year. Or maybe, if they were feeling particularly extravagant, have one in the hall and a second in the Blue Drawing Room.

A few more minutes passed and then Bea thought it was time.

'There's something I want to show you all,' she said.

'What is it?' Nicole asked.

Bea put her empty mug down and left the room, coming back a moment later with the large wooden box she'd found in the priest hole under the stairs. She placed it on the floor in front of the fire and opened it.

'What's that?' Valerie asked, peering into the box.

'It's a Bible from the seventeenth century.' Bea took it out and showed them.

'It's amazing,' Nicole said.

'Not as amazing as what else is in the box,' Bea told them.

'What?' Nicole asked.

Bea felt around to release the catch and then removed the piece of wood to reveal the hidden jewels.

Valerie gasped.

'Are those *real*?' Nicole asked, her eyes wide.

'They are,' Bea said, unable to hide her smile.

Rose inched across the carpet, her hand delving into the box.

'Careful, darling!'

Rose picked out a gold brooch set with a huge amethyst, her little mouth open and wordless.

'How long have you had this for?' Valerie asked.

'I found it last week.'

'Where?'

'Under the stairs. There's a priest hole there – where they'd hide Catholics during the sixteenth century. So these must have been hidden for hundreds of years.' Bea bit her lip, feeling just a little anxious at not telling them the whole truth about the discovery.

'They must be worth a fortune!' Nicole said. Both she and Valerie had joined Rose on the floor and they were all rifling through the jewels.

'I know. I'm not quite sure what to do with them.'

'Well, you'll have to sell them,' Valerie said. 'Isn't that the obvious thing to do? You've said yourself that you're worried about all the costs of running this place. It seems to me as if you've been handed a lifeline.'

'I know. But I hate the thought of them disappearing into some private collection somewhere or being locked away in a bank vault, never to be seen again,' Bea admitted.

'Perhaps there'll be some millionaire who'll buy them for a local museum,' Nicole said. 'Actually, there's someone who did that recently. Remember that Saxon hoard that was found by a metal detectorist? It was all over the local news. They bought the treasure and donated it to the museum in Ipswich, I think.'

Bea felt her heart skip a beat. 'That would be wonderful if we could do the same. I'd love to keep the jewels in Suffolk if it's possible.' She picked up the gold and ruby necklace, watching the way it glowed in the light of the fire.

'Is the ring you're wearing from the box?' Nicole asked.

'Oh, this wasn't part of the collection,' Bea said. 'I actually found it in a gap in the floorboards.'

'Bea!' Nicole cried. 'You should invest in a metal detector of your own. There's no telling what you might find in this old place.'

'Is there more treasure, Mummy?' Rose asked, glancing up.

'I don't think so, darling. I might have found it all now,' Bea said with a grin as she looked at the ring. She loved that she was now wearing three rings from her two Georges. It was a wonderful way of keeping them both close.

'Well, whatever you do, keep it all safe!' Valerie said.

'Oh, I will, don't worry,' Bea said. 'But I also think we should enjoy the pieces – just for a little while.'

Her sister and mother looked confused, but Rose seemed to understand immediately and her little hands delved back into the box and picked out an enormous gold and emerald necklace.

'I want to wear this one!' she declared and everybody laughed.

'And so you shall,' Bea told her. 'This is Ketton's special Christmas present to us all.'

There were far too many presents under the tree, Bea thought on Christmas morning. Her mother did spoil them all so. Of course, the lion's share was for Rose and the true delight was watching her face as she opened them. There were plenty of gifts for everyone, but the most special was the fact that they were all wearing a piece from the Ketton jewel collection. Rose had chosen the emerald necklace, Nicole was wearing diamonds and pearls, Valerie looked resplendent wearing a huge sapphire pendant with matching earrings, and Bea had chosen her favourite gold and ruby necklace to complement George's ring. It was all so outrageously wonderful and the four of them took endless photos showing off their sparkles.

Lunch was to be served in the dining room and Bea had made sure that it was looking its very best.

'You've outdone yourself this year!' Nicole told Bea as they entered the room together. The table had been laid with a simple white damask tablecloth and decorated with a long table runner of ivy and red berries. White candles in elegant silver holders waited to be lit and Bea had decorated the great windowsill with evergreens and glistening red and gold baubles, and had even curled some pretty ivy around some of the picture frames.

Nicole noticed this and crossed the room to look at the portraits.

'I'm not sure I could live with these,' she confessed. 'Don't they scare you?'

Bea joined her and gazed up into the now very familiar face of seventeenth century George. She'd given him a particularly pretty garland of ivy, threading holly berries through it.

'I think they scared me a little when I first moved here, but I've grown very fond of them now. They're... family!'

'Well, I suppose one can get used to anything,' Nicole said.

Bea glanced at her sister. 'Nicole?'

'Yes?'

'Do you believe in ghosts?'

'You mean the pale floaty things?'

'I suppose so, yes.'

She shook her head. 'I think it's all nonsense. The imagination can play tricks on you – that's all. Why? Have you been seeing things?' She suddenly sounded concerned.

'No, it's just...' she paused. 'I've been reading about the family history. Did you know that George here died at the battle of Naseby during the English Civil War? He was married to Madeleine.' She pointed to her portrait. 'They had six children, but two died young.'

'Oh, that's sad.'

Bea nodded. 'It was she who hid the jewels from Oliver Cromwell's men.'

Nicole frowned. 'How do you know that? Did she leave a diary?'

'Not exactly, no. But I've... well, I've been working things out. Timelines. Family history. That sort of thing,' Bea said, keeping things nice and vague.

'It all sounds fascinating.'

'It is!' Bea looked up into George's face. 'History's alive, isn't it? It surrounds us all the time.'

'Maybe it does in a place like this,' Nicole said. 'Talking of family history, has horrible cousin Simeon bothered you again?'

'No, thank goodness.'

'Good.' Nicole put her arm around her. 'You've been through a lot this last year.'

Bea nodded. 'Yes.'

They stood side by side, arms around each other, looking up at the portrait of George. There was a part of Bea that wished she could confide in Nicole and tell her all about her recent adventures, but Bea knew her sister wouldn't believe her. In fact, it would probably just worry Nicole. And so Bea didn't say anything. It would be her and George's little secret.

'Do you think there's time before lunch for me to have a walk?' Bea asked.

'I should think so. Mum's got everything under control in the kitchen and Rose is helping her. Do you want some company?' Nicole asked.

'No. I just need some air, you know?'

Nicole nodded. She knew.

A few minutes later, Bea had wrapped up warm and left the house, crunching across the thick snow that had fallen silently in the night. She headed towards the lake before taking the footpath to the church. Aptly named St George's, it was Saxon in origin and much beloved by the local community. Bea opened the great wooden door and stepped inside, feeling the chill of the building. It actually felt colder inside than it did outside even on this snowy December morning, as if centuries of cold had been locked inside, unable to escape. Bea shivered and pulled her scarf a little higher so that she could tuck her face into it.

While reading about the Civil War, Bea had learned that the church was one of many in East Anglia that had come under attack from the Puritan, William Dowsing. He'd seen it as his job to eradicate all evidence of popery. Two things were always top of his list and they were stained glass and brass inscriptions, and Bea looked for evidence of damage now. Sure enough, there were two windows in the tiny church which had clearly been made up using fragments of old glass which Dowsing and his men had smashed. It was odd to see the jumble of images. A couple of displaced heads floated in leaded isolation among fragments of coloured glass. How beautiful it all must once have been and Bea wondered at the conviction of the men who'd had the nerve to break such a piece of art.

She turned away from the window. The men doing all this damage had been here when George was away fighting and Madeleine was at Ketton alone. Bea shivered at the thought of how terrifying that time must have been.

But it was really the tombs she'd come to see. The church was home to many of her husband's ancestors and she approached the monuments now. The brass inscriptions had been destroyed by Dowsing, and the figures of the great Elizabethan tomb had had their hands, previously held in prayer, cruelly hacked away. Bea shook her head at the wanton destruction.

Bea turned from the Elizabethan tomb to the later, seventeenth century one. George and Madeleine. They almost seemed like friends to her now and her gaze softened as she looked at them, sleeping through eternity together, their carved stone bodies touching, their hands held in prayer. How peaceful they looked, she thought.

She took her gloves off, her fingers reaching out to touch the pale stone of George's shoulder. It felt almost intrusively intimate, but she felt as if she needed to do it – to make physical contact with him.

For a brief moment, the sun broke through the steely clouds and a shaft of light hit the stained glass window, casting a rosy glow on the tomb. Bea gasped; it was as if the faces of George and Madeleine had come to life. There was colour in their cheeks and she wouldn't have been a bit surprised if they'd both sat up and started a conversation with her. She smiled at the thought, removing her hand and saying a little prayer for them both.

There was one other George she wanted to visit. He was buried in the churchyard in a corner with some of the more recent of his Beaumont relatives. It was a special place with a lovely outlook from which you could glimpse Ketton Hall. In spring, it was full of violets and primroses, but there was nothing but snow today.

Bea walked towards the headstone which had been erected back in the summer. Again, she removed her gloves and reached out to touch it, needing that physical contact. She didn't quite know what to say. Her throat felt thick with emotion and she didn't trust herself to speak. Perhaps it was enough to simply be there, she thought, standing for a few solitary moments with only the icy winter wind to keep her company.

'Merry Christmas, George,' she whispered at last. 'I miss you so much.'

And then she turned to go, heading home across the Ketton estate to where her family was waiting for her.

CHAPTER THIRTEEN

Christmas was over much too quickly and it was sad to watch her mother and sister leaving Ketton after the holidays. The old hall seemed so very different when it was just home to Bea and Rose, but this was their life now, as much as Bea wished she could change the past and have her George back.

Perhaps she was a little like Madeleine Beaumont. During the Civil War, Madeleine hadn't given in to fear and turned her back on the house when her George had left to fight, nor even when he'd been killed. Well, Bea wasn't going to give up either. The years ahead might be difficult. There might be problems to face that she hadn't even thought of yet. But she would face them and she would raise her daughter to face them too. If there was one thing she'd learned over the last few weeks it was that the Beaumont women were strong and they didn't quit.

Bea still hadn't decided what to do with the Ketton jewels. There was time enough for that, she reasoned. Anyway, she wanted to enjoy them and welcome them back. They'd been hidden for so long and deserved their time to shine in the light.

One January evening, Bea sat at her dressing table with the

jewellery box. She was holding one of the gold necklaces that she'd previously overlooked. It was a simple chain, but it held a locket and Bea was thrilled to discover a portrait miniature inside it of a woman with dark ringlets wearing a yellow gown edged with lace. Bea gasped as she noted the similarity to the portrait in the dining room. It was George's wife, wasn't it? It was Madeleine.

Bea gazed into the beautiful face held inside the gold locket.

'I wish I could talk to you, Madeleine,' she whispered as she held the cold necklace in the warmth of her hands, staring into Madeleine's bewitching eyes. 'I wish you could hear me.'

As soon as the words were out of her mouth, Bea felt a sudden chill in the room, as if the winter breeze had somehow found its way inside. And there, in the corner of her bedroom, was a beautiful woman in a yellow gown edged with lace, her dark hair long and ringletted. Her face was pale and she had that magical translucency that Ghost George had had, and Bea knew immediately who it was.

'You must be Madeleine,' she said with a welcoming smile.

ACKNOWLEDGEMENTS

To Louisa Flavell at Otley Hall for showing me her beautiful home and giving me an insight into life in an ancient building – ghosts and all!

Thanks to Lynsey Coombs at the National Trust at Oxburgh Hall for letting me venture into the priest hole and for answering all my questions. Also, to Phil at Harvington Hall in Worcestershire for his wonderful videos of the priest holes there. And to Marie Wiik for her beautiful floristry videos which helped to inspire Bea's.

And, as ever, to Roy who lives each of my stories with me and provided the initial inspiration for this one!

A NOTE FROM THE AUTHOR

After finishing writing this novella, my husband and I visited Blickling Hall in Norfolk. I'd been a volunteer there the summer after I graduated from college, working in the estate office and room stewarding in the hall, and I'd been meaning to revisit ever since. How I loved my time there! It was a true privilege to get to know the rooms and the collection so well and a real pleasure to see it all again.

One thing that struck me was how it had stayed with me over the years and had even found its way into my latest story – *The Wrong Ghost*. I write about English country houses a lot – they are endlessly fascinating to me. But there were details at Blickling like a portrait of a gentleman from the English Civil War called Georges Villiers whom I'd discovered while researching my story and who influenced my descriptions of Ghost George. There was also a portrait of Charles the First and another of his wife Henrietta Maria who are both mentioned in this novella. There were also windows with views of the lake, and the local parish church was full of memorials to Blickling's owners.

But a house is always more than its architecture and collection. It's a place where people live and work and there's one person I remember with great fondness. Howard Eaton was the custodian there in the early nineties and he made me very welcome when I began working there. I remember being invited on a tour he was giving of the hall. He was passionate about the history of Blickling and I have a vivid memory of him standing under the portrait of Lady Constance, wife of the eighth Marquess of Lothian, tears in his eyes as he told us of how she was a widow for thirty-one years after losing her beloved husband, William. Howard also allowed me to accompany him one evening when he performed the delightful duty of locking up for the night. I followed him from room to room as he checked and locked each one, using the biggest bunch of keys I have ever seen.

Sadly, Howard died some years ago, but I often think of him. I only spent a short time in his presence, but he was the sort of person you meet and never forget. His kindness, humour and enthusiasm will stay with me forever.

Victoria Connelly

The
CHRISTMAS
ROSE

Bestselling author of *The Rose Girls*

VICTORIA
CONNELLY

To Michael and Brian with love

CHAPTER ONE

There were fewer sights more beautiful than Suffolk's Stour Valley in the snow. The gentle hills and little pockets of trees, the thatched cottages and the brick and flint churches were made all the more magical with a sprinkling of snow.

The two rows of mature horse chestnuts which lined the driveway to Little Eleigh Manor were bare and seemed almost black against the white landscape. In the garden, the rose bushes slept, their flowers long over although Honorine de Brabant and New Dawn had thrown out a few surprise blooms at the beginning of December, but the bitter rain had forced their delicate petals into retreat. Now, the bare rose bushes looked like rows of squat skeletons and it was hard to imagine that they would ever flower again.

The moat that surrounded the ancient manor had frozen days ago and, towering above it, the fourteenth-century red-brick turrets were fur-topped with snow.

It was hard for a family of rosarians to truly embrace the winter, but the three Hamilton sisters could see the beauty of the season and had made the very best of it by bringing armfuls of evergreens into their beloved home, and it was looking resplendent. Ever since her return home, Celeste Hamilton had insisted that the hallway and the living room were decorated for Christmas. One of the benefits of owning a medieval manor house, she'd said, was that the high ceilings could easily accommodate a large tree and so the sisters had ordered a ten-foot one.

'Are you sure we've got enough decorations for it?' Celeste had asked in panic, wondering if they'd been a little too ambitious.

'We can always buy more,' Evie had said extravagantly.

'Or *make* them,' Gertie had said.

There had then begun a long debate over the colour scheme with Celeste favouring traditional colours like gold, red and green, but Evie wanting to go for a winter wonderland palette of silver, white and icy pink.

Gertie, the middle sister, who usually found herself mediating between Celeste and Evie, had pointed out that the tree was so big they could easily accommodate both chosen colour schemes and would probably need to use every single Christmas decoration they could find. But, seeing Evie's woebegone face, Celeste had backed down. So, now, the enormous tree shimmered and sparkled in pale elegance, its silvery ornaments catching the light and making it glow against the dark woodwork of the hallway. However, Celeste had drawn the line at tinsel.

'Everywhere *except* the tree,' she'd insisted, and so there was tinsel wrapped around the handrail of the stairs and adorning the longcase clock. There'd been a spot of mild chaos when they'd first opened the box where the tinsel lived during the long months when it wasn't needed. They'd just started pulling out the sparkling strands when Celeste's terrier, Frinton, had dived in and had run away with a long silver rope. Celeste had been beside herself, envisaging all sorts of horrors and appointments at the vets. But they'd managed to get hold of the little dog and order had been restored, with Celeste insisting that tinsel was placed above Frinton level.

Coming in from a quick march around the garden with Frinton at her heels, Celeste surveyed the glory of the hallway with its twinkling lights and great swags of evergreens which Gertie had done such a marvellous job with. It really did look very festive indeed. There was even a sprig of holly on the barometer which was still refusing to read anything but "Change" on its old silver face. Celeste's partner, Julian, had offered to get it looked at by an expert, but Celeste had refused.

'It's kind of a *thing*,' she'd told him.

He'd frowned. 'Kind of *a thing*?'

'Part of the house. It wouldn't be the same if it actually worked.'

Julian seemed to understand her sentiment although, being very interested in antiques and seeing things restored to working order, she could sense that he was itching to get the barometer fixed.

Celeste took off her coat and boots and then unwound her long scarf before checking Frinton's paws for mud. The ground was iron-hard outside, but she wouldn't put it past the little terrier to have found a muddy patch somewhere amongst all the snow and ice. Inspection complete, she walked through to the living room but, despite the lamps being switched on, there was nobody around. Frinton quickly grabbed his current favourite soft toy which used to be a bunny rabbit but, after repeated chewing, looked more like a snake. He then trotted to his little basket, turned around three times and flopped down.

Dog settled, Celeste went in search of her sisters, walking out into the hallway just as Lukas was coming downstairs with baby Alba in his arms.

'How's my favourite niece?' Celeste asked, kissing the little girl's rosy cheek and stroking her fine blonde hair.

'A little bit grumpy this morning,' Lukas told her. 'That's probably why Evie went to work early.'

'I'm sure it wasn't,' Celeste said, naturally defending her sister. 'She just knows what a brilliant dad you are and that you can cope with absolutely anything!' Celeste kissed Alba again, delighting in the tiny laugh that escaped from her. 'I can't believe how much she's grown already.'

'And she's getting quite heavy now!' Lukas said with a laugh. He had such a wonderful laugh and it was hard to imagine life at Little Eleigh Manor without him. Things hadn't always been easy between him and Evie. Lukas had been far more intent on a relationship than Evie had, but she'd finally realised how wonderful he was and they were engaged now, and Celeste truly couldn't imagine a lovelier family.

'Evie in the study?' Celeste asked.

'I think so.'

'I'll go and find her. See you later my rosy-cheeked girl!'

Celeste watched as Lukas walked into the living room with his daughter and then she turned down the hallway for the short walk to the study. Since their mother's death, the study had been completely refurbished and was now a beautifully light room full of new furniture. The three sisters had truly made it a room which was a pleasure to work in and Celeste could hear their happy voices as she walked towards the door.

'You two hard at work already?' she said as she went in.

Gertie looked up from the computer and laughed. 'I can't believe the original workaholic is last in to the office these days.'

'Yes, well I've learned how to be more balanced,' Celeste said. 'I've been out walking Frinton. It's freezing, but so beautiful out there. There are icicles hanging from the thatch.'

Evie, who loved to try out different hair colours and was now sporting chestnut curls, looked up. 'I can't seem to get Alba interested in the snow.'

Gertie looked at her sister, perplexed. 'She's not even a year old, Evie! She's hardly likely to want to build a snowman yet.'

'I guess,' Evie said, pouting before returning her attention to her computer screen. There were three monitors set up in the study, one each for the sisters. 'Hey, tell Celeste who you got an email from last night.'

Gertie sighed and shook her head.

'Who?' Celeste asked.

'Aled!' Evie announced. 'He says he's really sorry and that he wants to visit at Christmas.'

'Yes, well that's not going to happen. Not after what he did to me in Turin!'

'What did he do again?' Evie asked with a giggle.

'You know full well what he did! I made the mistake of thinking that we were a couple, but then I saw him smooching with that ice cream seller. He tried to deny it but his chin was smothered in *her* strawberry ice cream.'

'Oh, Gertie! You do seem to have the most appalling luck with men!' Celeste said with a sympathetic smile.

'Yes, well, I'm not making *that* mistake again. I hereby dedicate my life to roses.'

Celeste smiled at that. Was there anything lovelier than a room full of rosarians?

'We've just been sent some of the images for the new catalogue,' Evie said. 'Come and see them.'

'Oh, how lovely!' Celeste cried as she peered over Evie's shoulder. 'I've never seen such a beautiful photo of Madame Alfred Carrière before.'

'Yes,' Gertie said. 'You can almost feel the creamy softness of her petals.'

'It's particularly hard to photograph white roses, isn't it?' Evie said. 'I've tried and I've never had any success.'

'I can't wait to see the finished catalogue,' Gertie said. 'It's ages since we had a new one.'

'Yes,' Celeste agreed. The Hamilton Roses catalogue was something that their mother, Penelope, had always been in charge of and it had been a kind of rite of passage for Celeste to take it over, but it was a job she'd fully embraced, welcoming the input of her sisters instead of guarding it jealously as her mother always had.

'We're just looking at ideas for the cover,' Evie added. 'What do you think? I'd like something pink.'

'You always like something pink!' Gertie teased.

'That's not true!' Evie said, but then pursed her lips. 'Well, it's mostly true, I suppose, but I embrace *all* colour.'

'Just don't dye your hair pink, will you? Alba's already known two – or is it three – different mothers since being born,' Gertie pointed out.

Celeste took a seat by her own computer and switched it on.

'Is Julian here yet?' Evie asked, looking at the clock on the wall.

'He should be now that it's ten,' Celeste said. 'The roads aren't bad between here and Nayland, are they? You don't think he's stuck somewhere, do you?'

'No. I saw a snow plough go by before so I shouldn't worry if I were you,' Evie said. 'Hey, how come antiques stores get to open later than other shops and businesses?'

Celeste smiled. 'I once asked him that and he didn't seem to have a good answer.' She logged onto her computer and went straight to her email, downloading the images that had come through for the new catalogue. 'I think we should have one of our own.'

'One of our own what?' Gertie asked.

'One of our own roses. On the cover.'

'Which one?' Evie asked.

'Summer Dawn?' Gertie suggested.

'I'm not sure yellow's right for the cover,' Celeste said.

'But we've got a wonderful photo of it.'

Celeste pulled up the photo of the pale yellow rose. It was, indeed, a beauty. 'But think about what Hamilton Roses stands for. Tradition, the beauty of old roses. I just don't think yellow is traditional enough.'

'I like Queen of Summer,' Evie said, 'and not just because it's pink!'

Celeste nodded. 'Yes, it's a beauty all right. It has all the wonderful qualities of Comte de Chambord, but without that infuriating balling in the rain.'

'Or quite as many thorns,' Evie added.

'But is it right for the cover?' Gertie asked.

The three of them each brought up the lovely image of the Queen of Summer on their computer screens. It was one of Hamilton Roses' best-sellers and, for a few moments, the three sisters gazed at its pink perfection in tender silence.

'It's perfect,' Evie said at last.

'I agree,' Gertie said. 'Celeste?'

Celeste looked at the delicate pink petals and the way the photographer had captured it so perfectly against the verdant green background of the garden. She could almost smell summer as she looked at it.

'Yes,' she said at last. 'That's our cover girl.'

CHAPTER TWO

There was no denying it, Julian Faraday was cold. The cavernous room in the north wing which had been converted into Rose Garden Antiques was seemingly impossible to heat. Not that you wanted an overly warm room where antiques were kept, but something above minus two would have been acceptable.

Esther Martin, who often worked alongside him in what was now affectionately known as 'The Fridge', was wearing a pair of fingerless gloves and a massive grey shawl which gave her a funny round shape. She never seemed to be warm enough even though one of the first things they'd done was to buy a plug-in radiator, but they were loath to use it too often as they didn't want to eat into the money they had yet to earn.

Still, Julian couldn't help smiling as he watched Esther moving around the showroom, a duster in her hand. There was something about Esther that was decidedly different these days. There was a spring in her step and a sparkle in her eyes. Since she'd moved into Little Eleigh Manor she'd become a different woman. Celeste had told him that it had taken some time for her to reveal the warm and loving human being who had been hidden away for so many years after the death of her only child, Sally, but the sweeter side of Esther had surely emerged. She was particularly close to Evie, Celeste said, and often babysat Alba.

'My little treasure,' she called the baby, and it was always a delight to see Esther with the child in the shop while Evie and Lukas worked together in the garden.

But Julian was becoming anxious that his idea to open an antiques centre had been a little too ambitious even in a county famed for its antiques, with tourists coming from miles around to browse in the shops at Lavenham and Long Melford.

He looked around the large room they'd converted. It was a beautiful space with its massive mullioned window, which overlooked the moat, and its large fireplace. It truly was the perfect backdrop for antiques. There was still restoration work to do on the sixteenth-century linenfold panelling and the window frames too, but the room was at least safe and habitable now and no longer posed a threat to human life as it had done such a short time ago when it had been jokingly known as The Room of Doom. Julian was truly proud to call this his workplace. It had its own entrance across the moat which, he believed, provided a unique shopping experience. He didn't know any other shops in England that you approached by crossing a moat.

Having handed over some of his responsibility at his London auction house to other members of staff, he was able to spend more time in Suffolk these days, which he delighted in. He could think of nothing better than getting to drive around the Suffolk countryside, finding antiques. Of course, it also meant that he got to spend more time with Celeste. Meeting her had been one of the great joys of his life, even though it had been under difficult circumstances for her family and she'd been forced to sell some of their beloved rose paintings. But, if it hadn't been for the Hamilton sisters' financial difficulties, he would never have met Celeste and she'd confessed to him that, although she'd dearly loved the paintings and had been sorry to see them go, she loved him more.

But how long would Julian be able to live his dream if the dream wasn't actually making any money? He still had a good income from the auction house, but that didn't mean he could afford to run the antiques centre at a loss.

Walking across to the little plug-in radiator, which was hidden behind the desk, Julian smiled at Esther as she sat down on a stool to polish an old silver candlestick.

'Cup of tea?' he asked.

'Lovely.'

He left the room, walking down the dark corridor which was lined with the same oak panelling as the antiques centre. Julian loved this little journey. He had been going to make do with a small table and a kettle in a corner, but Celeste had insisted that he shared the family kitchen and it made for as good an excuse as any to catch up with the Hamilton girls whom he was delighted to see when he entered now.

'Ah, Julian! I was just about to bring you and Esther some tea,' Celeste announced.

'I'm glad you didn't,' he told her. 'I needed the walk here to warm up.'

'Oh dear. Is it still horribly cold in there?' Gertie asked as she took a sip from a rose-covered mug.

Julian rubbed his hands together. 'It's beyond Arctic.'

Celeste crossed the room and gave him a hug.

'Now, that's warming me up nicely!'

Evie laughed. 'Is that sort of thing allowed in the workplace?'

'We're not in the workplace now,' Celeste declared. 'The kitchen is neutral territory.' As if to prove the point, Celeste then dared to kiss Julian fully on the mouth.

'Well!' he said. 'I'll be sure never to miss a morning break.'

Everybody laughed and Julian went to the cupboard and reached in for two mugs.

'How are things in the antiques world?' Gertie asked.

'Slow,' Julian said. 'I'd hoped for a bit more business what with

Christmas only a week away, but we're just not getting the footfall I'd hoped for. I mean, I know we're off the beaten track here and Little Eleigh isn't in one of Suffolk's antique hot spots...' his voice petered out and he sighed.

'Don't most businesses lose money for the first five years?' Evie asked.

'*Five?*' Julian sounded horrified. 'I thought it was the first year.'

'Yes, I don't think it's that long, Evie,' Celeste said.

'Well, you've only been open three months. You can't expect miracles,' Evie told him.

'I know,' he said, re-boiling the kettle. 'It's just...' He shrugged. What was he going to say to them? That he didn't want to let them down? That he knew how much work it had taken to get the north wing ready to use as a fully operational antiques centre? A lot of work and a lot of money. Most of the money from the sale of the rose paintings had gone on restoring that wing of the house. It was a job that had been long overdue. Celeste had told him it had been the best ever decision to put the room to good use. But what if it turned out to be a really bad decision? What if they couldn't turn a profit?

'Things will pick up,' Gertie told him. 'You're selling beautiful things in a beautiful place. Word will soon get around.'

'Just don't look at us to give you anything to sell. We're still getting over having to part with all those beautiful rose paintings,' Celeste said.

'It's not items to sell that we're short of,' Julian said. 'It's people to buy them!'

'Here, have a cookie,' Gertie said. 'And take a couple for Esther too. Chocolate chip cookies always make things better.'

Julian grinned. 'You know, your home-baking is having an adverse effect on my waistline.'

'That's easily amended,' Celeste said. 'All the paths could do with a shovel. There was more snow in the night.'

Julian gave a little salute. He liked to pull his weight around the place and enjoyed spending time out in the garden. It was a luxury not afforded to him when he was staying at his place in London.

Returning to the north wing and handing Esther her mug of tea and her cookies, Julian looked around the room at his beloved antiques, his gaze resting on the four-poster bed which filled the whole of the west corner. It was an impressive piece and Julian had fallen in love with it as soon as he'd seen it, but it had been a costly purchase and he was beginning to wonder if he'd been a little too ambitious in buying it. Did the people of Suffolk really sleep in such grand beds? Or had he let his heart rule his head with that particular piece?

The rest of the day passed with a slow trickle of people through the door. Browsers mostly, eager to see the old building and what they'd done with it as much as its contents. But there was one curious buyer who caught his attention. He was tall, with long dark hair which curled around his neck and he was wearing sunglasses which Julian found a little odd seeing as he was indoors. But the youngsters liked that sort of thing, didn't they?

'Anything particular you looking for?' Julian asked him.

The young man looked up. 'Erm, not sure. Just at the looking stage.'

'Feel free to ask any questions,' Julian told him, giving him the space and privacy that he himself liked when shopping, but Julian couldn't help glancing at the customer a moment later when he saw the young man's hand gently caress the back of a seventeenth-century chair. So, he has good taste, Julian thought, smiling to himself.

~

Motherhood changed you. There was no denying that, Evie thought as she sat down on the sofa having just put baby Alba to bed.

'I'm exhausted,' she told Lukas who was sitting beside her. 'I mean, *bone* weary. I shouldn't be bone weary at my age, should I?'

Lukas grinned. 'Let me give you a shoulder massage. I bet you're all tensed up again. You spend too many hours on the computer.'

'It's hard not to at this time of year,' she told him. 'Oh, how I miss the summer! I hate being cooped up indoors like this. It isn't natural.'

'I agree.'

She sighed. As much as she loved to see the snow, it infuriated her not to be able to feel the bare earth under her boots. She wanted to be out in the garden, sharing her love of it all with Alba. She'd already started telling Alba the names of all the roses, whispering them musically in her ear. Evie's sisters had laughed at her, telling her it was a bit early, but Evie was quite sure her young daughter was taking it all in.

Evie sighed, picking up her phone and scrolling through the photos she'd taken of the garden in the summer. All those colours, all those scents. Long over now as the rose bushes slept, but just waiting to return with a fanfare of beauty when May arrived. The pristine white snow might be very lovely, but it couldn't hope to compete with the radiant pinks, the sunset yellows and the passionate reds of the roses.

Evie logged into her Facebook page.

'What are you doing?' Lukas asked.

'Just catching up on my social media.'

'No wonder your shoulders are so tense. If you're not hunched over your laptop, you're scrolling on your phone.'

'I don't like to miss out on the gossip. Look – Kate's just put the twins to bed. Isn't that a cute picture?' She held the phone up to Lukas to show him her friend's photo.

'It's not good for you spending all this time looking at screens. You're tying yourself up in knots! What's so important about Facebook anyway?'

It was then that Evie screamed, causing Lukas to flinch.

'What is it?' he yelled in alarm.

Evie's hand was covering her mouth as she stared down at her phone.

'What on earth's going on?' Gertie said, appearing at the living room door.

'What's happening?' Celeste asked, joining her a second later.

'I don't know!' Lukas said. 'Evie?'

'He was here!' she said, her eyes fixed on her phone.

'Who was here?' Gertie asked.

'Scott! Scott Fabian!'

'Who on earth is that?' Celeste asked.

Evie gasped, looking up from her phone in undisguised horror. 'How can you *not* have heard of Scott Fabian?'

'Erm, can I just point out you'd never heard of Doris Day until last week?' Celeste said.

'Oh, you know I don't watch all those old films like you do,' Evie said.

'And *I* don't watch all the modern stuff,' Celeste said.

'Well, you should. Scott Fabian's only the star of the biggest show on TV!' Evie went on.

Gertie nodded. 'I think I might have heard of him. What's that thing he's in? Something set in space?'

'*Planet X*,' Evie said. 'It's a sci-fi adventure set in the future when all the prisons are so overrun that they send a group of prisoners out to colonise a new planet.'

'You mean like when we used to send convicts to Australia?' Celeste said.

'We used to do that?' Evie asked.

Julian appeared at the living room door with Esther by his side.

'We heard a scream,' he said. 'Everything okay?'

'That's what we're trying to establish,' Celeste said. 'What's so special about Scott Fabian, Evie?'

'That's what I'm trying to say – *he was here!*'

'Here where?' Esther asked.

'In the antiques centre – look!' Evie turned her phone round and they all peered at the screen.

'Somebody took a photo of him shopping right here and it seems to be all over the internet!'

Celeste turned to Julian. 'Did you see him?'

Julian took hold of the phone and looked closely.

'You really couldn't have missed him,' Evie went on. 'He's gorgeous!'

Lukas cleared his throat.

'Not as gorgeous as you, obviously,' Evie quickly added and then turned to Julian. '*Please* tell me you didn't miss him.'

'He was here all right,' Julian said.

Evie leaped off the sofa in excitement. 'What did he do? What did he say?'

'Well,' Julian began, 'he didn't say a lot really. Just wanted a look around. He showed a bit of interest in a couple of items, but he was in and out very quickly.'

'Did you talk to him?' Gertie asked.

'Just the usual welcome.'

'Was he wonderful?' Evie asked, a dreamy expression on her face.

Julian laughed. 'He was polite enough. He didn't make me swoon, though.'

Celeste batted Julian's arm.

'Did he make *you* swoon, Esther?' Evie asked.

'Can't say that I noticed him,' Esther said. 'I must have been having a dust.'

'Oh, this is *so* disappointing! We had a *huge* star right here at Little Eleigh and nobody noticed!'

'Maybe he'll come back,' Esther said.

'Yes, he was definitely eyeing up one of the chairs,' Julian told her.

'Oh, my goodness!' Evie suddenly said. 'This could be amazing for the shop!'

'It could?' Julian asked.

'He has a massive tribe of fans,' Evie explained.

'*Tribe?*' Celeste said, wrinkling her nose.

'His female fans. It's from his show. They follow him everywhere.'

'And you think they'll now be spending hundreds of pounds on nice antiques because their favourite star popped in here?' Gertie said. 'Come on, Evie! That's not going to happen.'

'I didn't say that, but this sort of publicity helps spread the word about a place,' she said. 'Don't you see? He's a huge star. If he's been seen somewhere, other people are going to want to go there too – to walk in his footsteps. Look!' Evie fiddled with her phone again. 'The antiques centre is being talked about on all these sites. Hundreds if not thousands of people have seen this and shared it. That photo someone took of him here is all over the country now.'

'Really?' Celeste said, turning to Julian who was looking a little sceptical about the whole thing.

'I'm telling you,' Evie said, 'this could be the making of Rose Garden Antiques.'

CHAPTER THREE

Nobody really believed Evie but, by the next morning, there was a crowd of young women outside the gates of the manor, waiting for the antiques centre to open. The snow and the biting wind hadn't seemed to put them off.

'Are they really all here because of Scott Fabian?' Celeste asked.

'You think they've suddenly acquired a taste for antiques?' Evie said. 'They're here for Scott!'

As soon as Julian unlocked the heavy oak door, they all trooped inside. There were at least a dozen of them.

'Is it true?' one of them asked breathlessly. 'Was he here?'

Julian smiled. 'Scott Fabian?'

The girls sighed and gasped at the mere mention of his name.

'He was, wasn't he? He was right here in this room! I saw it on Twitter!'

'He was indeed,' Julian confessed.

'What was he like? What did he say?'

Julian felt a little taken aback as the young women circled around him, their phones clicking as they took photos.

'He was very polite,' Julian said, rubbing the back of his neck.

'Did he talk about the show?' someone asked from the back.

'Well, he–'

'Is he engaged yet?' somebody else asked.

'I really couldn't say if–'

'When is the next season of *Planet X* out?'

'He didn't talk about it,' Julian said, noticing the look of disappointment on the girls' faces.

'He doesn't know a lot, does he?' one of the girls said with a tut.

It was then that Esther made an appearance.

'He admired these candles,' she told them, pointing a persuasive finger.

Suddenly everybody was grabbing handfuls of candles.

Julian sidled up to her. 'Esther,' he whispered, 'I'm not sure how ethical that is.'

'What? It'll keep the till happy and it's the cheapest thing in the shop. If they can have a little piece of their hero for under a tenner then I'd say they were winning.'

Julian shook his head at her logic, but thought it would probably be in their best interests if they ordered some more candles.

By the end of the day, all of the candles had been sold and they'd even managed to sell a few of the smaller items in the shop as well including a silver Art Nouveau photo frame and a beautiful inlaid box.

'Remind me to send a thank you card to this Scott Fabian,' Julian told Esther.

'I told you!' Evie said when she heard the news later that evening at dinner.

'Yes, it was quite something,' Julian said. 'We had a steady stream of visitors all day, all asking if Scott Fabian had been here and what did he buy and what did he say. Quite amusing!'

'Someone asked me what he smelled like!' Esther revealed.

Celeste almost choked on her spaghetti. 'What on earth did you say?'

'I said he smelled like beeswax and promptly sold her a tin.'

'Oh, Esther, you didn't!' Celeste laughed.

'Yes, I'm not sure about the ethics of all this,' Julian said.

'I say, make the most of it,' Esther said. 'It won't last forever.'

It was then that Julian's phone buzzed in his pocket. He took it out and looked at it, moving away from the table as he didn't like to interrupt dinner by taking a call, especially when he didn't recognise the number.

'Hello?' he said a moment later, feeling quite sure that it was somebody trying to sell him something.

'Hello?' said a hesitant voice that Julian didn't recognise. 'Is that Julian Faraday?'

'Yes it is. How can I help you?' Julian had now left the kitchen and was in the hallway.

'I was in your shop the other day and took one of your business cards from the desk.'

'Oh, yes?'

'Yes and I spotted a bed. Well, I spotted a lot of things and I'd really like to come back and look again but, well, I think I might have caused a bit of a problem. I drove by today and there seemed to be quite a crowd of people.'

Julian smiled. 'Yes, it seems we've had a bit of interest after...' he let his voice peter out as he realised just whom he might be speaking to.

The caller cleared his throat. 'I'm Scott Fabian and I'm really sorry if I've caused you any trouble.'

Julian paused as it sunk in. 'Erm, no trouble. We had a few more shoppers than usual, which is excellent. I should thank you really.'

Scott gave an uneasy laugh. 'That's kind of you.'

'So, would you like to come over? We could make an out of hours appointment if that would suit you better.'

Scott didn't answer at first and Julian hoped that he hadn't somehow scared him off.

'Actually,' Scott cleared his throat again, 'I think it might be easier if you came out to me. I mean, I really don't know what will go in my home.' He paused. 'You see, I've just bought it and it's – well – it's old. I've never had an old place before. I could use some help. Would that be all right? Is that the sort of thing you do? Because I really liked your stuff.'

Julian tried not to blanch at his fine antiques being referred to as *stuff*.

'I'd be happy to help if I can,' he told him.

'Great! Look, I know it's the run-up to Christmas and everything and you must be really busy,' Scott went on, 'but it would be really cool if I could get some things before then. Half the rooms here are empty and it would be nice to, you know, fill them a bit.'

Julian had spent the last few days worrying that he'd bought too much stock and now, for the first time, he was worrying that he might not have enough.

'That sounds great,' Julian told him. 'When would you like me to come over?'

'I think the sooner the better. I'm a bit sick of sleeping on the airbed. How would tomorrow suit you?'

'That would be fine.'

'Ten o'clock? I'm not an early riser when I don't have to be.'

'Ten's fine.'

'Right, I'd better tell you where I am.'

Julian reached into the inside pocket of his jacket, retrieved a small notebook and fountain pen and began to write down the address and directions.

'It's outside the village,' Scott was saying. 'In between the church and the green. The track's a bit treacherous with the snow and the potholes so be careful.'

'Okay,' Julian said, mentally trying to locate the village. He knew roughly where it was, but hadn't driven out that way for quite some time.

'Come round to the back door. I won't hear you at the front.'

'And is there anything you'd like me to bring from the shop? I mean, anything portable?'

'There was a chair I spotted that I really liked.'

Julian instantly remembered the chair Scott Fabian had been admiring. 'The seventeenth-century one?'

Scott laughed. 'I'm not sure to be honest. It kind of looked like a throne.'

'I know the one you mean. I'll bring it along.'

'Great! I'll look forward to it.'

'I'll see you tomorrow.'

'Cheers!'

Julian popped his phone in his pocket and walked back into the kitchen.

'Who was that, Jules?' Evie asked.

Julian looked at her and grinned. 'You're not going to believe who it was.'

'Who?' Celeste asked.

'Scott Fabian.'

A strange squealing sounded from the table, the like of which Julian had never heard before.

'What did he say?' Esther asked, waving her hand to quieten the three excitable Hamilton sisters.

'It seems he's bought a big old house right here in Suffolk–'

Evie screamed. 'I knew it! There've been rumours about it for a while now, but I didn't dare hope!'

'Let Julian finish, Evie!' Gertie said.

'So, he's bought this old house and wants to fill it with antiques.'

Celeste's mouth fell open. '*Fill* it?'

'Well, he wants my advice as to what might suit the place.'

'You're going over there?' Evie cried.

'Tomorrow morning.'

'You have his *address*?'

'Well, I couldn't very well go round there without it.'

'Oh, Julian – you have to take me with you,' Evie said, on her feet now. 'I can be your assistant for the day. I won't even charge you!'

Julian laughed. 'I don't think that's a very good idea, do you?'

'Why not?'

'Well, what would Lukas say for a start?'

'Oh, he won't mind,' Evie said, answering before Lukas could. 'He'll be glad that I'm getting it all out of my system. Honestly, I just need to meet Scott Fabian and maybe shake his hand or take a quick selfie. Maybe he'd even put his costume on for it. What do you think?' Evie shook her head as soon as she'd asked the question. 'No, that's going too far.'

'Evie, Julian can't possibly take you. He's professional and this is his work,' Celeste told her.

'Oh, you won't mind, will you, Julian?'

'Well, I don't think it would be wholly appropriate.'

Evie pouted and sat back down and Lukas put his arm around her in sweet consolation.

'Sorry,' Julian added with an apologetic shrug. 'I'll tell you all about it, though, I promise.'

'Yeah, well, you'd better!' Evie said with a smile that was only half begrudging.

Thick, fluffy flakes of snow were swirling in a pearly white sky as Julian got ready to leave Little Eleigh Manor. Since opening his antiques business, he'd bought an all-wheel drive as Celeste had warned him that he could easily get stuck driving his MG around the winter countryside. Looking at it now, he was glad he'd made that decision although he'd kept the MG for fun days out. Not only would he feel a lot safer heading out on this particular day in the all-wheel drive, but also the boot size allowed him to easily fit the seventeenth-century chair inside.

'Are you sure it's safe to go?' Celeste asked as he put on his coat and hat.

'It isn't that far and I'll be home before it's dark.' He bent to kiss the worry lines etching their way across Celeste's forehead.

'Drive carefully,' she told him.

'Of course.' He smiled and bent to pat Frinton. Then he turned to crunch his way through the fresh layer of snow that had fallen in the night.

Celeste watched until Julian's car was out of sight and then she closed the front door and returned to the warmth of the fire in the living room where she plumped a few cushions and straightened Frinton's bed.

She had to admit that she didn't like Julian venturing out. The roads around the Stour Valley were treacherous enough at the best of times but, under a layer of snow, they could prove lethal. Approaching the mantelpiece, she looked at the photo Evie had taken of her with Julian in the garden back in the summer. They were right in the middle of the rose garden, surrounded by enormous blooms. Celeste could almost catch their scent now and she closed her eyes, trying to recapture that wonderful, summery moment.

Julian had come into her life at such a strange time. She still couldn't believe that she'd been given the chance to fall in love again. After her failed marriage to Liam, she'd resigned herself to being one of those women who moved through life on their own, but then Julian had crossed the moat and walked straight into her heart.

Now, just as with Esther and Lukas, Celeste couldn't imagine Little Eleigh Manor without Julian. For a long time, she'd never thought it possible that she could ever make a home at the manor, but she and her sisters, Julian, Esther, Lukas and Alba had made a very special family there. Of course, there were still dark days when she would feel the presence of her mother and all her old anxieties would rise inside her, but she had only to walk into another room and find Evie bouncing Alba on her lap or take Julian and Esther a cup of tea in the antiques centre and her mood would lift. How lucky she was, she thought, to be surrounded by so much love.

She was just about to venture into the office when there was a knock at the door. It was probably Julian having forgotten something, she thought, but then he had his own key so surely he wouldn't knock.

Frinton started barking and came running through into the hallway after his mistress which pretty much told Celeste that it wasn't Julian on the other side of the door.

'Let's see who it is, shall we?'

She opened the door to the frigid world outside and gasped at the ruddy complexion that greeted her.

'Hello Celly, my dear!'

CHAPTER FOUR

'Uncle Portland!' Celeste exclaimed. 'What a surprise!'

'A pleasant one, I hope!'

'Come in – come in! What on earth are you doing here?'

'Come to see my three beautiful nieces, of course!' he said, a chuckle reverberating from out of his great white moustache. 'Very nearly didn't make it.'

'You drove all the way from Kent in this dreadful weather?' Celeste said, ushering him inside and taking his hat and coat as he stepped out of his boots.

'No bother, really.'

Celeste smiled. Their Uncle Portland had always been the world's most uncomplaining person.

'How lovely! I wish we'd known to expect you.'

'Then it wouldn't have been a surprise!' he said.

'I know, and it's a lovely one! But we could have got some of your favourite things in. Do you still have a passion for honey-roasted cashew nuts?'

He nodded and laughed and it was a lovely big, bubbling sound that came from the very centre of his being.

'Give your Uncle P a hug!'

Celeste sank happily into his massive embrace, her face enveloped in her uncle's tweed jacket and matching waistcoat while Frinton's little legs scratched at them both, eager not to be left out.

'And who's this little fellow?' Uncle Portland asked, bending down to scoop the dog up in his large hands.

'Frinton.'

'And a mighty handsome chap!'

'Just wait until you meet my other handsome chap,' Celeste said. 'And Evie's too and her daughter. You got the photos we sent you of Alba? Gosh, there's *so* much to catch up on.'

Uncle Portland looked a little uneasy.

'Is everything all right?' Celeste asked.

'Before everyone – you know – descends, I just want to have a quiet word with you.'

They walked through to the living room and Celeste threw a log onto the fire and they both sat down, Frinton curling up by Uncle Portland's feet.

'What is it?' Celeste said.

'I want to apologise, my dear. The fact is, I've been a terrible uncle.'

'No!'

'Now, you know I have,' he said, shaking his head gravely. 'I should have been here for you more. I know what a difficult time you had coping with your mother. She wasn't an easy woman to get on with.'

'It's okay, Uncle P.'

'No, no! I feel bad about it. But you know your mother and I never had a good relationship.'

'I know.'

He nodded. 'You know better than most, I think, what it was like to truly feel her wrath.'

Celeste gave him a tiny smile. 'Oh, yes.'

'I had to distance myself.'

'You don't need to explain, really you don't,' Celeste assured him. 'I did the same thing. I ran away from here. I had to get away and I made a dreadful mistake by getting married. I ran from one terrible problem right into another.'

Uncle Portland sighed. 'But you're all right now?'

'Never better.'

'Well, you look good. Healthy. Happy.'

'I am. I truly am.'

They exchanged smiles, their strange interwoven past silently acknowledged. They understood one another.

'Now, for goodness' sake, let me get you something warm to drink. I still can't believe you drove all that way. You must have left while it was still dark!' Celeste got up and led him out of the room.

'Always good to beat the traffic,' he told her.

'But to drive in these conditions.'

'It was nothing. Needed to see my rose girls.'

She smiled. 'Well, it's wonderful to see you. Evie? Gertie?' she called down the hallway. 'Come and see who's here!'

There then followed a mad few minutes of happy shrieks and warm embraces as Gertie and Evie ran through from the study and welcomed their uncle.

'It's so good to see you!' Gertie cried.

'Come and meet Alba and Lukas,' Evie said, grabbing him by the hands.

'He's going to have a drink first, Evie,' Celeste told her sister.

'It's going to be so much fun having you here for Christmas,' Gertie told him.

'Oh, I'm not staying for Christmas!' he said.

'What?' Evie shrieked. 'But you *have* to!'

'I wouldn't dream of putting you to all that bother.'

'But it's no bother, Uncle P,' Evie said. 'We've got bags of room here and you've *got* to spend time with your great-niece.'

'Yes, you can't come all this way and not stay for Christmas,' Celeste said, genuinely puzzled.

Uncle Portland stroked his moustache, looking uneasy. 'I hadn't planned on...'

'But we'd love to have you,' Gertie said.

'Yes,' Evie added. 'And maybe you could grow a big white beard to match your moustache and then you could be Santa. Alba would love that!'

Uncle Portland laughed. 'Well, let's see, shall we? I suppose I could be persuaded to stay a little while.'

'You absolutely can!' Celeste said. 'Now, let's get this drink and I'm sure there's some of Gertie's homemade flapjack hiding somewhere. That's worth staying for if nothing else!'

Julian was right. It wasn't far to travel, but the icy conditions made it a far longer journey than normal. Just before he'd left the manor, he'd placed a garden spade in the car in case he had dig himself out of any snowdrifts, and Celeste had given him a flask of hot tea, a bag of cookies and a blanket. He'd never felt so cherished.

Leaving the Stour Valley, he drove the short distance to the village where Scott Fabian lived. Julian had dared to look up the star on the internet the night before, marvelling at the amount of coverage there was on the young actor. He was only twenty-nine and the TV series, *Planet X*, was his first major role. Talk about landing on your feet, Julian had thought. Prior to the hit TV show, Scott had done a bit of stage work and a couple of low-budget horror films which were best not talked about. But he was obviously flavour of the month, gracing the covers of international magazines, doing a spot of modelling work and appearing at a hundred red-carpet events. It was a very different world from the quiet one Julian inhabited.

Entering the village and passing the church, Julian started slowing down, looking for the track that would lead to Scott Fabian's home. It wasn't difficult to find although, if he hadn't had instructions, he would most likely have never guessed that there was a house down there at all. It was probably the very reason Scott Fabian had bought the place. It was the perfect hideaway from a manic world where everybody seemed to want a piece of him.

As promised, the track was full of potholes as well as being covered in snow. Julian took his time, thankful that he wasn't in his MG. Then, just as he thought the track would never end, it dipped and turned a bend, revealing the most beautiful of homes.

It was the kind of house that graced the pages of luxurious lifestyle magazines. It was a black and white, timber-framed building dating back to at least the fifteenth century, Julian estimated, and it had the largest thatched roof he had ever seen.

He parked his car and got out, crossing the driveway in search of the back door. It didn't take long to find and he rang the bell. A moment later, the door opened and there was Scott.

'Mr Fabian? I'm Julian Faraday.'

'Please, call me Scott,' he said. 'And come inside before you freeze to death.'

'I'll just get the chair you wanted to see,' Julian said.

'I'll give you a hand,' Scott said, stepping into a pair of boots by the back door. Julian was glad of the help, not just because the chair was heavy, but because the ground was slippery and he'd have hated to have dropped the beautiful piece of furniture. It didn't take long for them both to get it indoors.

'Blimey, it's cold,' Scott said. 'I've just had a stack of logs delivered, thank goodness. But let's take a look at this chair.'

Julian gave him some space, watching as Scott ran his fingers over the woodwork.

'You must think I'm a philistine not knowing much about antiques, but I appreciate them.'

'But that's the most important thing,' Julian told him. 'If you can see the beauty in them, you can then go on and find out more about them. But it all starts with having that eye to spot something unique – something that speaks to you from another time and place.'

'And this chair spoke to me!'

'You've got good taste. It's one of the finest pieces in the shop.'

'I'll take it!'

Julian grinned. 'Yes?'

'Sure! Would a bank transfer be okay?'

'Of course.'

'Great. Now, let's get you something to drink and then I'll give you a tour. I'll be needing more chairs and anything else you can recommend to fill these empty rooms.'

'Okay,' Julian said, trying not to laugh at the young man's enthusiasm and the possible sales he had coming his way.

'You know, it might just be easier if you bring your whole shop over here. This old house could easily swallow it up.'

'I'll be happy to advise you on the pieces I think would suit this place.'

'Brilliant!' Scott said, clapping him on the back.

Evie, Julian thought, would surely have passed out by now.

CHAPTER FIVE

'How's this room for you, Uncle P?' Celeste asked as she opened the door into one of the spare rooms in the east wing. It wasn't terribly big, but it was a lovely cosy room with linenfold panelling and a casement window which looked out towards the walled garden.

'It's splendid!' he told her, nodding furiously.

'The bed's just been made up and we've got a little plug-in radiator for you. I hope it's not too cold.'

'No, no! Absolutely perfect.'

'Good,' she said. 'We've put some towels out for you over there and the bathroom's just along the hallway. I'll let you get settled in. We tend to spend a lot of time in the study so you'll know where to find us if you need us. Failing that, the kitchen or the living room. I'll introduce you to Esther later. She's running the antiques centre while Julian's out for the day.'

'Esther Martin?'

'Yes.'

'Wasn't it her daughter who was in love with your father?'

'That's right.'

'Bad business that. All ended in tears, didn't it?'

'I'm afraid so. But she's living here with us now,' Celeste informed him.

'Who is?'

'Esther. She's got a suite on the ground floor.'

'What?' Uncle Portland barked. 'Well, I never!'

Celeste laughed. 'I *told* you we've got a lot to catch up on.'

'It certainly sounds like it!'

Celeste smiled, leaving him to it as she returned downstairs.

Julian watched as Scott carefully placed his newly acquired chair in the hallway.

'I want this to be the first thing I see every time I come home.'

'It certainly looks the part,' Julian said.

'Looks like it was made for this house.'

'A little bit later in date, but it does look at home here.'

Scott clapped his hands together. 'Okay, how do you want to do this?'

'Well, if you tell me the pieces you're most in need of when you show me the rooms.'

'Sure – good plan,' Scott said. 'We'll start downstairs. Apologies for the cold. I'm only heating the rooms I'm using at the moment.' He led the way along the hall, opening a door into an impressive room. 'Dining room, I think.'

Julian nodded. 'Beautiful.' He noted the plasterwork ceiling and the enormous fireplace, the flagstone floors and the mullioned windows. But, boy, was it cold in there.

'Better have a dining table and chairs,' Scott said, sticking his hands under his arms in an attempt to keep them warm.

Julian took his notebook out from his jacket pocket and then retrieved his trusty fountain pen which accompanied him everywhere.

'I've got a table that might just do the job,' Julian told him, thinking of the piece he'd got stored in the room adjacent to the main shop. 'Mind if I take some measurements?'

'Please,' Scott said.

Julian got out his tape measure and made some notes and they moved on.

The rest of the rooms were equally as impressive as the first and the hours slipped happily by as the two men moved from room to room, discussing and dreaming and making notes and plans. The house was virtually empty save for a couple of beanbags, a leather chair and a sofa.

'I didn't really think it through,' Scott confessed, scratching his head. 'I'm going to have to get someone in to help at some point because I just haven't got the time at the moment, but I do want to choose at least a few pieces myself. That's why I was so pleased to find your place. But I knew I had to have this house when I saw it and I couldn't chance it slipping away.'

'If you don't mind me saying, you're a very unusual young man,' Julian said, hoping he didn't sound patronising. 'I mean, I thought – erm – someone like you – I mean, someone in your position, would want a modern place in London or New York or somewhere.'

'Oh, I've got a flat in London,' Scott said. 'I need a base there, but I don't want to be there all the time.'

'So what drew you to this place?'

Scott shrugged. 'I was flicking through one of those big glossy magazines. Someone had left it on set and I was hanging around so I took a look. I seriously didn't think it would lead to me buying a house!'

Julian laughed.

'But there was something about it that drew me to it, you know? I can't explain it. It was like I knew my fate was somehow tied up in it. Does that make sense?'

'It does,' Julian said, remembering his first visit to Little Eleigh Manor and meeting Celeste. 'Sometimes you just know, don't you?'

They exchanged a smile.

'My fiancée thought I was crazy,' Scott went on, 'but she totally fell for the place when I showed it to her.' Suddenly, his face took on a look of horror.

'What's the matter?' Julian asked.

'It's not exactly public knowledge that we're engaged,' he said.

'Your secret's safe with me,' Julian said, eager to reassure him.

Scott breathed a sigh of relief. 'I'd be grateful,' he said.

'Really, you don't need to worry.'

'That's good to know.' He shook his head. 'It's a nightmare trying to keep any sort of privacy these days. Everybody wants something from you and we've been trying to keep just a little bit of our lives private. I only proposed last week and we wanted to tell our families at Christmas. The press will find out soon enough. Once my agent gets wind of it, it'll be all over the papers and magazines.'

'It must be a strange life for you.'

'Yeah,' Scott agreed. 'That part of it is. It's the bit nobody warns you about. They're so eager to tell you how difficult it is to make a living, but they don't warn you about the pitfalls of when you actually do become famous.'

'I can only imagine what that must be like.'

'Hey, I shouldn't complain. Not when I've got so much be grateful for.' He looked around the room they were standing in and then his gaze focused on the view from the window. They'd barely noticed the weather had turned and that there'd been quite a blizzard since Julian's arrival. The outside world was one of black and white. Julian could barely tell where the ground ended and the sky began.

'It's looking quite dangerous out there now,' he said.

Scott walked across to the window. 'And it'll be dark soon. How were the roads when you drove here?'

'Not good.'

Scott nodded. 'They'll be worse now.'

'Yes.'

'I think you'd better stay.'

'I wouldn't want to put you to any trouble.'

'No trouble,' Scott said. 'It's just, well, you've seen the place. It's not cut out for inhabitants at the moment, but I have got an airbed and you're welcome to it. I can sleep on the sofa easily enough and it might be better than you getting stuck in a snowdrift.'

Julian nodded, seeing the wisdom of that.

'Then you'll stay?'

'If you're sure it's okay.'

'You'll be my first guest,' Scott said with a laugh. 'Hey – are you hungry? I'm starving! We didn't stop for lunch, did we? Tell you what, you ring whoever you have to ring to explain what's going on and I'll rustle up something in the kitchen. What say you to an omelette?'

'That would be great.'

'I'll get on with that then. Come and join me when you're ready. You remember where the kitchen is?'

Julian nodded and watched as Scott left the room and then he pulled his phone out of his pocket.

'Celeste?' he said a moment later.

'Julian! How's it going?'

'Good, but it looks like I'm stuck.'

'Are you all right? Where are you?'

'I'm still at Scott's. He's invited me to stay.'

'You mean *at* Scott Fabian's?'

'He said it would be all right. There's an airbed and a sofa.'

'But you don't have any – any–'

'I don't have my toothbrush, I know.'

'Or any spare clothes.'

Julian laughed. 'I didn't really expect this today, but I dread to think of the state of the roads now.'

'Yes, don't even attempt them. Stay safe,' Celeste told him. 'Hang on a minute. Evie's just come into the room.'

Julian heard Celeste talking to her sister and then heard a scream.

'No, I'm not going to tell him to take photos!' Celeste said and Julian had to stop himself from laughing. 'Evie's threatening to sledge herself over so she can stay there too.'

'Tell her I'm probably sleeping on an airbed in an empty room.'

'She'll still be jealous.'

'I'd rather be with you,' he told her.

'Just be safe and get home when you can,' Celeste said. 'And enjoy it! It's not every day you get to stay with a movie star!'

When Celeste came off the phone, she went to switch on the lamps in the living room. Dark was closing in at the manor and she felt relieved that Julian hadn't attempted to drive back. She'd been worrying about him all afternoon. When she'd taken Frinton out for a quick run, the snow had begun to fall heavily and she'd found it difficult enough making it back to the front door, never mind negotiating the country roads.

Looking around the cosy living room, it occurred to her that she hadn't seen Uncle Portland for a little while. True, she and her sisters had been working, but she didn't want to appear rude and so went in search of him.

Climbing the stairs, she called softly as she approached his room just in case he was having a doze.

'Uncle Portland?' She knocked lightly on the door, but there was no answer. She waited a moment and then tried again, knocking a little louder this time, but no reply came and, as she had no wish to disturb him, she left.

She tried again later, imagining that he would more than likely want something to eat.

It was as she was heading towards the stairs that she saw him coming out of one of the disused bedrooms.

'Uncle Portland!'

'Celeste!' He looked startled at seeing her.

'Are you all right?'

'Ah, yes. Quite all right. I was looking for the bathroom.'

'It's the next door down,' she told him.

'That's right. Silly me!' He waved a hand and disappeared into the bathroom and Celeste thought no more of it.

CHAPTER SIX

Julian looked around Scott Fabian's kitchen. It was the most complete room in the house in terms of usability. There was a large range, a beautiful old Butler sink, a sturdy table and chairs and endless shelves and racks ready to be filled with beautiful crockery.

'Well,' he told Scott across the table, 'that was the best omelette I've ever had. If the acting business doesn't work out, you should think about opening your own restaurant. Not that it hasn't already worked out for you. Acting I mean.' Julian could feel himself blushing but, luckily, Scott didn't seem to notice his embarrassment.

'My mum gave me a few quick recipes before I went to drama school,' Scott confided. 'I think she was worried I was going to starve.'

'It's a good skill to have.'

'I did a bit of cooking on set a couple of months ago. The caterer suddenly took sick so I stepped up with the help of some of the extras. It was great fun. Exhausting, but fun.'

'Was that the set of *Planet X*?'

'Yes. Do you watch the show?'

'I'm ashamed to say that I don't,' Julian admitted. 'But, then, I don't watch a lot of TV.'

Scott grinned. 'It makes a nice change to talk to someone who's not badgering me for plot reveals or asking me whether Monica Shay's character's ever going to return.'

'It's doing well, isn't it? What's that like – being in a big TV show?'

Scott shrugged. 'It's pretty cool,' he said. 'I got lucky. There was no telling from the pilot we shot. I remember getting the script and wanting to throw it back at my agent, but I was new in the business and it was a job so I took it. I've never been much of a fan of sci-fi and I really had no idea the show would be so big.'

'Do you watch it yourself?'

'Not the bits I'm in,' Scott admitted. 'But there are other storylines I like to keep up with. There are several crews, you see, and we all do our own thing with parallel storylines, but I hate watching myself on screen.'

'I can only imagine how that must feel.'

'But tell me about your job.'

Julian was genuinely surprised by this request, but was thrilled to tell Scott a little something about the work he did at his auction house in London and how his dreams of opening an antiques centre had recently come true.

'I feel very lucky,' Julian told him.

'I know that feeling!' Scott agreed as his phone rang. He took it out, checked it and then switched it off and threw it onto the table where it landed with an angry clatter. 'Two months old and it's already got a crack in the screen.'

Julian wasn't surprised if he threw it around like that regularly.

'I sometimes hate technology,' Scott went on. 'Everything's always moving forward and there's this constant demand to replace and renew. Maybe that's why I'm drawn to antiques and this old house.' He looked around the kitchen, at the deep stone windowsill and the flagstone floor. 'There's just this feeling of permanence, of something *real*. Like that old chair you brought round. That's so *solid*. It's not flimsy and brittle like that phone.'

'I love that about antiques too.'

'Then you'll work with me? You'll help me fill this place?'

Julian smiled. 'I'd be absolutely delighted to.'

~

'When are you going to switch that thing off?' Lukas asked Evie from the other end of the sofa.

She looked up from her laptop screen. 'In a minute. I've just found this interview with Scott Fabian where he's talking about a new film he's going to be shooting soon.'

'You're becoming obsessed with that guy,' Lukas said.

Evie sighed, noticing Lukas's pout. He wasn't normally one to pout, which told her she'd probably got herself a little too excited about Suffolk's latest resident. Happily, she closed down her laptop and put her arms around her fiancé's shoulders.

'You know you're the only man for me,' she told him, snuggling up next to him.

'Yeah? Are you sure?'

'Totally!'

'What if Scott Fabian arrived in his rocket from *Planet X* to sweep you off your feet?'

'I'd tell him I was very flattered, but that he'd better return to space because I'm already spoken for.'

'Really?'

'You bet!' Evie said, kissing Lukas's cheek. 'I bet he wouldn't know his way around a garden or how to prune a rose.'

'All important things.'

'Exactly,' Evie said and he kissed the top of her head.

'Hey, where's your Uncle Portland got to?'

Evie frowned. 'I'm not sure. He's probably with Celeste.'

~

But Uncle Portland wasn't with Celeste. In fact, Celeste had been looking for him again.

It had to be said that Portland was the perfect picture of an uncle: kind, jovial and slightly rotund. The girls had always been fascinated by the wonderfully old-fashioned way he dressed with a tweed waistcoat from which hung a gold chain attached to a watch in a pocket. His jackets were also of a hard-wearing tweed and always felt prickly when he embraced you.

But perhaps it was his laugh they loved the most: rich and fruity like a good wine. How they'd missed it over the years. Like with most people, he'd found it impossible to sustain a healthy relationship with his sister, Penelope. She had all but chased him away from the family home, Celeste realised that now. But they were going to make up for lost time.

'If only I could find him,' she thought. He'd disappeared shortly after dinner. She'd given him some time and space, but it seemed odd that he hadn't joined them in the living room. The fire was lit and the room was cosy.

Venturing upstairs, she soon saw that his bedroom door was open and that he wasn't inside.

'Uncle Portland?' she called down the hallway.

The bathroom door was also open and he wasn't in there or in the room she'd seen him come out of earlier. Where could he be, she wondered? In a house the size of Little Eleigh Manor, it wasn't always easy to locate somebody.

She checked the rest of the rooms on the first floor.

'Uncle P?' she called. 'Are you there?'

He couldn't have gone outside. It was dark and freezing cold. Besides, she'd seen his boots in the hallway. He must be inside but where?

It was then that she heard a noise coming from above. She looked up. That was definitely the sound of footsteps coming from the attic. Could he really have gone up there? Well, she guessed it was either Uncle P or a ghost with very big feet.

But then the footsteps stopped. She listened intently, wondering what he was doing. Perhaps she should leave him to it. After all, this had once been his home and perhaps he was just reacquainting himself with it in his own unique way.

She was just about to return downstairs when her uncle appeared at the end of the hallway.

'Celly, my dear!'

'Uncle! I was worried about you.'

'You were?'

'You disappeared,' she said, hoping he might reveal what he'd been up to.

'Just stretching my legs,' he said.

'You've got cobweb in your hair,' she told him, moving to brush it away as he came closer.

'Ah!' he said, 'I think perhaps I'll have a shower.'

'Everything okay?'

'I'll join you anon,' he said, not answering her question and she watched as he returned to his bedroom and closed the door behind him.

It was a confused Celeste who entered the living room a moment later. Evie and Lukas were cuddled up on the sofa, Esther was knitting under the light of a lamp and Gertie was sitting in a chair reading a book. It was a cosy scene with candles lit on the coffee table and fairy lights twinkling on the mantelpiece.

'The strangest thing just happened,' she told them.

'What?' Gertie asked, looking up from her book.

'I just caught Uncle P coming down from the attic.'

'What was he doing up there?' Evie asked.

'That's just it – I don't know and he didn't say.'

'Didn't you ask him?'

'No,' Celeste admitted. 'I wasn't sure if I should. It felt, I don't know, awkward somehow.'

'Perhaps he was just having a look around – reminiscing,' Gertie said.

'Perhaps,' Celeste said, but she wasn't convinced. There'd been something in her uncle's face that she couldn't quite pinpoint. Something that seemed unsettled and uneasy.

It was a full twenty minutes before he came downstairs to join them. He'd showered and changed and smelled of that wonderful citrusy scent that the girls remembered from their childhood.

'Well, look at this!' he said as he sat down next to Evie. 'It's like a scene from *Little Women*.'

Everybody laughed.

'Is Alba in bed?' he asked.

'Oh, a long time ago,' Evie said. 'We've got a baby monitor here, but she's usually no bother.'

'I still can't believe I'm a great-uncle,' he said with a chuckle.

'I can't believe I'm a father,' Lukas said.

'Nothing stays the same for long, does it?' Celeste said.

'So, let me see if I've got this right,' Uncle Portland said, sitting forward on the sofa. 'Celeste – you're with Julian and Evie is with young Lukas here.'

'That's right,' Evie said.

'So who's Gertie with?'

Esther's knitting dropped to her lap and Gertie almost did a double take while Celeste gasped and Evie laughed.

'She's not found the right man, yet, Uncle P,' Evie said. 'She has the world's worst luck when it comes to men.'

'Bad luck can change,' Uncle Portland said. 'Never give up on that.'

Celeste looked at him as he spoke. There was a dreamy sort of look in his eyes as he gazed into the fire.

'But you've never married, have you, Uncle P?' Gertie said.

All eyes turned to the old bachelor in their midst.

'That's true. My life in the Navy made it tricky.'

'Did you want to marry?' Celeste asked, curious now.

He sat for a moment, his great big hands on his knees as he looked into the dancing flames of the fire.

'It wasn't meant to be for me,' he said at last.

'It's not too late, though,' Evie told him. 'You're still a very handsome man.'

He guffawed. 'Well, thank you, my dear.'

'I think it's all about meeting the right person and we never know when that's going to happen, do we?' Evie went on.

'You're absolutely right,' he said.

Esther nodded, putting her knitting down in her lap. 'There's nothing quite like finding that right person. I was lucky with my husband. And I miss him every single day, even now after all this time.'

'Poor Esther,' Evie said.

'Oh, no,' Esther said, her pale blue eyes gazing down at the large ruby ring and the slim gold wedding band she still wore on her left ring finger. 'Not poor Esther at all. We had many, *many* good years.'

The room fell quiet again with just the gentle hiss of a log which Gertie had thrown onto the fire.

Celeste gazed around the room. It was so lovely to have it full of the people she loved, she thought, and it felt especially cosy with the snow softly falling outside. It was just a shame that Julian wasn't there to share the moment. But at least they'd persuaded Uncle Portland to stay for Christmas so there would be more evenings to enjoy together. She smiled at the thought. This was going to be the loveliest of Christmases.

CHAPTER SEVEN

It took Julian a moment to work out where he was when the first rays of morning light pierced the thin curtains. He sat up, rocking slightly on the airbed. It has been a surprisingly comfortable night and he'd slept well. Scott had found an extra blanket and had taken up home on a sofa in the living room and Julian had been given the luxurious privacy of a large bedroom with its very own en suite that looked like something from a hotel with its roll-top bath and his and hers sinks.

Julian got washed and dressed. Scott had lent him a T-shirt and some jogging pants to sleep in and he neatly folded them now. Then, crossing the room, he drew back the curtains and looked out onto a white landscape. The grounds were extensive with large topiary bushes which looked like great fat clouds upon the lawn. There was a pond which was frozen over and a tennis court which wouldn't be in use for some time, he guessed.

Finding his way downstairs and back to the kitchen, he was delighted to see Scott at work with a frying pan.

'I wasn't sure what you'd like so I've cooked a little bit of everything,' he told Julian. 'The kettle's just boiled so help yourself to tea or coffee.'

'Thank you.'

'Sleep well?' Scott asked.

'Very well.'

'Good! The forecast said it was actually a mild night and it looks like it's been thawing out there,' Scott said.

'So I'd better enjoy my first and last breakfast cooked by a star,' Julian teased.

'Yeah, don't get used to it!'

They laughed and got on with the serious business of eating a very fine full English breakfast.

~

Celeste had just eaten her breakfast when her phone rang. She took the call in the hall and came back a moment later.

'That was Julian,' she told everybody. 'He's on his way back and it sounds like he's made a sale or two.'

'That's great news!' Gertie said.

'Esther, I think you might have some work ahead of you.'

'I'll get my duster out,' she said.

~

Julian returned a little while later, his face flushed with colour as he kissed Celeste and then told her all about his adventures.

'He wants me to furnish the whole place,' he told her.

'That's wonderful!'

'It is, but it'll mean getting a lot more stock and he wants a delivery before Christmas so he can celebrate in style at his new place.'

'Then you'd better get a move on,' Celeste said with a laugh.

They walked through to the antiques centre together and Julian related the good news to Esther.

'He's taking the bed, that table, those six chairs, the mirror, wardrobe and dressing table.'

'They've all been cleaned this morning,' Esther informed him.

Julian grinned. 'He'll be wanting to take you away from me next!'

'Well, tell him I'm not for sale,' Esther said with a rather chuffed smile.

Celeste watched as Julian made a call.

'I know it's short notice,' he said, 'but I've got some pieces that need moving. Would you guys be able to handle that? It's only a few miles, but there are some big pieces. Okay. Yes, come on over and I'll show you. Thank you.' He hung up. 'It looks like we might just make somebody happy in time for Christmas.'

The next few days were a flurry of activity as Julian toured the local antique centres, looking for pieces that were suitable for Scott. Before he'd left Scott's home, they'd made sure Julian had a list of pieces Scott was looking for. How strange it was to have a movie star's wish list in his pocket, Julian thought. Scott had put his trust in Julian's judgement although Julian had assured him he would photograph the larger, more expensive pieces and text the photos to Scott for his approval before purchasing them on his behalf.

Julian had never had so much fun. If this was what it meant to be an antiques dealer then he never wanted to do anything else. Although he was acutely aware that a job like this might never come his way again.

Slowly but surely, Julian collected a number of pieces together that he thought would be to Scott's taste. He'd taken some photos of Scott's home, asking him to imagine the kind of furniture he could see in each of the rooms, and this proved invaluable to him as he toured the antique centres of Suffolk. Some of the bigger pieces he found on his travels would be delivered to Little Eleigh Manor and, from there, they'd be taken to Scott's together with the pieces he'd chosen from Rose Garden Antiques.

Once a good collection had been put together, there followed a period of feverish activity as furniture was pulled out of corners and checked over and made ready for removal. Julian had to admit that it would be a bit of a wrench to see some of the pieces go. Each beautiful antique had been hand chosen by him and had found its way into his heart, and parting with them would be a little like mourning. But at least he knew that they would be loved and appreciated and it charmed him immensely knowing how perfect they would look at Scott Fabian's house.

'Is he really going to sleep in this bed?' Evie asked, her hand caressing one of the great carved posts as the bed was slowly dismantled to get it out of the room and into the van.

'Well, I think it's too good for a guest room, don't you?' Julian said.

'The bed of a movie star,' Evie whispered dreamily.

Julian laughed. 'He has very good taste.'

Celeste couldn't have been happier for Julian. She'd seen his anxiety earlier in the week when he'd been worrying about the antiques centre, but this recent order had really boosted his confidence and she hoped that this piece of luck would help spread the word about the place. Certainly, the local papers had been talking about Scott Fabian's recent move to Suffolk and that he'd been spotted shopping in Rose Garden Antiques. It could only be good news for Julian's burgeoning business.

It was a couple of days later, and just three days before Christmas, that the large removal van arrived for the furniture. Julian directed everything, advising on which pieces to put into the van first and which pieces were the most delicate. Everybody stood by the living room window watching the progress.

Finally, when everything was safely packed away, Julian came inside to kiss Celeste.

'Well done,' she said.

'I just hope he likes it all once it's in place.'

'He'll *love* it!'

Julian smiled. 'Yes, I think he will!'

Celeste watched as Julian left to follow the furniture's progress. He'd promised Scott that he'd supervise the move and help arrange things so that they'd look just perfect, and Celeste knew that he was going to enjoy that job immensely.

Gertie joined her by the window and Celeste turned to smile at her.

'Isn't it exciting?'

Gertie nodded, but there was something in her expression which caught Celeste's attention.

'What's the matter?' she asked her sister.

'I'm not sure, but I've just seen Uncle P coming up from the cellar,' Gertie told her.

'Really? What do you think he was doing?'

'I don't know and he didn't see me so I pretended not to see him.'

Celeste sighed. 'He's been poking around a lot,' she said. 'I don't think he's just reacquainting himself with his old home. I think he's looking for something.'

'What could he be looking for?'

'I'm not sure.' Celeste led her sister into the privacy of the dining room. 'You don't think he's going to stake a claim, do you?'

'Stake a claim? What do you mean?'

'I can't help but think how he and Aunt Leda and Aunt Louise never made a fuss about the house and the rose business being handed to us.'

Gertie laughed. 'None of them wanted the responsibility. They knew how much work this house requires and knew they were well out of it by walking away.'

'But what if they've changed their minds? What if they realise the value of this property and want a slice?'

'You really think that's what this is about? You think Uncle Portland's come to spy on us and throw us out? Wouldn't he have said something before?'

'I don't think he'd ever have dared challenge Penelope,' Celeste said, thinking how difficult her mother had always been to get on with. It'd been another reason why they'd never seen much of their uncle or aunts over the years.

'But the house is ours, isn't it?'

'Yes, of course it is.'

'He can't challenge that.'

'Well, not legally, but morally, he might try to,' Celeste said.

'Do you think he's in some kind of financial trouble?'

'I really don't know. He hasn't said anything if he is.'

'But would he have said anything? I mean, it's not like we've been close over the years, is it?' Gertie pointed out.

'I know, but I think he might say something if he is planning on asking for a share of the house or business.'

Gertie looked thoughtful. 'Perhaps he could move in – like Esther did.'

'Perhaps,' Celeste said. 'But what if that isn't enough? What if he's after money?'

'We don't have any. We spent all the money we got from the paintings, and the business is only just beginning to pay the bills and our salaries.'

'We still have that painting Evie retrieved,' Celeste said, thinking about the beautiful rose painting that their stepmother had stolen from the manor and hung in her own ugly modern bedroom. Celeste still shuddered when she thought of that hateful act.

'Should we ask him?' Gertie said.

'Ask him what exactly? "What is it you've really come here for, Uncle P? Because we're not selling the house so you can retire to a villa in the Canaries!"' Celeste pushed her dark hair away from her face. She was feeling more and more anxious by the minute.

'No!' Gertie said. 'You can't say that, but I think we should at least try to find out–'

Her sentence was cut off as the large figure of Uncle Portland entered the room.

'Ah, there you are!' he said. 'I've been looking for you. There's something I need to ask you.'

Celeste and Gertie glanced at one another, their fear and dread visible in their eyes.

'What is it?' Celeste asked, swallowing hard, but ready to stand her ground.

He scratched the centre of his moustache, prolonging the agony of the sisters.

'How does one go about getting a daily newspaper here?' he asked. 'I'm missing my morning crossword.'

Julian was a bag of nerves following the removal van through the snowy landscape. A lot of the snow had melted now, but the roads were still slick with black ice and he tried not to have visions of all of those beautiful antiques strewn across the winter landscape. But he need not have worried. The van made it safely to its destination and it wasn't long before the furniture was being unpacked.

'Christmas is here!' Scott said with a grin as the work began. 'Wow! Bella's going to be so surprised. She's coming up here for Christmas Eve, but she has no idea that I've been so busy. I mean, that *you've* been so busy!' he said, welcoming Julian with a handshake.

'Well, it's not everything you've asked for, but I've made a good start and I can continue looking for the other pieces after the craziness of Christmas is over. Anyway, I hope you like what we've got here.'

'I'm sure I will. I loved the photos you sent through.'

Julian followed him inside and saw that an enormous Christmas tree had been put up in the living room and was already partially decorated in silver and gold.

'So there's the Cromwellian chest to go in here and the little table,' Julian said. 'We've got the dining room table and chairs coming in next. Is the room ready?'

'Sure thing. I had one of them nice rugs delivered yesterday. You know with all the swirly patterns?'

'Persian?' Julian asked.

Scott nodded. 'That's it!'

'Nice. Can I take a look?'

Scott led the way into the dining room and Julian admired the beautiful carpet with its deep blues and reds. It looked perfect in the oak-panelled room and would set off the table and chairs he'd bought for Scott perfectly.

The next couple of hours flew by. It was the four-poster bed that took the most work. The headboard and canopy were the heaviest pieces, but the removal men took it in their stride and the many component parts were soon in place in the main bedroom.

'Make sure it's where you want it,' Julian said, 'because it'll take an army to move it once it's put back together again.'

Julian watched as the men moved the pieces into place. How strange it looked dismantled. Scott looked on in fascination, his mobile phone at the ready to take photos.

When it was finally put together with its magnificent headboard, canopy and four intricately carved posts, Scott let out a long, low whistle of appreciation.

'Like it?' Julian asked, quite unnecessarily.

'I don't know what to say except I don't feel worthy of it. It'll certainly be a change from the airbed.'

'Yes, it's quite a promotion.'

Scott laughed. 'It certainly is.' He turned and shook Julian's hand. 'I'm glad I stumbled across your place.'

'I was going to ask you how you found us.'

'Just taking a look around,' he said. 'It looked nice and quiet.'

'Well, it's been a bit busier since your arrival.'

'Ah, sorry about that.'

'Don't apologise!' Julian said. 'It's been good for business.'

'Really? I wasn't sure if my fan base had the budget for antiques.'

'Maybe not, but we've done a roaring trade in beeswax candles.'

Scott laughed again.

'And it all helps get word out there. We've not been open long, you see, and I know we're a bit off the beaten track.'

'But you've got a website?'

'Oh, yes.'

'Then I'll make sure any of my friends who admire these pieces know where to find you.'

'That's very kind of you.'

'No problem.'

'I hope you enjoy your first Christmas here.'

'I'm sure I will. Merry Christmas, Julian.'

'Merry Christmas,' and the two men smiled and shook hands again and Julian felt immensely grateful that Scott Fabian had just happened to pass Little Eleigh Manor when he had.

Pulling into the driveway of the manor later, Julian breathed a sigh of relief. It had been an exhausting day – good but exhausting. Scott had loved every last item of furniture and had even remembered a few other items that he'd hoped Julian could hunt down for him.

Getting out of the car, he stood for a moment, looking up at the beautiful red-brick facade of the manor with its two soaring turrets. Lights glowed warmly from the windows, beckoning him inside as great fat flakes of snow began to spiral out of the sky. Crossing the driveway and moat, he opened the front door and was immediately greeted by Celeste who ran to kiss him, and Frinton who barked his doggy welcome. The lights from the Christmas tree twinkled and he could hear the gentle roar of the fire from the living room. Life, he thought, was very sweet.

~

There was a special little slot in the day at Little Eleigh Manor. Just after the antiques centre had closed and before dinner was served, Evie would take her young daughter to visit Esther in her suite on the ground floor, and the two women would catch up on the day together before Alba was taken upstairs to bed.

Esther would tell Evie about any amusing moments from the antiques world and Evie would tell Esther what was happening in the rose business. During the winter months, the curtains would be drawn, the heating on and the lamps would cast a cosy, golden glow that seemed particularly conducive to easy conversation.

Evie loved these quiet moments and often remembered that it wasn't so long ago when she'd actually been scared of Esther. Now, though, they were the very best of friends and Evie felt immensely grateful to have this very special relationship.

'Her first Christmas,' Esther said as she cradled Alba in her arms. Alba was looking blissfully sleepy now after her feed.

'Yes. I'm still trying to get Uncle P to dress up as Father Christmas, but I'm not sure Alba would really appreciate it.'

'It's going to be a special enough Christmas without the need for anybody to get dressed up.'

Evie agreed as she looked around the room which she and her sisters had helped decorate with fat bunches of holly and sprigs of mistletoe in celebration of the season. It was then that her eye caught the oval photo frame on the little mahogany table. Sally Martin, Esther's daughter. It was the one of her taken in Africa. She was holding a straw hat and her hair tumbled over her shoulders so beautifully.

Esther saw where Evie was looking and gave a sad smile.

'Christmas is always a little tricky,' Esther confessed.

Evie nodded.

'I always knew that losing Sally must have been the most heartbreaking thing ever for you,' she said, 'but I didn't really feel how devastating it must have been until I became a mother myself.'

She paused, looking across at her daughter, her peachy cheeks so soft and cherubic.

'I remember that first time I held Alba in the hospital and that great swell of love I felt for her.' Tears welled up in Evie's eyes now as she recalled the moment. 'It was so powerful – like I knew that I'd sacrifice anything for her and that I'd protect her with my whole being.'

Esther nodded. 'Oh yes. It's a magical feeling, isn't it?'

'How did you cope, Esther? I can't imagine what it must have been like and what you went through.'

Esther took a deep breath. 'I don't think I did cope. I just shut down and hid myself in a place where nobody could reach me. Not for the longest time anyway. My husband didn't know what to do and it drove a wedge between us that might have been the end of us. But time passes, doesn't it? That horrible old cliché. And your life moves forward.'

She stared down into the sleepy face of Alba and seemed to find contentment there.

'You know,' Evie began, 'becoming a mother's also helped me realise the strange relationship that me and my sisters had with our mother. Growing up, you just think everything is normal, don't you? It sometimes takes a bit of time to gain perspective.'

'But you're in a good place now, aren't you?'

'Oh, yes!' Evie said. 'I don't think I could be happier. I just wish I can be the best mother ever for Alba.'

Esther looked up at her. 'If you wish it then it shall be.'

Evie smiled. She liked that. She liked that a lot.

CHAPTER EIGHT

Rose Garden Antiques closed at four in the afternoon on Christmas Eve and everyone headed down to the kitchen for a much-deserved tea. It had been a group effort in those last few hours because it had been so wonderfully busy. Word had definitely spread about the place since Scott Fabian's visit and the shop was virtually empty of stock by the end of the day.

'I'm going to have to do some serious shopping before we open again,' Julian said. It was evening now and they were all sitting around the fire in the living room, roasting chestnuts. 'But I'm really looking forward to that and I forgot to tell you that Scott said he'd pass on the word about the antiques shop to his friends.'

'What – *movie star* friends?' Evie asked.

'I guess we'll have to wait and see,' Julian said, 'and, of course, he'll be wanting roses too,' Julian added.

'What?' Celeste said.

'He saw the sign for the rose business and said he'd definitely be wanting some for his garden. I'm sure that's something Evie could handle.'

Evie leaped up from the sofa and ran to hug Julian.

'Thank you, thank you!' she cried.

'Well, you'll probably be dealing with his gardener,' Julian warned, 'but I'm sure Scott will want to say hello in person at some point.'

Celeste smiled at him and mouthed a silent thank you, knowing that he'd done that especially for Evie.

She then turned her gaze towards the orange flames of the fire.

'It's hard to believe Dad's in Florida, isn't it?' she said.

'Didn't he want to spend Christmas here?' Uncle Portland asked.

'No, he likes a bit of sun at Christmas,' Celeste explained.

'I think Christmas should be cold,' Evie said. 'You can't roast chestnuts over the fire in Florida, can you?'

'Not comfortably,' Esther said, looking up from her knitting.

A few moments of companionable silence passed.

'I feel we should be telling stories or something,' Evie suddenly announced.

'Anyone know any good ones?' Julian asked. 'I think you're meant to tell ghost stories on Christmas Eve.'

'Well, I don't know any good ghost stories and I suppose you all know the legend of the Christmas rose,' Uncle Portland said.

'What's that?' Gertie asked.

'You've not heard it?' he asked in surprise.

'No!' everyone said at once.

'Tell us!' Evie said.

Uncle Portland shifted in his seat, getting comfortable, and gazed into the fire. 'The Christmas rose,' he began, 'is pretty much like all the other roses. To begin with. It has a strong squat base. Its stems have an average number of thorns and its leaves come bright and green, deepening to a dark gloss. It's a lovely thing which would sit well in any garden but, unlike its companion roses, it remains completely without bud.' He paused before continuing. 'Now, the gardener waits patiently for the rose, thinking, perhaps, that it may just be a late bloomer, but all through the summer, no bud appears and no flower comes.'

'Was the gardener sure it was a rose?' Gertie asked.

'Oh yes. It was a rose all right,' Uncle Portland assured them. 'But the gardener got so frustrated with it that he very nearly dug it up. After all, it was taking up space where a more productive rose could grow.' Once again, he paused.

'Go on!' Evie told him, her eyes fixed intently upon him. 'What happened?'

'The months passed by. The gardener walked up and down his borders, admiring the blooms and smiling, and then stopping in his tracks at that single flowerless rose bush. He'd shake his head, vowing to dig it up and put it on the fire the next day if it didn't bloom, but something kept stopping him from doing that. Then autumn came and his roses began to fade after their second flush and still that one bush hadn't flowered. October turned into November and then December arrived with its icy, grasping fingers. The light faded early and then something happened.'

'What?' Gertie asked, moving forward in her chair.

'On the shortest, darkest day of the year, the gardener noticed something. A single bud was beginning to unfurl. He couldn't quite believe it at first but, by the end of the week, a perfect crimson rose had blossomed.'

'Just in time for Christmas!' Evie cried.

'Exactly so.'

Esther smiled. 'What a lovely story. Is it true?'

'I'm not entirely sure,' Uncle Portland confessed. 'The girls' grandfather told it to me a long time ago and I never thought to ask him.'

'I've never come across a rose that only blooms in the winter,' Gertie said. 'Imagine if we could breed one. A Christmas rose with a really good scent.'

'It would be worth a *fortune!*' Evie said.

Lukas kissed her cheek. 'Something to work on in the New Year,' he said.

'You think I couldn't do it?'

'I didn't say that,' he told her.

'Evie could do anything she set her mind to,' Esther said.

'I know she could,' Lukas said, 'but not before she sets a date for our wedding.'

'Oh, Lukas! I've said it'll be in the summer.'

'Yes, but we need to be more precise than that,' he insisted.

Evie laughed. 'I love it when you use such English words as *precise!*'

He shook his head, clearly exasperated by his bride-to-be.

'You'll come, won't you?' Evie asked Uncle Portland.

'I wouldn't miss it for the world,' he told her.

'We're holding it here,' Gertie said proudly. 'We've been working on getting a licence to hold wedding ceremonies in the garden and Lukas is going to build a gazebo.'

'I'm quite tempted to get married again myself!' Esther said and everyone laughed.

'It's going to be quite an occasion,' Uncle Portland said. 'I can't wait to come back here again.'

Celeste caught Gertie's eye and she read an unspoken message there. Uncle Portland might be returning for the wedding, but what if he was planning to come back for good and turf them all out of their home?

Christmas Day dawned bright and clear and oh-so-white. Celeste had got up as soon as it was light and had dressed and taken Frinton outside. The snow was at least a foot deep in the garden and the little dog had trouble walking in it and his fur was soon encrusted with tiny snowballs.

Taking him back inside, she rubbed him down with a towel and gave him his breakfast. She then walked through the house, switching on the Christmas tree lights and the lamps in the living room.

The house soon filled with the happy noise of family. Evie came downstairs wearing a beautiful gold necklace Lukas had bought her and he was sporting a new jumper she'd bought him.

Julian lit the fire and presents were exchanged. There were the usual delights of new books and handmade scarves, cosy gloves and boxes of chocolates. Frinton got a new squeaky toy and a bone, and Esther had made him a little woolly coat in handsome stripes. Alba had a new doll and teddy bear and the sweetest dress covered in roses. Even Uncle Portland had bought presents for everyone – delicious tins of biscuits and boxes of Turkish Delight.

Once everything was tidied away, Celeste, Julian, Esther and Gertie went to prepare lunch while Evie and Lukas laid the table in the dining room. It was spread with a white linen tablecloth, and red candles were lit in silver candelabras. Esther had bought luxury crackers and they were placed next to the napkins. It all looked splendid.

When everybody was sat around the table later, Julian cleared his throat and stood up.

'I just want to say a few words before we begin this glorious meal. A couple of years ago, I was living the single life in London. I had a job I liked and I thought things were pretty good. But then I met Celeste and all of you.' He paused, gazing around the table. 'Now, I can't imagine any other life. You welcomed me and helped me realise a very special dream. You're my family and I love you all.'

Celeste could feel tears pricking at her eyes.

'So, let's raise our glasses,' Julian said, picking up his glass of wine. 'To friends and family.'

'To friends and family!' everyone chorused.

Was there anything more wonderful than the post-dinner slump on Christmas Day? The Hamilton sisters had it down to a fine art. Julian was snoozing in the armchair closest to the fire, Lukas was cradling

Alba in his arms and Esther was reading a new novel Evie had bought her. There was just one person missing. Uncle Portland.

Celeste motioned to Gertie and the two of them left the room.

'He's gone again,' Celeste said.

'Maybe he's having a lie down after all that food,' Gertie suggested.

'I somehow don't think so,' Celeste said, 'but we can go and look if you want.'

The two of them went upstairs and approached Uncle Portland's bedroom. As Celeste had predicted, the door was open and the bedroom was empty. And then they heard the sound again. The sound of footsteps coming from the attic.

'I tell you, he's definitely looking for something,' Celeste said.

'I think you're right,' Gertie agreed. 'Every time we see him, he's poking around in cupboards and looking under furniture. Yesterday, I saw him coming out of one of the rooms in the north wing which hasn't been used in ages.'

'Well, this time, he's going to tell us what he's up to.'

They made their way to the little flight of steps which led up towards the attic and there, standing in the doorway, was Uncle Portland, looking decidedly dishevelled.

'What on *earth* are you doing, Uncle?' Celeste demanded.

His hair was covered in a light dust and his hands looked grubby too.

'I'm going to,' he paused, trying to catch his breath, 'need some help.'

'Are you all right?' Gertie stepped forward and lifted his hand as if to check his pulse.

'No – not me, my dear. There's nothing wrong with me, but I need some help with something.'

Celeste shook her head. 'Uncle, this has gone far enough,' she told him, her hands on her hips. 'You've been sneaking around, hunting in rooms that you've really no business at all to be in. *What* is it you're looking for?'

CHAPTER NINE

Uncle Portland walked forward.

'Celeste, my dear. Could you call Julian and Lukas to help me move something downstairs?'

'What is it?' Gertie asked.

'It's a trunk and I think you should take a look at what's inside.'

Celeste stepped forward. 'We can manage a trunk,' she insisted, trying not to panic at what might be inside it.

'Are you sure?'

'We're not weaklings, Uncle P,' Gertie said.

He smiled. 'All right then. Let's give it a go.'

The two of them followed him into the attic, passing by bits of broken furniture and old suitcases until they came to a trunk. It wasn't very big, but it looked heavy with its rounded lid and metal studs.

'There are handles on either side. You two take that side and I'll take this. Ready?'

'Ready!' Celeste and Gertie said in unison.

'Heave!' Uncle Portland cried. He wasn't kidding. The chest was heavy and Celeste soon began to wish that they had called Julian and Lukas for help.

'What's inside this?' Gertie asked as they reached the steps leading out of the attic and onto the landing. 'A ton of Tudor bricks?'

'You're not going to believe it when you see it,' Uncle Portland said, stopping to mop his brow with a handkerchief from his pocket.

'Try us,' Celeste said.

'Let's get it downstairs first.'

They all took deep breaths and then lifted the trunk up once again, managing to get as far as the main stairs.

Evie, Julian and Lukas came running out of the living room when they heard the commotion.

'Give the girls a hand!' Uncle Portland cried and the three of them bounded up the stairs to take the trunk from them.

'What is this?' Evie asked.

'We don't know yet,' Celeste said.

'Get it into the living room,' Uncle Portland said.

'I'll get a duster,' Gertie told them and, a few minutes later, the trunk was dusted off and placed in the centre of the living room.

'Well, I never!' Esther cried when she set eyes on it, baby Alba in her arms. 'Would you look at that?'

'We are, Esther!' Julian said. 'It's beautiful. It wouldn't look out of place in the antiques centre.'

'You are most definitely *not* going to sell this!' Celeste told him and he grinned at her.

'Of course not,' he said, 'but it's a beautiful thing. Whose was it?'

'I have no idea,' Celeste said. 'I've never seen it before.'

'You know what's inside it, don't you?' Gertie asked Uncle Portland.

'Oh, yes,' he said.

'It's like Christmas morning all over again!' Esther said. But Celeste wasn't so sure. What if there were papers Uncle Portland had been looking for like some codicil to their mother's will, perhaps, or documents proving he had a rightful claim to the manor and the

Hamilton Roses business? She almost wished that it had a huge padlock on it and no key.

'Come on, then – let's open it!' Evie cried, clearly frustrated by the hold-up.

They all crowded around as Uncle Portland bent down to open the curved lid of the trunk.

Celeste gasped at the sight and Frinton trotted forward to take a look, sniffing with a nose full of curiosity. The trunk was filled with photograph albums. Lots of them.

'Go on,' Uncle Portland said. 'Take a look!'

Gertie leaned forward and pulled one out.

'I had a feeling your mother wouldn't have just thrown them out,' he said.

'What are they of?' Evie asked.

'They're of everything,' Uncle Portland said. 'Births, weddings, parties, holidays. Me and your mother as children – your aunts too. Baby photos of you girls.'

The three sisters glanced at one another. 'But I didn't think there were any of those,' Celeste said. 'I mean, we've only seen a few photos of us over the years.'

'They're all here,' Uncle Portland said.

All at once, everybody started taking albums from the trunk, gently turning the pages and gasping at the contents.

'Look at this one of Evie!' Gertie cried.

'That's *me?*' Evie said in surprise.

'It certainly is. Look – that wide-eyed expression is unmistakable!' Gertie said.

Evie gasped. 'But – but – I look just like Alba.' She looked at her daughter who was still asleep in Esther's arms.

Everybody crowded around the album and stared at the photo in quiet wonder. It was true: it was as if they were looking at a recent photo of little Alba.

A magical few moments passed as hands dived into the trunk. As well as albums, there were old envelopes in there too – stuffed full of black and white and sepia photographs, some large and some barely bigger than postage stamps.

'Look! This is when Grandma and Grandpa first laid out the beds for the roses,' Celeste said.

'And look at the state of the house here!' Gertie said. 'How on earth did they live in it like that?'

'It was a wonderful adventure,' Uncle Portland told them.

'Uncle P – who's this?' Celeste asked, handing him a black and white photo a moment later. He took it from her and examined it, his eyes lighting up in an instant, but then filling with tears.

'It's her,' he whispered.

'Her who?' Evie said, coming forward.

'Belinda,' he said, making the name sound like the most precious thing in the world. 'Belinda Crammond.'

'Who was she, Uncle P?' Gertie asked, her voice gentle as she gazed at her misty-eyed relative.

'Yes, tell us about her,' Evie pleaded.

Uncle Portland sank deeply into the sofa by the fire and looked down at the photo he was still holding in his hands.

'She was, perhaps, the love of my life,' he told them as he looked at the sweet face of the girl in the photograph.

Everybody gathered around him.

'She used to live in the house along the valley – the little thatched one that overlooks the river – and she used to come and play here during the holidays. I was a couple of years older than her and had a bit of a crush on her. She was friends with your Aunt Leda as they were the same age, but we all used to play together. All the usual things like hide and seek and make-believe battles and things.' He smiled at the memory. 'We were so young.'

'What happened to her?' Lukas asked.

'She moved away when she was ten,' he told them. 'She and Leda wrote letters to each other for a while, sending photographs and things. I used to read the letters when my sister was out.' He chuckled. 'I remember the summer she came to visit her grandmother who was still living in the thatched cottage.'

'Marnie Crammond?' Esther said.

'That's right.'

'I remember her.'

'Belinda was here for a couple of weeks and Leda went to visit her at the cottage. It was six years since I'd last seen her, but I hadn't forgotten her. She was sixteen then and what a beauty! I rode up and down the lane on my bike, hoping to catch her out in the garden and one day I did. She waved to me and I stopped my bike and went in and we talked and laughed. I'd never felt so...' He stared down at the photo of Belinda again, 'so easy around a girl before. I'd always been so tongue-tied. But, with Belinda, it felt so natural. Anyway, we spent more time together. I'd take her roses, getting shouted at by your grandfather for picking his favourite blooms, and–' he stopped.

'What?' Evie asked.

'She left.'

'You didn't keep in touch?' Celeste asked.

'I was never one for writing letters,' he said. 'It was harder in those days. None of this social media to keep in touch.'

'And you never saw her again?' Gertie said.

'No,' Uncle Portland said. 'At least, not until this summer.'

'*What?*' Celeste said.

'I met her in a garden centre of all places. I'd decided to buy some roses for my garden.'

'Uncle! You don't need to *buy* roses – you should have called us!' Evie told him.

'Well, I'm very glad I didn't because I might never have met Belinda again.'

Everyone was very excited about this and started asking him questions all at once. Uncle Portland held his hands up and laughed.

'She didn't recognise me at first, it has to be said. I had to tell her my name – *twice!*'

'And you have such a wonderfully unique name too!' Evie said.

'Yes, it isn't everyone who's called Portland!' Gertie said, sounding indignant on behalf of her uncle.

'And she didn't believe me when I told her she used to play here as a child,' Uncle Portland went on. 'She'd forgotten all about it.'

'But you've got proof now,' Celeste pointed out.

'Oh, yes! Actually, that's why I came here. I mean, I wanted to see you all, of course, but I had a feeling there were photographs of her somewhere.'

'You mean, *that's* what you've been looking for?' Celeste asked.

He nodded. 'I just prayed that your mother hadn't thrown all the old photographs out.'

'But why didn't you tell us what you were looking for?' Gertie asked. 'Why all the creeping around, scaring us half to death?'

'I *scared* you?' Uncle Portland looked mortified.

'We thought you might be trying to find some old will that would push us out of the manor,' Gertie confessed.

'You didn't!'

'The thought did cross our minds,' Celeste admitted.

'Oh, my dears! Why didn't you say something? I feel terrible!'

Celeste looked at Gertie and then, quite suddenly, they both burst out laughing.

'*You* feel terrible?' Celeste said. '*I* feel terrible! I genuinely thought you were up to something.'

Uncle Portland shook his head, his face quite red now.

'Can you ever forgive me?' Celeste asked.

'Nothing to forgive, my dear!'

Celeste turned to hug him.

'I'm so sorry.'

'And I'm sorry too,' he said. 'No more sneaking around, I promise.' And then he sighed. 'But seeing this photograph again and meeting my Belinda, I feel like I've wasted so much time. There've been so many empty years.'

'So she never married either?' Esther asked.

'She never did, no.'

'She's been waiting for you, Uncle P!' Evie said.

He laughed. 'I doubt that. She had a very successful career in the city. I don't think she was pining over me.' His eyes took on a dreamy look. 'But I wish we'd kept in touch all the same. Who knows what might have been?'

'But it's never too late!' Gertie cried.

'That's right!' Evie said. 'Just like your story about the Christmas rose that only blooms in the heart of winter. It's the brightest of them all, isn't it?'

Uncle Portland chuckled.

'Yes, you've found each other again now,' Celeste said.

'That must give you hope too, Gertie,' Evie said, rather undiplomatically, Celeste thought.

'Thanks!' Gertie said.

'Well, we'll see,' Uncle Portland said. 'It's certainly good to have a bit of female company.'

'And you must bring her here,' Evie said, 'because we all want to meet her, don't we?'

'She must come to our wedding,' Lukas said.

'But come before that too,' Celeste said.

Uncle Portland nodded and Celeste couldn't help thinking how very happy he looked. Happy and, perhaps, hopeful.

It was later on Christmas Day when Celeste and Julian entered the living room again. Alba was in bed and Esther, Evie and Lukas were tidying the kitchen. Frinton had been out for his last walk and Uncle Portland was snoozing in the chair by the fire, the photo of Belinda in his lap.

Celeste knelt down on the floor, gazing into the chest of forgotten photographs.

'These could have been lost up there forever,' she said to Julian. 'We might never have known about them.'

Julian knelt down beside her and put his hand on her shoulder, instinctively feeling her pain. Penelope Hamilton might well be dead, but her legacy of damage still lived on.

'Look at this,' she said, opening one of the albums to see a photo of her and her sisters playing in the rose garden. 'I remember that dress,' she said, her fingers gently touching the past as she admired the yellow and white checks she had once worn as a child.

Uncle Portland slowly stirred in his chair and blinked his eyes open.

'Was I asleep?' he asked in surprise.

'Just a little,' Julian said with a smile.

'Uncle P?' Celeste said. 'Can I ask you something?'

'Ask away, my dear. Ask away.'

'Were you never mad that Grandma and Grandpa didn't leave the manor and rose business to you? I mean, you were their only son.'

He stroked his chin and looked thoughtful for a moment. 'That's been worrying you, hasn't it, Celly?'

'Yes, a bit,' she admitted.

'Then let me put your mind at rest. This notion of automatically leaving things to a male heir is nonsense, don't you think? I had no real interest in the rose business. It never would have done for me to stay here in Suffolk. Your grandparents knew that and they also knew that your mother was passionate about roses and, of course, she'd started making a family, hadn't she? I couldn't compete with that!' He chuckled. 'This house needs a family in it, not an old bachelor like me.'

'But you might have married and had children if you hadn't gone away,' Celeste pointed out.

'Not me,' he said. 'The Navy was calling. I couldn't have been shackled to this old place.'

Celeste got up and walked towards him, bending to kiss his warm cheek.

'We've missed you,' she told him. 'You should have visited more.'

'I know, my dear, I know. But your mother never made it easy over the years.'

'But it's easy now.'

He smiled at her. 'Yes,' he said. 'It's easy now.'

And so it was, Celeste thought, as she hugged her uncle close to her and gazed into the bright flames of the fire. Life at Little Eleigh Manor was so very different now. Today, it was a place of comfort, a place filled with love and joy – a place to call home.

*Christmas with
the Book Lovers*

VICTORIA
CONNELLY

A very Merry Christmas to all my readers!

CHAPTER ONE

When Callie Logan met and fell in love with Sam Nightingale she'd had no idea that she'd be welcomed into his family so wholeheartedly. As an only child, with parents who always seemed rather surprised by her presence, it was a unique experience to be made welcome each Sunday for lunch by his parents, grandparents, brother and three sisters. She took part in their conversations and joined them on their rambling country walks with the family dogs and truly felt like an honorary member of the family when she became the butt of one of Josh's jokes.

Wrapping Sam's Christmas present now, she felt so lucky to be a part of life with the Nightingales. It amazed her that she'd only known Sam since September, and how she counted her blessings that she'd walked into his bookshop that day and been caught sniffing one of his books. It had been a little joke between them ever since.

'Of all the books in all the bookshops in all the world, she came and sniffed mine,' he'd tease. She loved that.

Sealing the wrapping paper and writing the label, she smiled. This, she thought, was the perfect present. She'd known the instant she'd seen it on the shelf of the tiny bookshop in the backstreets of

Cambridge. Her eyes had watered at the price but it was a first edition. A first edition of a very special book. She'd simply had to buy it and she couldn't wait to see Sam's face when he unwrapped it.

She'd been a little tempted to keep it herself, she had to admit. Indeed, she'd placed it on her shelf of beloved hardbacks just to see what it looked like. But wasn't that the test of a really good gift? If it truly hurt you to give it away then you knew that it was a good present.

She'd chosen some beautiful cream and gold paper which complemented the old cloth cover and its buttery-white pages, and had placed acid-free tissue paper around it first. She'd never felt so excited to give a present in her life.

She looked out of the living room window of Owl Cottage. The Suffolk countryside was locked down under a layer of frost, the ground had hardened to iron and the air was filled with the delicious scent of wood smoke from the cottage chimneys that jostled around the green at Newton St Clare.

Sam was picking her up in a few minutes and they were off to spend Christmas Eve at his parents' home, Campion House. Christmas was always a special time at the Nightingales', Sam had told her, and Callie couldn't wait to experience it. She'd finished writing the latest chapter of her new children's novel that morning and was now ready to embrace Christmas full on.

And there he was. Callie waved a hand in excitement as Sam pulled up outside her cottage. A moment later, after checking her blonde hair was neat and tidy, she opened the door to him and they kissed – a long, loving kiss that lingered like a beautiful dream.

'You ready for the onslaught?' he asked, his warm brown eyes gazing down into hers from behind his glasses.

'Absolutely ready.'

'Are you sure? You've not seen my family once the mulled wine starts to flow.'

'I'm sure they're delightful.'

'I'll remind you of that when Grandpa Joe gets up on the coffee table and starts singing bawdy songs!'

Callie laughed. 'I'm looking forward to it.' She put her coat on and grabbed the bag that contained her present for Sam and the box of homemade goodies from a local farm shop which she'd bought for his family.

They drove through the country lanes which were mud-splattered and full of potholes, but so very beautiful with their berry-bright hedgerows and views across the ploughed fields. A hare ran across the road in front of them and a dizzy pheasant almost got himself run over as they turned a corner.

'Did you ring your parents?' Sam asked.

'Yes.'

'And?'

'The usual,' she told him. 'They're not doing much and they didn't ask me what I was doing.'

'*Really?*'

Callie nodded.

'I can't believe they didn't invite you to spend Christmas with them. I mean we're happy that they didn't, of course, because it means *we* get you for Christmas. But it's a bit odd, don't you think?'

'It's hard to say,' Callie confessed. 'I grew up with odd, so it seems normal.'

Sam reached out a hand and squeezed her gloved ones.

'I remember sneaking downstairs one Christmas Eve,' she told him. 'I must have been about six or seven. My parents were in the front room. We had a little tree that year. We didn't always have one. I think they stopped buying them once I went to high school. Anyway the tree lights were on and I could see them sparkling through the door which had been left open a little. And I could hear Mum and Dad talking and the unmistakable sound of Sellotape being ripped and I knew they were wrapping my presents. Or rather *present.*'

'Present? You mean just one?'

'Yes, I heard Mum say, "One present is adequate. We don't want to spoil the girl."'

'You're kidding?'

Callie shook her head. 'And Dad murmured something in agreement.'

Sam looked shocked by her story and she smiled at him. 'I hope it was a good present,' he said.

'It was a doll.'

'A doll that you wanted?'

She sighed. 'Not really. But she was the biggest seller that year and was in all the shops. I guess it was an easy present to get.'

'And what did you want?'

'A different doll. A friend of mine had this other doll. She wasn't as well known as the famous doll in all the shops. Her hair wasn't as bright and her clothes weren't as fancy but I liked her better. She had a sweeter face.'

'So your parents never asked you what you wanted?'

'They never asked and I never dared tell them.'

'You never wrote a letter to Santa?'

'Oh, no! They told me quite plainly that he didn't exist.'

'No way! You grew up without Santa Claus?'

'And the tooth fairy. They said they didn't want my head full of nonsense.'

'Perhaps that's why you became a children's writer,' he said. 'Rebellion.'

Callie laughed. 'Yes. I spent years secretly reading fairy tales and then started writing my own.'

Sam shook his head. 'I don't know how you survived such a childhood. It couldn't have been much fun. Being on your own as well.'

Callie looked out of the window as they passed a row of thatched cottages, their windows twinkling with Christmas lights.

'It's funny but I never felt lonely. I read a lot and I guess all those fictional characters kept me company.'

'Your childhood made you the writer you are today.'

'Exactly,' Callie said, 'so I can't exactly be cross or sad about it, can I?'

Sam smiled. 'You're amazing,' he told her. 'You see the positive in everything.'

'Well, I'm feeling very positive today,' she told him. 'I've been looking forward to Christmas with your family.'

'Good.'

'So, tell me about *your* Christmases,' she said, eager to turn the attention away from herself.

Sam took a deep breath. 'Well, after a special Christmas Eve tea, we all sit around the fire in the living room and take it in turns to read all those wonderful old Victorian ghost stories by the likes of M R James, Sheridan le Fanu and W W Jacobs. Sometimes we dip our noses into a bit of Bram Stoker or Mary Shelley, choosing the spookiest passages.' Sam gave a laugh.

'What?'

'I was just remembering – we have to finish with something lighter like Charles Dickens. Mum and Bryony always complain that the dark stuff gives them nightmares. Bry says, "I can't go to bed with Dracula's fingernails or that monkey's paw in my head!"'

They both laughed.

'And you read out loud?' she asked.

'Of course.'

'It must be really special to read to one's family like that. To all gather around and share stories.'

'There's no getting away from it in our family,' he confessed. 'We all went through that awkward teenager stage where we'd rather have been doing our own thing, usually involving a computer, but Mum and Dad would drag us into the front room and force feed us fine literature.'

'I bet you're glad they did now.'

'I guess I didn't really mind at the time either. I gained so much from it. There are so many wonderful passages I remember by heart because of reading them aloud. Take the opening from Sheridan le Fanu's *The Dead Sexton*: "The sunsets were red, the nights were long, and the weather pleasantly frosty".'

'Ooooh, gorgeous!'

'Isn't it? I love the rhythm of that sentence. You'd be able to enjoy it reading it in your own head, but there's far more joy by reading it aloud.'

'That's one of the things I wish I could enjoy more as an author,' Callie said, 'reading aloud. I'm always asked to do it for audiences and I get so nervous.'

'You just need to practise,' Sam told her.

'Maybe,' Callie replied, 'but I don't know if I'll ever be able to shake that awful knot-in-the-stomach feeling when I have to do something like that.'

Sam slowed the car down and turned into the driveway of Campion House. The Georgian home looked splendid with each of the sash windows glowing with lights, and a large evergreen wreath hanging on the front door tied by a red ribbon.

'Take a deep breath and, with any luck, you'll emerge alive in a few hours,' Sam said, giving her cheek a kiss before they got out of the car and knocked on the door.

They didn't have to wait long. The door opened to Sam's mother's warm smile and the sound of excited dogs barking from the depths of the house.

'Sammy! Callie, darling!' Eleanor chorused, ushering them inside. She was wearing a pretty red cowl neck jumper and her dark hair was swept up and held with a diamante pin. 'Come on in out of the cold. Hasn't it turned bitter? I took the dogs out this morning and I swear my fingers turned blue.'

'I've just had an extra pile of logs delivered,' Callie said. 'I thought I could get away with buying the odd bag from the local garage.'

'Says someone who's never spent a winter in the country,' Sam laughed.

'I'll have you know that I've spent plenty of winters in the country, only we never had a wood burner and I didn't realise how greedy they were,' Callie explained as she took off her boots and Sam helped her with her coat.

'But there's nothing like a real fire, is there?' Eleanor said, linking arms with Callie. 'Come and sit by ours. The living room's lovely and toasty.'

Carrying her bag of presents with her, Callie gasped as she entered the room. The large Christmas tree – which was easily eight foot in height – sparkled in the far corner, its decorations a pleasing mix of traditional colours: silver, gold, green and red. Underneath lay heaps of beautifully wrapped presents, all tied with silky ribbons and glittery bows.

As Eleanor had promised, a fire blazed, instantly warming Callie, and lamps glowed around the room giving it a cosy, intimate feel, perfect for storytelling, she thought. She couldn't imagine a place she'd rather be.

'Where is everybody?' Sam asked as he followed them into the living room and walked over to the fire to warm his hands.

'In the kitchen stealing mince pies,' Eleanor said. 'I'd better go and rescue a few so there's some left for you two. Have a seat, now, and I'll get you a cuppa.'

'Not opened the mulled wine yet?' Sam asked.

Eleanor tutted. 'Tea first. Wine later.' She left the room and Sam pulled Callie into his arms.

'Careful! Don't crush the presents.'

'What have you got in that bag of yours?' Sam asked, trying to peer inside.

'You'll have to wait and see,' she told him, leaving the warmth of his embrace to place her presents under the tree.

'Hmmmm,' he said, going to take a look. 'Would that be a book?'

'Sam Nightingale! You wouldn't be the sort to spoil a present now, would you?'

He held his hands up. 'Not going anywhere near it,' he said with a chuckle. 'At least, not until you're out of the room.'

She gave him a warning glance.

'It's all so beautiful,' she said. 'I've never seen such a big tree in a home before.'

'Mum loves Christmas. Dad too. They go and pick the tree together and Mum and Grandma spend hours decorating it together. We all used to – not just the girls either. Even Josh and I would get to choose some baubles to put on the branches.'

'SAM?' Eleanor's voice called through from the kitchen. 'Come and grab a mince pie before Josh eats them all!'

Sam laughed and they both went to rescue their treats.

After a tea in the dining room which included cinnamon scones oozing with butter, mince pies and copious cups of tea during which everybody talked themselves hoarse, they all gathered around the fireplace in the living room. Callie looked at the glowing faces of the Nightingale family. There was Grandpa Joe and Grandma Nell sitting in the upright armchairs which had been pulled closer to the fire. Callie had to confess to having a soft spot for Grandpa Joe. He'd been instrumental in bringing her and Sam together and she would always feel a huge debt of gratitude towards him.

Sam's parents, Frank and Eleanor, were sitting on the smaller sofa, holding hands and laughing about something. Josh, Sam's younger brother, was sitting next to them, texting something on his phone, his face earnest.

Callie and Sam were sitting on the large sofa along with Polly. Archie, Polly's son, was at a friend's house. He was too young for their ghost stories, Polly told her as she'd refastened her long dark hair with a tortoiseshell clip. No doubt he'd join in soon enough, though, Callie thought. It seemed you couldn't be a Nightingale without reading your fair share of ghost stories around the fire at Christmas.

Bryony, the middle sister, who ran the children's bookshop in Castle Clare, was sitting on a large cushion on the floor in front of the fire. She was wearing a long, silver scarf around her neck which caught the light, giving her an ethereal look. Callie adored the way Bryony dressed – she was all floaty fabrics and bold colours.

Beside Bryony was Lara, the youngest Nightingale, home from university. She was sitting cross-legged on the carpet, her long curly hair tumbling over her shoulders and her face full of smiling mischief as she told Bryony all about her latest boyfriend.

'Right, then!' Frank's voice boomed through the chatter. 'Who's up first?' He looked around the room. 'Come on. Let's have a taker!'

Eleanor caught Callie's eye. 'They're always a bit nervous before the first glass of mulled wine,' she told her guest.

'I'll go,' Josh said with the authority of a teacher taking charge of a classroom.

'And what have you chosen?'

'My favourite M R James,' he said. '*A Warning to the Curious.*'

There was a murmur of approval around the room.

'Do you know it, Callie?' Josh asked her.

'I don't,' she confessed, feeling her cheeks flush as the Nightingale clan stared at her. 'I mean, I know a little about M R James, but I've never read him.'

'*Never* read...' Frank began, only to have his wrist slapped by Eleanor in warning. 'But he's one of East Anglia's most celebrated writers.'

'Oh, I know,' Callie said, 'and I promise I'll rectify that really soon.'

'Well, you're in for a treat,' Josh told her, 'because this is James at his best.'

'At his *spookiest* best,' Lara said from the floor. 'This is the one with the "lungless laugh", isn't it?'

Bryony gave a shudder. 'It's creeping me out already.'

Josh laughed and picked up the book, which had been resting on his lap, and opened it.

CHAPTER TWO

Callie had enjoyed her fair share of audio books in her time, but nothing could compare to the pleasure of being read to aloud, and Josh Nightingale was obviously a connoisseur. He read with a passion, an intensity, but also with a lightness of touch which allowed him to highlight the more humorous or poignant passages of the story.

When he'd finished, he closed the hardback to rapturous applause and acknowledged his family with a smile and a modest nod of his head.

'Mulled wine, I think,' Eleanor said, getting up from the sofa.

'At last!' Josh cried.

'Have to make a good start and earn it first,' she said.

'How many stories do you read in an evening?' Callie whispered to Sam.

'Three or four. Some are longer than others and are shared around the room. Although Grandma doesn't read them anymore. Her eyesight isn't terribly good.'

Callie glanced towards Grandma Nell who was smiling at Josh from her chair, obviously enjoying the evening in her own quiet way.

'Sometimes,' Sam continued, 'we'll get together beforehand and choose who's going to read what. At other times, it's more informal and we pick and choose on the night, sharing the book between us all.'

'Well, I'm loving it,' Callie confessed. 'You were brilliant, Josh!'

'Thank you, kind lady!' he said with a grin.

'Chuck another log on the fire, Dad,' Lara said from the carpet.

'You're closer than I am,' Frank said.

'Yes, but I've just had my nails done – look!'

'I thought you were a poor student,' Polly said.

'I am! We do each other's nails.'

'When you're meant to be studying?' Josh teased.

'You can't study *all* the time,' Lara protested.

Frank got up, shaking his head good-naturedly at his daughter. For a few moments, everyone watched in happy silence as he threw a couple of fat logs onto the fire and gave it a good stoke. The logs crackled and the flames rose. It was a wonderful sight.

'Didn't we ban M R James at Christmas?' Eleanor asked as she came back into the room a few minutes later with a tray full of mulled wine in crystal glasses.

'Are you kidding?' Josh said, standing up to help pass the glasses around. 'Nothing beats a bit of M R James at Christmas.'

'Josh is right,' Grandpa said. 'It wouldn't be Christmas without the master of the ghost story.'

'Hey, Sam,' Lara said. 'Remember that old edition you had of M R James's *Ghost Stories of an Antiquary*?'

'Of course I do. It was a first edition.'

'What happened to it?' Frank asked.

'I sold it. Under pressure from you lot,' he said, wagging a finger at them all.

'*What?*' Frank said.

'You don't remember?'

'Tell Callie about it, Sam,' Polly said.

'Oh, must we remember that horrible time all over again?' Eleanor said. 'I still have nightmares about it.'

Bryony shook her head. 'You've never known a book cause so much trouble.'

'I think it was haunted,' Lara said.

'Don't be daft!' Josh said. 'A book can't be haunted.'

Lara frowned. 'Why not?'

Silence fell. Nobody seemed to have an answer to that.

'Grandpa Joe, didn't you used to have a paperback copy of the book?'

'Not as nice as that volume you managed to get your hands on,' Grandpa Joe said. 'And it wasn't haunted.'

'Oh, Grandpa!' Sam cried. 'My edition wasn't haunted!'

Grandpa Joe gave a naughty chuckle. 'That's what you say.'

Sam shook his head and then smiled at Callie. 'When we were young, Grandpa read the stories from a paperback edition out to us, sitting around the fire at Christmas just like we are now.'

'They used to scare me to death!' Bryony said.

'Me too,' Polly said. 'All those demons with hairy hands, and strange eerie laughter coming out of the mist.' She gave a theatrical shudder at the memory. 'But we've kind of got used to them now.'

'M R James himself used to read his stories to a few invited guests each Christmas Eve in his rooms at King's College in Cambridge,' Frank told them. 'That might have been where our fascination for ghost stories at Christmas began. It's known that the carbon-monoxide from gas lamps in Victorian times produced hallucinations and that led to a rise in the popularity of ghost stories.'

'Really?' Callie said. 'I never knew that.'

'Well, luckily, we've got electricity today,' Eleanor said.

Callie rested her hand on Sam's arm. 'Are you going to tell me about this haunted book, then?'

'Yes, tell Callie about how you came to have the book,' Frank said. 'I kind of wished I hadn't retired from the family business and that I'd been given this job myself.'

'Yes,' Sam said taking a sip of mulled wine. 'I got really lucky with this one. 'It was a day in early February when Mr Roache first got in touch with me at the shop. He was eighty-seven and lived in a hamlet between Castle Clare and Foxearth. It was pretty tricky to find, actually. I thought it might be some sort of elaborate joke by the time I'd turned down the third dead-end lane and been chased off by an angry Labrador, but I eventually found the place. It was a magnificent sixteenth-century property. All beams and leaning walls. He was having to leave it. Moving to Devon to be closer to his family, I think. Anyway, he was selling off a lifetime's collection and the library was extensive. It was quite a job.'

'Tell her about Mr Roache,' Bryony said.

Sam grinned. 'He was a character straight out of Dickens. He was tall and wiry and had these long bony fingers which would grab me by the elbow and steer me towards the shelves. "This one," he'd say. "This one."'

Lara laughed. 'So funny!'

'Yes, for months after, this lot would keep grabbing me from behind and hollering "*This one, This one*"! Very unnerving!'

Callie giggled.

'Anyway, he was obviously passionate about his books and seemed anxious that they find good homes. It took several months to catalogue them all and we did get good homes for them. Many of them stayed together which seemed to please him.'

'Get to the good part – go on!' Grandpa Joe urged, sitting forward in his chair.

'Yes, one afternoon, after I'd packed up the last box of books, I felt Mr Roache's bony fingers on my elbow again but instead of whispering, "This one," he said, "This way." So I followed him into a room that he'd been using as a study. It was a beautiful room with this enormous Victorian desk and a massive globe and wonderful old framed maps on the wall. Anyway, there on the desk was the book. I recognised it at once. M R James's *Ghost Stories of an Antiquary*. Beautiful. First edition from 1904. Lovely thing.' Sam paused.

'What happened next?' Callie asked.

'Mr Roache moved to the desk and picked up the book and

handed it to me. At first, I assumed he'd just found it and wanted me to sell it as I had the other books but he said, "This one. For you."' Sam shook his head at the memory. 'I told him I couldn't afford it and he assured me it was a gift. He'd been watching how I handled his other books. He said I did it with "a particular care" and he said he knew I'd appreciate this one.'

'A very nice gift,' Frank said.

'If it wasn't haunted!' Eleanor said.

'Yes, tell me more about the haunted bit,' Callie encouraged.

'Let me tell you about the book first,' Sam insisted. 'What a book. It's the one with those four fine illustrations by James McBryde. You know the artist died before completing the rest?'

'A great shame,' Grandpa Joe said. 'Beautiful pictures.'

'Yes, they have a lovely light feel about them. Totally unique,' Polly said. 'Although the one of the demon with the long hairy hand still gives me nightmares.'

'Yes, much too spider-like for me,' Bryony said.

'McBryde was a friend of M R James's and it's thought that James only published the book as a showcase for his friend's artwork. Well, the illustrations alone are worth buying the book for.' Sam paused. 'As books go, it's very plain to look at on the outside, but that's something I've always rather admired. It's beautiful in its simplicity. It's a beige-coloured cloth cover – kind of the colour of wet sand – with the title *Ghost Stories of an Antiquary* at the top and "M R James" in capitals at the bottom and all this space in between which modern book covers simply wouldn't allow.'

'I've always wondered if McBryde would have illustrated the story called *The Mezzotint* had he lived. You know the one about the picture which keeps changing?' Polly said. 'I'd love to have seen a representation of that.'

'I'm kind of glad one doesn't exist. I think that would creep me out too much to see it,' Bryony said.

'Back to the book,' Sam said. 'The pages were butter-soft and wonderfully mottled with age as you'd expect from a book over a hundred years old. Part of its charm.'

'And the smell?' Callie prompted.

'Ah, I was just coming to that,' he said. 'It had a wonderfully comforting scent of familiarity. A woody, wholesome scent that makes you feel happy in an instant. It spoke of decades of wonderful reading, of moments of stillness by a good fire.'

Callie nodded knowingly.

'The dedication in the book is to "all those who at various times have listened to them". The stories are meant to be read aloud,' Sam explained. 'That's what James originally did at the Chit-Chat Club in Cambridge.'

Grandpa Joe cleared his throat. 'He writes so well about the English country house and the English country gentleman – the rather fusty old bachelor academic who spends most of his time poking around old churches or cathedral archives.'

'Fusty old bachelor – sounds like Josh!' Lara said.

Josh grunted and threw a cushion at her.

'Hey!' Eleanor warned.

Callie placed a hand on Sam's arm. 'So, are you going to tell me why your family thought this book was haunted?'

'Well,' Sam began, 'the first Christmas we read from the book, strange things seemed to start happening...'

CHAPTER THREE

Sam took a long sip of his mulled wine and continued.

'We started with the first story in the collection: *Canon Alberic's Scrapbook.*'

'It's about a fusty old bachelor,' Grandpa Joe said.

'Modelled on Josh,' Lara teased. Luckily for her, there wasn't another cushion near Josh for him to chuck at her.

'Throw in an historic building and an old book and you've got the perfect Jamesian recipe,' Sam said.

'That's the spidery hand one, isn't it?' Bryony said.

'It is.'

'Let's not talk about that hand again please,' Polly begged.

'So, what happens to this fusty old bachelor?' Callie asked, desperate to get on with the story.

'We turned all the main lights out that night,' Sam said. 'I'd always wanted to read by candlelight.'

'Bad for your eyes!' Grandma Nell cried.

'Yes,' Sam agreed.

'And bad for the imagination,' Bryony said. 'Like those gas lights in Victorian times. I kept thinking there were things crawling out of the corners of the room.'

'So I read the story. It's set in a tiny old town in the foothills of the Pyrenees in France where an academic called Dennistoun is poking around the cathedral. The sacristan is showing him around and won't leave his side.'

'Oh, isn't there some horrible laughter coming from somewhere in the cathedral?' Lara asked.

'That's right. The sacristan keeps his back to the wall and looks uneasy all the time.'

'And what does Dennistoun make of it all?' Callie asked.

'Well, like all idiots in stories,' Josh came in, 'he doesn't seem to be aware of the danger he's in.'

'Are you sure we're not spoiling the story for you?' Sam asked. 'I don't think I should tell you much more in case you want to read it.'

'I'm not sure I want you to go on after what happened last time,' Eleanor said.

'What happened?' Callie asked.

'Well, suffice to say that Dennistoun tempted fate and was visited by a demonic creature with hairy hands and piercing eyes,' Sam said.

Callie shivered.

'Why do these silly old academics poke their noses into the past all the time?' Bryony asked.

'Because there'd be no story if they didn't,' Josh pointed out.

Bryony nodded. 'Good point.'

'But the Christmas we read those stories, we began to wonder if some of those demons were real, didn't we?' Sam added.

'Yes, when you finished *Canon Alberic's Scrapbook*, Mum got up to warm up some mulled wine,' Josh said.

Eleanor shook her head. 'I really don't want to remember it again.'

'Go on, Mum!' Polly encouraged. 'Callie's going to spontaneously combust any second now if we don't tell her!'

It was true. Callie found that she was sitting on the edge of the sofa, her eyes wide and her mouth dry in anticipation.

'I would love to know,' she admitted.

'Well,' Eleanor said, taking a deep breath, 'I went through to the kitchen. I didn't put the main lights on. I just had the little one on above the Aga where I was warming the wine. I got the glasses out of the cupboard and put them on the tray and noticed one of the glasses had a smear on it so I took it to the sink to wash. You know there's a big window by the sink which looks out on to the garden? I noticed the security light had come on and I saw something moving in the shrubbery. I couldn't really make out what it was, but it was pretty large and...' she stopped, staring into the fire as she shook her head.

'What?' Callie prompted.

'It had these brilliantly bright eyes. They looked as if they were burning,' Eleanor said.

'You'd been at the wine ahead of everyone else, Mum!' Josh teased.

'I swear I hadn't touched a drop.'

Callie looked closely at Eleanor. Her face was pale as she recounted the story and she looked totally earnest.

'What happened next?' Callie asked.

'I waited to see if the creature would come out into the open but it didn't.'

'And that's when we heard you scream,' Josh said.

'I did not scream!' Eleanor insisted and Josh laughed.

'Just kidding, Mum!'

'It's not a matter to kid about. There was something out there in the dark.'

'But it turned out to be a stray dog, didn't it?' Lara said.

'A stray dog did show up the next day,' Frank said. 'We found it in the field when we were walking our two dogs and rang the local rescue who came to take it. But it came home with us and ate as if it hadn't eaten in days, poor thing. I really think that's what you saw in the garden that night, darling.'

Eleanor shook her head. 'I still think there was something else out there. The stray dog was white and what I saw was black.'

'It could have been Black Shuck!' Grandpa Joe cried, getting excited.

'Oh, what's Black Shuck?' Callie asked.

'The ghostly black dog that's said to roam around the countryside of East Anglia,' Polly explained.

'Most counties of England have a big black beast story,' Frank pointed out.

'I've never heard of Black Shuck,' Callie said.

'Well, there was something out there that night,' Eleanor said.

'What do you *think* it was?' Callie asked.

'Oh, I've had more than one sleepless night pondering that question,' Eleanor confessed.

'And she's kept me awake more than one night with her pondering and pacing,' Frank added and everyone laughed.

'But that's not the only thing, is it, Mum?' Lara said.

'Something else happened?' Callie asked.

'Oh, yes,' Eleanor said. 'But, first, more wine.'

She got up and left the room, coming back a moment later with a jug filled with mulled wine, the scent perfuming the room as everyone accepted a top up.

'Only a little for my Nell,' Grandpa Joe said.

'Spoilsport!' Nell said with a little giggle.

'See – you're getting merry already,' Grandpa Joe told her.

'If a person can't get merry on Christmas Eve, when can they?' Grandma Nell said.

Finally, when Eleanor was back on the sofa, she began.

'After everyone had left that night, I was tidying a few things away. I like that quiet time in the kitchen after a get-together, just pottering around, washing the glasses and loading the dishwasher. Anyway I was taking a tray of clean glasses to put away in the dresser in the room next to the kitchen. You know the room, Callie?'

'I've never been in there but I know where you mean.'

'I opened the door and put the tray on the table in there, ready to load the glasses into the dresser, when I realised how cold it was. Now, it's not a room we use a lot and it's a little colder than the rest of the house but it seemed unnaturally cold in there that night. As cold as a cathedral,' Eleanor said.

'Like the cathedral in *Canon Alberic's Scrapbook?*' Lara suggested.

'Was there a horrible laughter coming from the dresser, Mum?' Josh teased.

'No, there wasn't a horrible laughter but I did draw the curtains and I couldn't get over the feeling that I was being watched.'

'I've always found that room a bit eerie,' Polly confessed.

'It's just because we don't use it that much, that's all,' Josh said.

'And did you ever find out why it was so cold in there?' Callie asked.

'The radiator needed bleeding,' Frank said. 'That was all.'

Josh threw his head back and laughed.

'Was that it?' Callie asked.

'It was the radiator for sure,' Frank said but Eleanor was shaking her head.

'It was more than just cold I felt in there,' she said. 'I felt a presence.'

Callie swallowed hard. She didn't like the sound of that. 'What sort of presence?'

'A malevolent one.'

'Mice,' Frank said. 'We had mice in there, didn't we?'

Eleanor smacked his arm. 'It wasn't mice.'

'And it wasn't a stray dog,' Josh said, patting his mum's arm. 'We know.'

'Oh, you're impossible! I thought you believed in ghosts,' she said to Josh.

'No,' he said. 'But I do believe in a good ghost story. Now, who's up next?'

But nobody was listening to him.

'Sweetheart,' Frank was saying, 'you just let that M R James book get to you.' He turned to Callie. 'Sam let me keep hold of the book because I wanted to have a leisurely read of it, and I made the mistake of bringing it into our bedroom that night. I wanted to read *The Mezzotint* again. I think that's one of James's best stories. Anyway Eleanor came into the room and started screaming, "I can't sleep with that thing in here! Get it out!" and she took the book out of my hand and slid it across the floor out of the room.'

'Mum!' Sam cried. 'Tell me you didn't really do that with my first edition!'

'I was *not* having that book anywhere near me. Heaven only knows what nightmares I would have had with that thing in the bedroom,' Eleanor said.

Sam's mouth had dropped open.

'I couldn't stop her, son,' Frank said.

'It didn't stay on the floor all night, did it?' Sam asked.

'Of course not,' Frank assured him. 'Once I was certain your mother was asleep, I got up and rescued it.'

'You didn't bring it into the bedroom, did you?' Eleanor asked in horror.

'Why, did you have nightmares?' Frank asked.

'Yeah, what did you dream about that night, Mum?' Josh asked.

Eleanor moved uneasily on the sofa. 'I don't remember.'

Frank picked her hand up and kissed it. 'I think we should probably move the conversation on, don't you?'

'Yes,' Eleanor agreed.

'Are there any more mince pies, Mum?' Bryony asked.

'Yes, in a tin by the bread bin.'

'I'll get them,' Sam said. 'I need a stretch.'

'I'll help,' Callie said, getting up and leaving the room with him.

'Things were getting a little heated in there,' Sam said once they were out of earshot, 'and not just from the roaring fire.'

'You know, your mum doesn't strike me as the kind of person to just imagine these sorts of things,' Callie observed.

'She isn't. She's the most no-nonsense person you could ever hope to meet. But that book really upset her.'

'Oh, dear,' Callie said.

'Are you okay?' Sam asked, tilting his head to look at her. 'You're awfully pale. Don't tell me *you've* seen a ghost now.'

'No, I've not seen a ghost,' she said with a grin. 'I was just thinking how strange it is that a book could have had such an effect on her.'

'I suppose it's a good job I got rid of it,' he said. 'Much as I miss it.' He opened the tin and then reached into one of the cupboards for a plate, piling the mince pies onto it.

'Do you ever regret selling it?' Callie asked, biting her lip.

'Every single day.'

'Really?'

'It was a beautiful book.'

Callie nodded and swallowed hard. 'Yes, I can imagine.'

'Have you ever let go of a book and then regretted it?'

Callie thought for a moment. 'I once leant a book to a friend knowing, I suppose, that the odds of getting it back were pretty slim. She was so forgetful.'

'And you didn't remind her?'

'I didn't have the heart although I did take a quick look at her shelves when I went round to hers,' Callie confessed.

'And did you see it?'

'Yes. It was right there snuggling up to her own titles which she'd probably borrowed from other friends.'

Sam laughed. 'And you didn't just reach out and take it back?'

'No. I've got plenty of books. I couldn't begrudge her one.'

Sam leaned forward and kissed her cheek. 'You're an angel.'

'No I'm not. I made a mental note not to lend her any more books in the future.'

'Quite right,' Sam said. 'Now, I think we'd better get these mince pies back to the masses before they send out a search party.'

The mince pies were soon passed around and nobody spoke for a while as they were enjoyed. Callie gazed into the depths of the fire, thinking about the strange things Eleanor had told them all. Could a book really be haunted? Could ghost stories really transcend into reality? And, if so, how? Did the reading aloud have anything to do with it? Did the words have a power once they were shared aurally? These were things she'd never thought of until that night and it fascinated her.

'Hey, I think Callie should tell us a ghost story,' Lara suddenly said.

Callie gasped and quickly shook her head. 'But I'm hopeless at reading aloud.'

'You don't need to read one – just *tell* us one,' Polly encouraged.

'But I don't know any ghost stories,' she protested.

'Oh, nonsense! Everybody knows a ghost story,' Lara said. 'Especially a writer. Don't writers attract stories like filings to a magnet?'

Callie frowned, casting her mind back over the years of growing up in rural Oxfordshire.

'Well, there was a local legend about the snowdrop girl,' she said at last.

'Oooo! That sounds good and spooky,' Lara said, settling down to get comfortable. 'Go on, tell us her story!'

CHAPTER FOUR

Callie took a fortifying sip of mulled wine and gazed into the fire. Then she began.

'There's a valley not far from where I grew up. There's not much there – a small church, a wood and a row of old cottages. But it's very beautiful particularly in the winter months when the hills are frosty and the fields fill with mist.

'There's a stream there, a tributary of the River Thames, and its banks are white with snowdrops each year. Or rather *one* of its banks is white with snowdrops. It's strange because both banks are in the same dappled shade and yet the snowdrops only flower on one side.'

'Why's that?' Lara asked.

'Shush!' Josh hissed. 'No interrupting the storyteller.'

'Sorry!' Lara said. 'Do go on, Callie.'

'Well,' Callie continued, 'the story goes that there was a young woman who used to walk through the misty fields towards the stream. It's thought that she was looking for her lover who never came back from the war.'

'Which war?' Frank asked.

'Stories vary, but it's most likely to be the first world war,' Callie said. 'Nobody seems to know, but there's a solitary grave in the churchyard which is said to be hers. It's weathered and lichened with age and you can no longer make out the name or dates. But she can be seen in the misty fields of winter, her face as pale as frost as she makes her way to the stream, the snowdrops growing where she walks.'

Silence greeted Callie as she finished and she swallowed hard.

'It's not much of a story, I'm afraid. Not a lot happens,' she apologised.

'Are you kidding?' Lara said. 'It's one of the spookiest things I've heard in a long time!'

'Isn't that what ghost stories are, though? A big lot of spooky atmosphere and not much plot?' Polly asked.

'I think you should write it down,' Sam said.

'Maybe,' Callie said. 'I wonder if something more could be made of it.'

'If you throw in a fusty old bachelor academic and some kind of ancient treasure, it could rival M R James for sure,' Grandpa Joe said with a laughed.

Callie grinned. 'I don't know. I think I'd rather go down the romantic route and find out more about the girl's lover. What was their relationship like? Did they write to each other while he was away?'

'You're going to have to write that now,' Lara said.

'Did you ever see the snowdrop girl?' Bryony asked.

'I'm afraid not although I did once go there in February when the snowdrops were flowering, but it was a damp, grey day. Perhaps not very good for ghosts.'

'It's funny, isn't it?' Polly said. 'So many ghost stories are set in winter or on a cold, dark day.'

'It was a dark and stormy night!' Josh said.

'Exactly!' Polly said. 'But wouldn't it be spookier to have a ghost appear on a summer's day – say in a beautiful garden when you're least expecting it?'

'But dark, wintery days put us in the mood,' Lara said. 'Pathetic fallacy and all that – where the weather matches the action of the story. I think it builds tension.'

'I suppose it's whether you prefer a build-up of tension,' Sam said, 'or a horrific shock.'

'Suspense or surprise,' Frank said. 'Which is more important?'

'Suspense lasts longer as you're reading,' Bryony said, 'but surprise or shock will get more of a response.'

'I prefer shock,' Eleanor said. 'It gets things over and done with nice and quickly. Suspense lingers and frightens you for too long.'

Frank leaned towards her and kissed her cheek.

'Perhaps we should read something a bit lighter one Christmas,' she suggested.

'Oh, not *A Christmas Carol*,' Josh said. 'I mean Dickens is a classic and everything, but it's not exactly spooky, is it?'

'What's not spooky about seeing your dead business colleague's face in a door knocker or seeing your own grave?' Bryony cried.

'I guess,' Josh said. 'But I can't help picturing the Muppets whenever I read or hear it now. It's ruined it for me.'

Grandpa Joe chuckled from his chair.

'I love the conversations your family has about books,' Callie whispered to Sam.

'I'm not sure we ever talk about anything else,' he whispered back. 'Or, if we do, it usually swings back to books.'

'I like that.'

'Just let me know if you get bored and want to go home.'

'Are you kidding? I'm loving it.'

'Even though Bryony made you tell a ghost story?'

'At least I didn't have to read out loud from a book.'

'No, they're saving that task for next year,' Sam said, squeezing her hand.

'Hey – shush a min!' Frank suddenly said. 'Did you hear that?'

'Hear what?' Sam asked.

'I thought I heard footsteps on the driveway.'

Everyone was silent for a moment and then Eleanor laughed.

'He's just being silly,' she said.

'Oh, Dad!' Polly cried. 'You freaked me out.'

'Me too – that's not funny,' Lara said from the floor.

'I'm not joking, folks,' Frank said.

'Well, if you really heard something, we'd better take a look,' Sam said, on his feet in an instant.

Eleanor was shaking her head. 'If you're messing around...' she warned but she was on her feet too and heading towards the living room curtains.

'Let me,' Frank said, drawing one of the curtains back and peering out of the sash window. The dark evening glared back at them, solid and unyielding. Soon there were half a dozen Nightingale faces peering out into the dark, the orange flames of the fire reflected in the glass between them.

'I can't see anything,' Polly said.

'Doesn't mean there isn't somebody out there,' Frank told her.

'Absence of evidence isn't evidence of absence,' Josh said.

'Exactly,' Frank agreed. 'I'm heading out there.'

'I'd rather you didn't,' Eleanor said.

'It's as well to know for sure,' Frank said, heading out of the living room into the hallway. Everybody followed him and watched as he pulled on his coat and a pair of boots.

'I'm coming with you,' Sam said, finding his own coat as his father opened the front door. A gust of wind blew inside, reminding them that they might be nice and cosy inside but winter was still raging outside.

Callie watched as the two men disappeared into the darkness of the garden.

'I wish they hadn't gone out there,' Eleanor said.

'They'll be back in a minute,' Polly assured her mother. 'As soon as they realise how cold it is.'

Everyone waited anxiously by the front door, keeping it just a little bit open so they could see the moment the men returned.

'Come back inside, Frank!' Eleanor called into the darkness. The wind had picked up now and was howling through the tall trees on the other side of the road. Eleanor poked her head out and called again.

A moment later, Frank and Sam were back inside, stomping their feet and rubbing their hands together.

'Couldn't see anyone,' Frank said.

'Or anything,' Sam added.

'It was probably nothing, Dad,' Josh said.

'Who would be out on a night like this?' Polly observed.

'Nobody,' Grandpa said. 'Come on, Nell – let's get back to the fire.'

'Can we heat some more mulled wine, Mum?' Josh asked.

'I think I'd rather have a cup of tea,' Polly said.

'Polly, put the kettle on,' Lara chimed.

'Ha!' Polly said. 'I was going to give you a tenner if you hadn't said that.'

'Yeah, right!' Lara said.

'I think I'll have a tea too,' Eleanor said. 'Anybody else?'

Everybody nodded and made their way to the kitchen where a tea tray was soon laid with mugs.

Eleanor walked over to place a spoon on the draining board and let out a little scream.

'Frank! There's something out there.'

Everybody moved towards the window which overlooked the back garden.

'Wouldn't the security light come on if there was something out there?' Polly asked.

'It did come on,' Eleanor said. 'It's just switched off.'

'And now it's on again,' Josh said unnecessarily as the light flooded the garden and everyone moved closer to the window.

'I can't see anything,' Bryony said. 'Where was it, Mum?'

'In the shrubbery. On the left. I didn't get a very good look – it moved pretty fast.'

'Well, I can't see anything now.'

'Listen,' Eleanor said as Brontë and Hardy started to bark from the boot room. 'The dogs know something is out there.'

'They're probably just picking up on your fear,' Frank said. 'That's all. Come on now, let's have this tea. I need to warm up by the fire.'

'Come on, Mum,' Polly said, putting her arm around her mother's shoulder and giving her a squeeze.

They all trooped through to the living room and the mugs of tea were handed out.

'Maybe it's that stray dog come back again or Black Shuck come to wish us a Merry Christmas,' Grandpa Joe laughed.

'Don't even joke about it, Grandpa!' Polly said.

'Tell me more about this Black Shuck,' Callie asked as she settled back on the sofa.'

'Dad – you were actually told a story by a local about him, weren't you?' Frank asked.

'That's right, son,' Grandpa Joe said. 'We were out by the coast. Somewhere between Aldeburgh and Southwold. Beautiful heathland up that way. Lots of open space. A landscape of wind and light. Do you remember that day, Nell?' he asked his wife. 'The day we spoke to the old farmer's wife hanging out her washing?'

'Oh, yes,' Nell said. 'Old Shuck.'

'Old Shuck. Black Shuck. Sometimes Old *Shock*,' Grandpa Joe went on. 'The farmer's wife called him Old Shuck and told a fearful tail of a woman in her village some years before who'd been cycling home from work after dark when she was aware that something was following her in the gorse bushes that ran alongside the road.'

'Did she see anything?' Lara asked.

'At first, she just kept peddling. The old manor house she worked at was a good two miles from her village and she wanted to get home as quickly as possible but, no matter how fast she peddled, the beast kept pace with her. She couldn't shake it off.'

'You can't shake off Old Shuck,' Grandma Nell said.

'But she kept peddling,' Grandpa Joe continued, 'the thin beam from her headlamp lighting the road ahead. Then she made the mistake of looking behind her.'

'What did she see?' Bryony asked.

'A pair of huge red eyes watching her from the undergrowth,' Grandpa Joe said. 'But the beast made no sound as it followed her and the next time she turned to look it had vanished.'

'And what happened to the woman?' Callie asked.

'Nothing happened to the woman but her mother died the very next week. Shuck, you see, is thought to be an omen of death – maybe not of the person who sees him but of somebody close to them.'

'Well, that's got my spine good and tingling,' Lara said from her seat on the floor.

'And the farmer's wife told us that the woman gave in her notice at the manor house and took work in the village. She never went down that stretch of road again.'

'And did you and Grandma go down the road?' Bryony asked.

'We did,' he said proudly, 'only we drove. With the windows up and the doors locked.'

'There isn't actually any physical evidence for Shuck though, is there?' Josh asked.

'Don't you remember the church door?' Frank asked his son. 'I took you out to Blythburgh with me on a job and we stopped to look at the church on the way home.'

Josh frowned. 'You mean those marks on the door?'

'What marks?' Polly asked.

'Big black marks on the old wooden door,' Frank told them. 'Said to be Shuck's from an attack during a storm when he crashed into the church and killed a man and a boy.'

'Wasn't there a huge dog skeleton found recently in Suffolk?' Eleanor asked.

'That's right,' Sam said. 'Out at Leiston Abbey. The bones of a seven-foot-long dog were found in a grave. That's not far from

Blythburgh with those claw marks on the church door, or Bungay where there was another fatal attack.'

'You think those bones really belonged to some kind of hell hound?' Callie asked.

'Who knows?' Sam said. 'There are more things in heaven and earth...'

'Oh, my god!' Lara said. 'I don't like the thought of a seven-foot dog prowling in our shrubbery.'

'There's nothing out there,' Josh said.

Just then there was a loud bang on the front door, making everyone leap up from where they were sitting.

'What on *earth*?' Frank shouted, on his feet and out in the hallway quicker than you could say Ebenezer Scrooge.

Everyone except Grandma Nell followed him again. Sam grabbed hold of Callie's hand and she was glad of the comforting gesture because she couldn't help feeling a little nervous as Frank opened the door.

'There's nobody there,' he said.

'That was definitely a bang on the door. We didn't imagine that, did we?' Josh said.

'No, we didn't,' Frank said, stepping out into the night.

'Please come back in, Frank,' Eleanor called.

'This is beginning to freak me out now,' Lara said.

A handful of dead leaves chased each other through the door and made Callie shiver.

'I should go out after him,' Sam said, stepping forward to grab his coat again just as Frank came back inside.

'Couldn't see a thing,' he said. 'We could get torches and do a proper sweep of the garden.'

'We could call the police,' Lara said.

'Or we could all just go back to the fire,' Grandpa Joe said. 'If it's anything urgent I'm sure we'll hear about it in good time.'

'But who would knock on a front door on Christmas Eve and then run off?' Eleanor asked.

'It was a bang rather than a knock,' Polly said.

Grandpa Joe gently ushered everyone back into the living room.

'There's a gap in the curtains,' Bryony said, moving towards them to close them tightly.

'Well, that's ruined a nice cosy evening,' Polly complained. 'I feel all on edge now.'

'I was already feeling that way after Grandpa's Black Shuck story,' Lara admitted.

'I think we'd better get on with the ghost stories,' Josh said. 'That'll be the best way to forget whatever might or might not be going on outside. Who's next?'

'I'm not sure I'm in the mood anymore,' Bryony said.

'How about a nice cheery story?' Polly said.

'Do we know any of those?' Josh asked with a laugh.

'I know one,' Lara said. 'Actually, Callie's snowdrop story reminded me about it. It's a kind of romantic ghost story.'

'It's not scary, is it?' Eleanor asked her daughter. 'I think I'm done with scary for tonight.'

'It's not scary, I promise.'

'Well, let's hear it,' Bryony said and so Lara began.

CHAPTER FIVE

'There's a little church of brick and flint with a round tower that overlooks fields and woods,' Lara began. 'The church is deserted and the graveyard is overgrown with cow parsley, willowherb, brambles and ivy but it's still visited by those who know of its existence.'

'Where is it?' Polly asked.

'No interruptions!' Bryony reminded her.

'Sorry. Just curious.'

'Could be any number of East Anglian churches,' Frank said.

'And it doesn't really matter,' Lara said. 'But this one is special because there's a tomb in the church.'

'Oh, I don't like tombs,' Eleanor said. 'I thought you said this wasn't going to be scary.'

'It isn't scary!' Lara insisted. 'I promise.'

Callie watched Lara's bright eyes glitter in the firelight as she continued her story.

'The church is plain inside. The beautiful old stained glass windows are long gone and the wooden screen and statues too.'

'Basher Dowsing,' Grandpa Joe said, referring to the puritan soldier who'd done so much damage to the churches of East Anglia during the Civil War.

'But there was one piece he didn't touch,' Lara continued. 'The tomb of the fourteenth-century knight. Maybe it was because the knight was a fellow soldier. Maybe Dowsing took pity upon him and left him to his rest.'

'What does he look like?' Grandma Nell asked and Lara smiled.

'I was just getting to that. He lies by the altar, his head on a pillow and his feet resting on his faithful dog. He is wearing a helmet and there is chain mail around his face. He has a kind, gentle face with a long straight nose and full lips. He looks earnest, sincere,' she paused, 'handsome.'

There were collective sighs of appreciation from the women.

'His hands touch in prayer and there's a detail in his armour at the elbows which looks like a heart with a sweet seven-petalled flower at its centre.'

'He wears his heart on his sleeve!' Bryony cried.

'Oh, for goodness' sake!' Josh said, shaking his head in despair. 'Can't we read another M R James story?'

'No!' Lara told him.

'I like this one,' Eleanor said. 'Go on, Lara.'

'It is said that he had a sweetheart waiting for him at home but she was ill when he left her and died before his return. He never got over her death and he never loved another. The legend goes that he will rise again one day, but that it will take the kiss of a very special maiden at midnight on Christmas Eve.

'Scores of maidens have made their way to the church on Christmas Eve over the centuries, pushing each other aside so they can kiss those stone lips, but none has ever woken him. Then, one night, on a cold and frosty Christmas Eve, a young woman was visiting an elderly relative who told her the legend of the knight. The girl laughed at the story but she couldn't shake it from her head and lay awake in bed that night thinking about the little church and the knight who slept there.

'Finally, at half past eleven, she got out of bed and got dressed, leaving the house and walking across the fields towards the church. It was a bitterly cold night and she kept telling herself that she was crazy to even think of doing such a thing but it was as if she didn't have any say in the matter – she had to go there. She had to see the knight.

'She almost doubled back when she saw the church in the thin beam from her torch because its tower was wrapped in mist, but something kept her moving forward and she entered the porch and approached the big wooden door and opened it. Of course, it was pitch black in the church and she moved slowly to the altar where she'd been told the tomb was.

'Just then, a great light shone through one of the glassless windows. It was the moon. She hadn't realised there was a full moon out that night because it had been hidden behind cloud until that moment. Now, it guided her to the tomb of the knight to the left of the altar and she saw him for the first time.

'She reached a hand out and touched the carved belt of his armour, noting the beautiful round medallions on it, and then her fingers stroked the wavy lines of the chain mail and rested on his face.

'She looked at her watch. It was five minutes to midnight. Five long, cold minutes but they seemed to flash by in a heartbeat as she looked at the knight's gentle face.

'Finally, the time had come to test the legend and she bent forward and lowered her lips to the cold stone lips of the sleeping knight, closing her eyes and kissing him.'

Lara paused and glanced around the room at the rapt faces watching her.

'Go on!' Callie urged. 'What happened?'

'What she had been expecting to happen,' Lara continued. 'She'd been ridiculous leaving her bed in the middle of the night and traipsing across a cold field. Looking down into the lifeless stone, she couldn't help laughing at having dared to believe the legend. Even if the knight *had* somehow come to life, he was from the fourteenth-century. He'd probably speak a form of English which she wouldn't understand – something between Chaucer and Shakespeare. For a few brief moments, she'd truly let herself believe in a silly story. Maybe she'd watched *Sleeping Beauty* too many times as a child.

'Turning to leave the church, she gasped as she saw a man standing in the church doorway.

'What are you doing here?' she asked in panic, suddenly feeling very vulnerable alone in a church at midnight.

'I came to see the knight,' he said.

She gave him a quizzical look. 'Were you going to kiss him?'

'No!' the man cried. 'But I was wondering if there'd be a fair maiden here who was going to. I brought my camera,' he said, lifting it up from around his neck to show her.

She studied him for a moment.

'So, did you?' he asked her.

'Did I what?'

'Did you kiss him?' he asked.

She tucked a strand of hair behind her ear, suddenly feeling very foolish.

'I might have.'

The man, who'd walked out from the shadows so that the moonlight fell upon him, smiled at her.

'And what happened?'

'Nothing,' she confessed. 'I'd better get home.'

'The village?'

She didn't want to tell the stranger where she was heading in the dark but there was something about him that made her trust him.

He cleared his throat. 'I'm staying at my mother's for Christmas,' he told her. 'Maybe you know her. Isabel Knight?'

'Yes!' she cried. 'You're Isabel's son?'

'Alex Knight,' he said, giving her his hand to shake.

'Knight?' she repeated. 'Really?'

'As I live and breathe,' he said.

Lara gave a little bow from the waist and everybody applauded.

'Is that a *true* story?' Polly asked.

Lara smiled a knowing smile. 'Erm, not exactly.'

'Where did you read it?' Eleanor asked. 'I've never heard it before.'

'I didn't read it. I wrote it.'

'You made that up?' Bryony asked.

'Yes.'

'When?' Frank asked his daughter.

'This term at uni.'

'When you're meant to be studying?'

'It was in my spare time. I was all inspired after reading *Romeo and Juliet*. I couldn't help imagining a scene where Romeo kissed Juliet and she awoke in time. Wouldn't that have been a better ending?'

'Not better,' Sam said. 'Happier.'

'It wouldn't have been a tragedy then,' Grandpa Joe said.

'I don't like the tragedies,' Lara said. 'Give me a comedy that ends in at least three weddings!'

'Me too,' Eleanor said.

'And then I remembered something else. We'd read a bit of Chaucer and I remembered a knight's tomb we'd once seen in the church at Stonham Aspal. Remember him?'

'The legless knight?' Josh said.

'Yes, poor man had had his legs smashed.'

'Probably by Basher Dowsing,' Grandpa Joe said.

'Probably,' Lara said. 'Well, I wanted to make him all complete in my story. Give him his legs back.'

'Sweet girl!' Bryony said, giving her a little hug.

'But you made the church derelict,' Frank said.

'Atmosphere!' Lara said.

'Well, looks like you've got competition on the story writing front, Callie,' Sam told her.

'It sounds like I have!' Callie replied, smiling first at Sam and then at Lara.

'Oh, I don't know about that,' Lara said modestly.

'I tell you,' Eleanor began, 'Lara's wasted doing admin for the Castle Clare literary festival – she should be one of the guest speakers.'

'I think I'm a little way off that, Mum!' Lara said.

Polly got up from her place on the sofa and walked towards the window, drawing back the curtains a little and peering outside.

'What is it, Polly?' Frank asked his daughter.

'I can't see anything, but I thought I heard someone on the gravel,' she replied.

'Yes, I thought so too,' Frank said, joining her at the window. 'This is getting tiresome, isn't it?'

Bryony got up, poking her head through the curtains between them and gasping a moment later.

'It's a man!' she cried.

'Where?' Frank and Polly asked together.

'He just walked out from behind the beech tree – there!'

'What's he doing?' Lara asked, her voice raised in panic as she got up from the floor.

'I'm not sure,' Bryony continued as she fiddled anxiously with her silver scarf. 'Oh, he's heading this way. He's coming to the front door!'

Sure enough, there was a knock on the front door a moment later.

'What shall we do?' Eleanor asked, looking genuinely scared.

Frank turned to look at her. 'We answer it,' he said.

CHAPTER SIX

For the third time that evening, Frank Nightingale opened the door but, this time, Callie could see he was ready to give whoever it was who was disturbing their peace a good ticking off if need be.

As the light from the hallway fell on the interloper, they saw it was a tall, thin man with a pale face. He was wearing a woolly hat with a great fat bobble on the top and he looked anxious.

'Sorry to disturb you,' he began. 'I'm Mr Parker. I've been lookin' for Emily Parker's cottage. She's my sister.'

Eleanor came forward. 'You mean Honeysuckle Cottage? That's just along the road here. You're not far from it. About another mile.'

'Oh, dear,' Mr Parker said. 'I've been goin' round in circles for hours on these country lanes. Then Felix kept whining so I let him out and he ran off afta somethin'.'

'Felix?' Frank asked.

'My dog.'

'Would that happen to be a big black dog?' Grandpa Joe asked, coming forward.

'A black collie, aye. He just took off. I was chasing him round your garden, I'm sorry to say.'

'It was you who knocked on the door earlier?' Frank asked.

'Aye, but then I caught sight of Felix and ran to get him.'

Grandpa Joe started to chuckle. 'You gave us a bit of a start,' he told Mr Parker. 'We'd been reading ghost stories and we imagined Black Shuck was stalking our shrubbery.'

'Oh, dear! Oh, dear!' Mr Parker said, shaking his head. 'I didn't mean to scare anyone. I didn't knock at first because I was scared of disturbing you, what with it being Christmas Eve and everything, but then I was gettin' a bit desperate.'

'Where's Felix now?' Polly asked.

'Safe in the car with his blanket.'

'Where are you parked?' Frank asked.

'Just down the lane.'

'Why don't you come in and get warm for a moment?' Eleanor said. 'You could have frozen to death out there.'

'I thought I had at one point,' Mr Parker said, clapping his hands together as he came into the hallway. 'You sure I'm not disturbing you any?'

'No, no!' everyone insisted.

'Cup of tea?' Polly asked him as Eleanor offered to take his coat and hat.

'Very kind of you.'

Polly went to the kitchen to make the tea and everyone else went through to the living room with Mr Parker.

'Have a seat by the fire,' Eleanor said and Mr Parker sat down on the sofa.

'Where've you come from?' Frank asked as he put a couple more logs onto the fire.

'Yorkshire. Wensleydale'

'A fair old drive,' Frank said, returning to the sofa next to his guest.

'It is that.'

'Beautiful,' Eleanor said. 'We've had quite a few holidays in the Yorkshire Dales.'

'Aye, it's a popular spot,' Mr Parker said. 'Quiet at this time of year, mind. Not much in the way of tourists.'

'How's the weather been up there?' Grandpa Joe asked.

'We've had snow on and off since October.'

'Goodness!' Eleanor said. 'We're having our first little flurry tonight.'

'The perfect night to be sat around a fire,' Mr Parker observed.

'So, as Grandpa Joe was saying, we were just telling a few ghost stories,' Frank said. 'It's a bit of a tradition at Christmas by the fire.'

'And you mentioned Black Shuck,' Mr Parker said. 'Can I ask what that is?'

Grandpa Joe leaned forward in his chair, happy to have an ear as he told their guest about the legendary hairy black dog which rampaged through the East Anglian countryside.

'And you thought my Felix might be-'

'Yes, I'm afraid we did,' Frank said with a laugh, now that it was safe to laugh.

'We have our own big dog legend in the north. Gytrash,' Mr Parker said.

'Oooo!' Lara cried. 'Doesn't he get a mention in *Jane Eyre*?'

'That's right,' Sam said. 'The scene where Jane spooks Rochester's horse.'

'I wonder what is it about big black dogs that captures the imagination in legends?' Callie asked.

'Well, Gytrash is often thought to be a horse,' Mr Parker said.

'Really?' Callie said.

'He's sometimes thought to be feared, sometimes thought to be gentle. He can lead people away from a footpath or guide them to one from the moors. There are so many stories, it's hard to know what to believe.'

Polly came in with a teapot and mugs on a tray. Eleanor poured, giving a mug to Mr Parker first and then passing the others around to the family.

'So, have you had any experience of Gytrash yourself?' Grandpa Joe asked.

Mr Parker took a sip of his tea. 'Well, no.'

'Do you believe in him?' Lara asked.

'Now here's an interesting thing,' Mr Parker said. 'There was one point in me life when I would've said no to that question and answered it so quickly as to suggest there was no room for doubt. But now? Well, things ain't that simple.'

'How so?' Josh asked.

Mr Parker shifted a little on the sofa and took another sip of tea.

'I live in a house about a half mile from the nearest village. It's a modest-sized house built of the local stone. Lived there all me life. Like me parents and their parents afore 'em. Couldn't live anywhere else now.'

His gaze drifted towards the fire where a log crackled and spat fat flames and Callie wondered what he was thinking of and what he was about to tell them. It was, she realised, that delicious moment when you know you're going to be told a story and you're just waiting for it to begin.

'I've never married, never had children,' he went on, 'and yet I've never been alone in that house.'

Callie swallowed hard and glanced across the room at Eleanor who was looking at Mr Parker with an anxious expression on her face.

'Never alone?' Lara repeated, her face rapt.

Mr Parker nodded. 'That's right. Not with Elizabeth there.' He paused and then gave a little smile.

'Who's Elizabeth?' Grandma Nell asked. Callie looked up. She'd thought Nell had been dozing but, even though she had her eyes closed, it was obvious she hadn't missed a thing.

'Elizabeth,' Mr Parker said. 'She was the sister of my great-grandfather. She only lived to be nine years old before drowning in the river.'

'You mean she's a ghost?' Lara asked.

'Oh, aye. I remember the first time I saw 'er. It weren't until I was in me early twenties. Both my parents had died by then. Perhaps she didn't want me to be alone. Anyways, she was standing in front the fire one cold November evening and I remember bein' able to see the flames right through her. And the funny thing was, I wasn't afraid. I just stood and watched her to see what she'd do.'

'And what did she do?'

'She turned around and looked right at me,' Mr Parker said. 'I think she was warming herself up. Her dress looked wet see.'

'And you really weren't you scared of her?' Bryony asked.

'Nowt to be scared of,' Mr Parker insisted. 'She just sort of roams about a bit and then vanishes. It's kind of comforting in a way. Sometimes, she can be the only person I see all day.' He gave a little smile at that. 'She seems to favour the house, standing by the fire or near radiators as if to keep warm. But I've seen 'er in the garden too. I don't have much of a garden – it's just a bit o' rough grass with a potato patch and a raised bed for me greens. But I've seen her out there by the old apple tree, her pale hair blowing as she looks down the valley towards the river that took her life.'

'Do you talk to her?' Eleanor asked.

'Oh, aye. I tell her a bit about me day.'

'And does she ever talk back?' Lara dared to ask.

'Not with words,' Mr Parker said, 'but her eyes seem to speak to me. I do believe she hears me. There was one time a couple of summers ago. I had to have one o' me best dogs put to sleep. Heartbreaking day that. Had 'im for fifteen years. Picked him out from his litter and he was by me side every day since. Felt like I'd 'ad me heart ripped out that day.'

'Oh, we all know what it's like to lose a dog,' Grandpa Joe said. 'Terrible, terrible pain.'

'Aye, it is. And it was as if Elizabeth knew for she stayed with me that day. She was never far from me and her presence was a comfort, I have to say. Ghost or not. She was there for me.'

Callie could feel that her eyes were swimming with tears now and she did her best to blink them away, giving a little sniff and hoping she wouldn't betray herself. She could see that Eleanor and Bryony were equally moved by Mr Parker's story. Lara, however, was simply rapt.

'And does she always wear that same dress?' Lara asked him.

Mr Parker nodded. 'The dress that looks wet? Aye, she does. She never changes, never ages. She's the one constant thing in me life. I can always rely on Elizabeth.'

'That's the spookiest thing I've ever heard,' Lara said. 'I don't think I've ever met someone whose house is haunted.'

'Come an' visit,' Mr Parker said.

'Would she show herself to me?' Lara asked.

'Well, I couldn't make any promises. She's a bit shy when it comes to strangers.'

'Actually, I think *I'd* be the shy one,' Lara said. 'I've always thought I'd like a *Wuthering Heights*-type experience with the supernatural but it would probably really freak me out!'

'I don't know how you can live there,' Eleanor said.

'You get used to it,' Mr Parker said matter-of-factly. 'After all, it was 'er home afore it were mine.'

'That's a very interesting way of looking at it,' Sam said.

'It's the only way as far as I'm concerned.'

There was a pause as everyone seemed lost in their own thoughts and then Mr Parker stood up.

'I'd best be off,' he said. 'Thank you for the tea. I'm all warmed up now!'

'Would you like me to give Emily a call and let her know you're on your way – put her mind at rest,' Eleanor asked him.

'Aye, very kind of you,' Mr Parker said. 'I'm afraid me mobile isn't working. Mind you, I don't think it was working when I left home. I'm not very good with these modern gadgets.'

'I know how you feel,' Grandpa Joe said. 'I don't believe in mobiles myself. When I'm out of the house, I'm out of the house and, if anyone wants to talk to me, they can wait until I get back home.'

Mr Parker nodded in agreement. 'Well, thanking you again,' he said, pulling on his coat and bobbly hat. 'And sorry for disturbing you.'

'Not at all,' Eleanor said.

'You've made Christmas Eve all the more entertaining,' Frank told him.

'Do you want us to see you back safely to your car?' Sam asked.

'I can manage,' Mr Parker said.' I'm used to the dark where I live.'

'Goodnight, then,' Frank said.

They all stood in the hallway, watching Mr Parker as he disappeared into the lane and was swallowed up by the dark night.

CHAPTER SEVEN

'Well, that was unexpected,' Sam said.

'I don't think I'm ever going to visit Yorkshire,' Lara said. 'Or at least Wensleydale.'

'Ghosts are everywhere,' Grandpa Joe said. 'You'd never visit anywhere if you wanted to avoid them.'

'Do you really believe that?' Lara asked as they returned to the cosy warmth of the living room.

'I believe we should keep our eyes and minds open,' he said, winking at her before returning to his chair.

'I'm not at all sure about our Mr Parker,' Josh said, scratching his chin and looking thoughtful.

'What do you mean?' Sam asked.

'I mean, I don't think we should just accept what he told us.'

'Why not?'

'Why not? Because he's been talking to an apparition all his life!' Josh said.

'And you don't believe him?' Lara asked.

'I think we should definitely question it.'

'Says the man who reads M R James with such glee,' Bryony said.

'I know the difference between fact and fiction,' he told his sister.

'Ah, you see, that's where I struggle,' Sam said. 'I often blur the two.'

Callie looked at Sam who was wearing a big grin on his face at the joy of sparring with his siblings.

'Me too,' Callie said.

'Yes, but you're a fiction writer so you're pardoned,' Josh told her.

'Well, thank you!' Callie said.

'But the rest of us haven't got that excuse,' Josh continued. 'We should have cross-examined him some more.'

'You don't cross-examine a guest,' Frank stated. 'Besides, I was enjoying his story.'

'Story!' Josh pounced on the word. 'So you didn't believe him?'

'I didn't say that,' Frank said.

'But you questioned him in your own mind?'

'Perhaps,' Frank admitted.

Eleanor shook her head. 'Boys, boys! Enough arguing.'

'We're not arguing, Mum,' Josh said. 'Just debating. Isn't that right, Dad? Isn't that what you always say?'

Frank nodded. 'Nothing like a good healthy debate.'

'Yes? Well, keep me out of it,' Eleanor said. 'I'm going to give Emily a quick call and let her know her brother's on his way.' She left the room, going out into the hallway to use the phone.

Callie smiled at Sam and he picked her hand up and kissed it.

'What did you make of Mr Parker?' she whispered to him. 'I mean, *really*?'

'I thought he was very interesting,' Sam said.

'But did you believe him? About Elizabeth, I mean?'

Sam took a deep breath. 'He looked earnest enough. I don't see what reason he'd have to lie. Why? Didn't you believe him?'

'I don't know,' she said honestly. 'There was a part of me that wanted to. The writer in me, I suppose, who likes a good story. But I'm not sure if I believe in ghosts.'

They could hear Eleanor's voice as she spoke on the phone and, a moment later, she came back into the room, her face ashen.

'What is it, darling?' Frank asked.

'I've just spoken to Emily,' she said.

'Everything okay?' Bryony asked.

'No, not really,' Eleanor said, walking towards the sofa and sitting down. 'She said her brother died four years ago.'

Silence filled the room for a moment as everybody stared at Eleanor.

'Are you sure, Mum?' Sam asked.

'That's what she said.'

'You mean her brother as in Mr Parker?' Grandpa Joe said. 'Mr Parker who was sitting in our front room?'

Eleanor nodded. 'I – I can't quite take this in.'

'Is this some kind of hoax?' Josh asked. 'Mum, are you having a laugh?'

Eleanor looked at Josh and Callie saw the distress in her face.

'You think I would joke about something like this?'

Josh shrugged. 'I don't know.'

'I'm not joking,' Eleanor said.

'So who was Mr Parker?' Lara asked.

'If Mr Parker – the *real* Mr Parker – is dead, then who was the man who was sitting in our front room?' Bryony asked.

'A ghost?' Lara said, a shocked look on her face.

'The temperature did drop when he was here,' Grandpa Joe confessed.

'That's because the front door had been open,' Josh countered. 'Blimey, we've gone from M R James to J B Priestley this evening.'

'Yes, it is very like *An Inspector Calls*, isn't it?' Sam said. 'But I'm pretty sure Mr Parker was real.'

Frank shook his head. 'There must be an explanation. Mr Parker was flesh and blood. Look – you can see the dent in the cushion from where he was sitting. Ghosts don't dent cushions.'

'How do you know?' Grandpa Joe asked.

Frank rolled his eyes. 'I just have an innate sense of these things.'

'And he managed to drink a whole mug of tea,' Josh said. 'Surely ghosts don't drink.'

'This is very confusing,' Eleanor said shaking her head as if that might help her to makes sense of things.

'What exactly was said on the phone?' Frank asked.

'What do you mean?'

'Tell me what you said to her and what she said to you – word for word.'

'Well, I'm not sure I can remember it all.'

'Just try.'

Eleanor frowned. 'Emily answered and -'

Frank held up a hand. 'How do you know it was Emily?'

'Because I rang her number.'

'Are you sure? Did you say her name when you talked to her?'

'Well – I'm – I'm not sure now you mention it.'

'Okay. What next?'

'I said it was Ellie calling and that her brother was with us.'

'Did you say Mr Parker?'

'No. I don't think I did.'

'Okay,' Frank said, standing up. 'Let me check the number you rang, okay?'

Eleanor got up and the two of them went out into the hall together while everybody else listened intently from the living room as Frank redialled the number Eleanor had rung.

'Hello?' Frank's voice said a moment later. 'Is that Emily Parker?' There was a pause. 'Okay. Sorry to disturb you.'

'Frank?' Eleanor said as he hung up.

'You didn't ring Emily,' they heard Frank say.

'Dad?' Josh called through. 'What's going on?'

Frank and Eleanor walked back into the living room.

'Your mother didn't ring Emily. She dialled a wrong number.'

'Oh, thank goodness!' Eleanor cried, her hands clapped over her mouth. 'I'm so relieved! I thought we'd had a ghost in the front room. We'd have had to move house!'

Bryony laughed and Lara joined in. Callie too although it was a sort of nervous laughter because she was still processing everything.

Josh shook his head. '*Now* can we go back to our stories?'

'I'm sorry, Josh,' Polly said, standing up, 'but I've got to get going. I'm to pick Archie up.'

'Is it so late already?' Frank said, glancing at the clock on the mantelpiece. It was nearly eight o'clock.

'Well, we'll see you both tomorrow, okay?' Eleanor said. 'I can't wait to see my gorgeous grandson.'

'I just hope you're not going to spoil him,' Polly said.

'As if!' Eleanor said, glancing towards the Christmas tree where a myriad presents with Archie's name on awaited him.

Everybody got up and hugged Polly in turn.

'It's certainly been a memorable Christmas Eve,' Polly said. 'I hope we haven't put you off coming again, Callie.'

'Absolutely not!' Callie said. 'I've loved every minute of it.'

Polly left a moment later to a chorus of goodbyes and the front door was shut against the cold night once more. Eleanor then took a moment to ring Emily Parker, mightily relieved to get the correct number this time.

'Mr Parker's arrived safely at his sister's,' she announced to everyone.

'Good!' Grandpa Joe said.

'Glad to hear it,' Frank said.

Josh rubbed his hands together. 'How about another M R James, then?' he asked. 'Sam – what about you reading us *Canon Alberic's Scrapbook* to round the evening off?'

'You know, I think we've had enough spooky goings on tonight,' Eleanor said. 'And I'm not sure I ever want to hear another M R James again. Just having that Mr Parker incident tonight has reminded me of those strange things that happened when we were all reading from that haunted first edition.'

'Oh, Mum! It wasn't haunted,' Sam assured her. 'Anyway, I got rid of it.'

'Sam?' Callie said, resting a hand on his arm.

'What is it?' he asked, looking at her. 'Are you okay? I was going to say that you look as if you've seen a ghost, but I'd better not in the circumstances!'

'No, I'm fine, it's just...'

'What?'

She could feel that her heart was racing.

'I think you'd better open your Christmas present,' she told him, getting up and crossing the room towards the Christmas tree, picking his present out from where she'd placed it under the twinkling boughs. She was aware that everybody was watching her as she handed Sam the cream and gold gift a moment later.

'Callie, are you sure you want me to open it now?' he asked. 'It's not yet Christmas Day.'

'I really think you should,' she said.

He smiled at her. 'Well, thank you.'

'You might not be thanking me in a minute,' she warned him.

'Well, this is all very mysterious,' he said, leaning forward to kiss her before he opened his present.

'Oh!' he said as he tore into the paper and unfolded the delicate tissue. 'I don't believe it.'

'What is it?' Lara asked from the carpet, kneeling up to get a better look.

Bryony got up too and gasped as she saw it. 'Oh, blimey!'

'What is it?' Eleanor asked.

'I'm not sure you want to know, Mum,' Sam said, looking at Callie as he shielded the book against the eyes of his family.

'I'm so sorry,' she said. 'I had no idea when I bought it, but I've been so worried since you gave that description of the book earlier this evening.'

'Callie – this is – this is amazing!' he said, glancing down at the gift.

'Let me see!' Lara said, getting up from the carpet and reaching out to touch the gift. 'Oh, no!' she cried a moment later, turning to her mother.

Eleanor frowned but didn't get up.

'Who did you sell your book to?' Callie asked Sam.

He frowned as he tried to remember and then he nodded. 'It went to a bookshop owner in Cambridge, I think. Yes.'

Callie swallowed hard. 'I bought this in Cambridge – a little shop down an alley near King's College.'

Sam nodded again. 'That'll be it.'

'Oh, dear!'

'Don't worry,' he told her, wrapping her up in a hug. 'I love it! I never wanted to let it go in the first place.'

'Let what go?' Josh asked.

'The book!' Sam said, holding it up at last for everyone to see. The gesture was met by gasps of wonder and horror. It was the M R James first edition.

'The haunted book!' Grandpa Joe cried.

'What is it?' Grandma Nell asked, rousing from a little nap.

'Callie's bought Sam that haunted book!'

Callie looked at Eleanor whose eyes had almost doubled in size as she saw what it was Sam was holding.

'It's the same exact edition,' Sam declared a moment later, turning it over in his hands.'

'Are you sure?' Eleanor asked. 'Are you absolutely sure?'

'No mistaking it. It's the same book that I was given by Mr Roache.' He laughed. 'Callie – you're a genius! I never wanted to let this book go. I've regretted it ever since.'

'You get that book out of this house, Samuel Nightingale!' his mother warned.

'Oh, Mum! Don't be silly. It's just a harmless old book.'

'I don't want it anywhere near me. I'm sorry, Callie, but I can't have anything to do with that book. I'm sure your intention was good, but... but – *that book!*'

'I'm so sorry, Eleanor,' Callie said, moving towards her and placing her hand on her arm. 'If I'd had any idea at all, I'd never have chosen it.'

Eleanor nodded. 'I know, my dear. You weren't to know.'

'I can't believe it's the book!' Bryony said, daring to get a little closer to the copy of *Ghost Stories of an Antiquary*. 'It's like serendipity or something. Callie must have been drawn to this book knowing that Sam had a connection to it.'

'You think so?' Callie asked.

'I do,' Bryony said. 'I really believe that about books – there's something in them that can draw you to them.'

Callie smiled. She liked that idea and remembered the moment she'd seen it in the little bookshop and had held it for the first time, knowing that it was the right gift for the man she loved.

'Right,' Grandpa Joe said, getting up from his chair and clapping his hands together. 'I'll just let the dogs out. They've been nice and quiet tonight considering all the comings and goings. They'll be ready for a stretch no doubt.'

'Be careful,' Frank told his father, 'it'll be slippery.'

'I won't go far, don't worry,' Grandpa Joe said.

'Hey, let me just see that ghoulish illustration again,' Josh said, 'before Sam sells the book for the second time.'

'I'm not selling the book, Josh,' Sam told him. 'Which illustration?'

'The one with the hairy hand.'

Sam sat down with the book on his lap and carefully opened it, quickly finding the illustration which Josh was after.

'Just how I remember it,' Josh said. 'Look at the way that hand's bent – just like the legs of a spider.'

'That's pretty freaky,' Lara said.

'I do wish you'd close that book, Sam,' Eleanor said. 'It's giving me the chills.'

'What's that?' Lara suddenly asked.

'What?' Eleanor said.

'I thought I heard something.'

Everybody was quiet for a moment, listening intently. Sure enough, a light tapping could be heard.

'It's coming from the window,' Frank said. He moved to the curtains and quickly drew them back.

'It's Grandpa!' he cried and they all heard Grandpa's naughty chuckle from the other side of the window.

Eleanor shook her head in despair. 'Why, the rotten...! I'll give him what for, I really will!'

Grandpa was still chuckling when he came back into the room a few minutes later, giving Nell a big kiss on the lips.

'That was a mean trick, Grandpa!' Lara told him.

'Yes, and one I'll remember tomorrow when I'm serving the extra crispy roast potatoes you love so much,' Eleanor promised him.

'Aw, I was just having a bit of fun,' he said, bending to kiss his daughter-in-law.

'There's been rather a bit too much fun today,' Eleanor said.

'And I'm afraid I've contributed to it by bringing this book here,' Callie said.

'It's okay, Callie,' Frank assured her. 'It's been fun remembering the old book.'

'Fun for some of you,' Eleanor said. 'I'd have been quite happy to have forgotten it. It's brought back all sorts of memories.'

'Maybe we should take it home now,' Sam said. 'You ready to leave, Callie?'

'Oh, I didn't mean to send you packing, Callie, love,' Eleanor said.

'No, no – it's fine. I think it was time I was heading back. Actually, all these ghost stories have given me an idea I really should write down,' she confessed.

'You're going to work on Christmas Eve?' Josh said, astounded.

Callie laughed. 'I'm afraid writers don't switch off just because it's Christmas. I even managed to get a bit of writing done this morning.'

'Well, I'm personally very grateful to you,' Bryony said. 'My customers *love* your books so – go on – get back to that keyboard of yours!'

Everyone laughed and hugged and said their goodnights and the two of them left to a chorus of happy voices.

'We'll see you tomorrow, Callie!'

'Bye, Sam!'

'Merry Christmas!'

CHAPTER EIGHT

Sam drove Callie back to Newton St Clare and she invited him in for a hot chocolate which she made after jotting her ideas down in a notepad. Owl Cottage felt horribly cold after the warmth of Campion House but Sam soon got a fire going and Callie turned on a couple of lamps and switched on the lights of her little Christmas tree, turning the tiny living room into a cosy haven.

'I'm so sorry,' she told him again as they sat on the sofa with their hot chocolates. 'I had no idea about that book. I knew you were an M R James fan and I was pretty sure that you didn't have a first edition. When I saw it, I got so excited.'

'Callie – it's an amazing present. I love it! Although you shouldn't have spent so much.'

She gave a little shrug. 'I've had a pretty good year with my own books,' she told him, 'and I just couldn't leave it behind. I only wished I'd known about the history of the book.'

'I guess it's not something we talk about too often,' he said, 'although the subject does come up at Christmas as we're reading ghost stories.'

'So, what are you going to do with the book?' she asked.

'I'm going to keep it of course,' he said. 'I just won't be allowed to bring it within a five mile radius of Mum. I think she's going to take out a restraining order against it.'

Callie laughed but her smile soon faded. 'You don't really believe it's haunted, do you?'

'The book? No, of course not. Why, do you?'

She shook her head. 'Although the night I brought it home from Cambridge, I had a power cut for the first time ever.'

'Really?'

She nodded.

'Coincidence,' he said.

'Yes. Very likely.' And then she took a deep breath. 'All the same, I'd prefer it if you kept it at yours in the future.'

'Really? You don't want to borrow it for the night and read it in bed?'

'Erm, no. I really don't.'

Sam shifted on the sofa and cleared his throat.

'What is it?' Callie asked.

'You know, there might actually be something in this haunted book idea.'

Callie frowned. 'What do you mean?'

He turned to look at her, pushing his glasses up his nose. 'Promise me you won't say anything to the others. I wouldn't want to spook them and – well, you've seen how easily spooked they are.'

'You're spooking *me* now,' she told him.

'Well, I won't tell you if you think it'll upset you.'

'Oh, Sam! You can't say something like that and *not* tell me!' she cried, nudging him lightly.

'You sure you want to know?'

'Yes!'

He took a deep breath. 'Okay, then, but you can't unknow it once it's told.'

'Understood. Now, tell me.'

'Remember me telling you about Mr Roache?' Sam asked. 'The man who gave me the book?'

'The one with the bony fingers who kept saying, "This one! This one!"'

'Yes. Well, when he gave me the book, he told me a little bit about its history. He'd been a collector and his father had been one too, and it was his father who'd bought the M R James first edition. Mr Roache knew that I'd appreciate the book and I was delighted when he offered it to me, but he said that it wasn't altogether a gift. I asked him to explain, and he didn't answer for a moment, but asked me to sit down. He had this big old Knole sofa which was mostly threadbare and we sat on that together. Well, perched. I remember thinking I'd never get up again if I sat on it properly – it was so deep and had half-collapsed in the middle.'

Callie giggled. 'But what did he say about the book?'

'He told me that, if I was to take it, I'd have to remember his warning. It was a special book, you see. A book that could make people feel things.'

'*Feel* things?'

'Yes, those were his exact words and I still remember the chill I got when he said them. He told me his father had bought the book from an old man who'd studied at King's College, Cambridge.'

'That's the college M R James was at.'

'That's right.'

'Do you think the old man knew M R James?' Callie asked.

'There's no way of knowing now,' Sam said. 'I asked Mr Roache the same thing and he said it was possible. Just imagine if he'd been a student under M R James.'

'It would be a lovely link to the author. Wouldn't he have got the book signed, though, if he'd known the author?'

'Maybe,' Sam said, 'but I've seen quite a few authors at our literary festival and I sometimes get so dumbstruck that I daren't even approach them to get a book signed!'

Callie smiled at him.

'Anyway,' Sam went on, 'that's not all. The man Mr Roache's father bought the book from believed that it might not only be a first edition, but the *first* first edition. Can you imagine? The very first to have been printed. And he sincerely believed that that made everything all the more *vital*. He believed that the emotions in the writing were stronger, the images more real and the terror more horrifying, and – all those feelings – all those emotions – are felt by the reader. Or rather, they're felt by *some* readers. Those attuned to such things.'

'Like your mother?'

'Exactly.'

'Do you believe that?'

Sam took a deep breath. 'I don't know. But I suppose it could be like a fine art print or etching – you know, the lower the number of the artwork, the more valuable it is, the sharper the image. Perhaps it's the same with the first print run of a book.'

'But how do we know it *is* the *first* first?'

'I don't think there's any way of knowing for sure. It's something I'd never really thought about before this book.'

Callie gazed into the flames of the fire. 'There is always this special quality about a first edition, isn't there?'

'Oh yes. Remember how keen you were to get a copy of your own first edition after you realised you'd given the last one away?'

'Yes!' Callie said. 'I couldn't bear not to have one.'

Sam put his arm around her and they sat still for a moment, watching the fire and listening to the sound of the wind in the chimney.

'You know, I think you should have your present now, seeing as I've already opened mine,' Sam said after a few minutes.

'You've got it with you?' Callie asked as he stood up and went to get his coat, returning with it and rifling in one of the deep pockets.

'Here we are,' he said, handing her a red and gold package tied with a red ribbon.

'Oh, Sam!'

'Go on – open it.'

Callie didn't need to be told twice, tearing an end of the pretty paper and sliding out a red box and opening it to reveal a pretty gold locket in the shape of a book.

'Sam! It's beautiful!' she cried.

'I saw it in a little shop on my travels and couldn't resist.'

'It's lovely. Will you put it on for me?'

'Of course.'

He took the necklace out of its box and she lifted her hair up for him to fasten it, his fingers brushing the soft skin of her neck.

'Please tell me this little gold book isn't a haunted first edition,' she said.

He laughed. 'I think this is definitely a book with a happy ending,' he told her and she nodded.

'I do too,' she said as they kissed.

'Merry Christmas, Callie,' he whispered, holding her close.

'Merry Christmas, Sam.'

ACKNOWLEDGEMENTS

Thank you to Ellie Mead for lending me her wonderful M R James editions and to Robert Lloyd Parry for his marvellous M R James performances.

ALSO BY VICTORIA CONNELLY

Christmas at the Cottage

The Christmas Collection (A compilation volume)

The Christmas Collection Volume Two

A Summer to Remember

Wish You Were Here

The Runaway Actress

Molly's Millions

Flights of Angels

Irresistible You

Three Graces

It's Magic (A compilation volume)

A Weekend with Mr Darcy

The Perfect Hero (Dreaming of Mr Darcy)

Mr Darcy Forever

Christmas With Mr Darcy

Happy Birthday Mr Darcy

At Home with Mr Darcy

One Perfect Week and Other Stories

The Retreat and Other Stories

Postcard from Venice and Other Stories

A Dog Called Hope

Escape to Mulberry Cottage (non-fiction)

A Year at Mulberry Cottage (non-fiction)

Summer at Mulberry Cottage (non-fiction)

Finding Old Thatch (non-fiction)

Secret Pyramid (children's adventure)

The Audacious Auditions of Jimmy Catesby (children's adventure)

ABOUT THE AUTHOR

Victoria Connelly is the bestselling author of *The Rose Girls* and *The Book Lovers* series.

With over a million sales, her books have been translated into many languages. The first, *Flights of Angels*, was made into a film in Germany. Victoria flew to Berlin to see it being made and even played a cameo role in it.

A Weekend with Mr Darcy, the first in her popular Austen Addicts series about fans of Jane Austen has sold over 100,000 copies. She is also the author of several romantic comedies including *The Runaway Actress* which was nominated for the Romantic Novelists' Association's Best Romantic Comedy of the Year.

Victoria was brought up in Norfolk, England before moving to

Yorkshire where she got married in a medieval castle. After 11 years in London, she moved to rural Suffolk where she lives in a pink thatched cottage with her artist husband, a springer spaniel and her ex-battery hens.

To hear about future releases and receive a **free ebook** sign up for her newsletter at www.victoriaconnelly.com.

Printed in Great Britain
by Amazon

11423365R00150